HEARING EVIL
Cycle of Evil: Book 2
Jason Parent

Hearing Evil

Cycle of Evil™: Book 2

A Red Adept Publishing Book

Red Adept Publishing, LLC

104 Bugenfield Court

Garner, NC 27529

http://RedAdeptPublishing.com/

First Print Edition: May 2018

Cover Art by Streetlight Graphics

This is a work of fiction. Names, characters, places, and incidents either are the product of the author's imagination or are used fictitiously, and any resemblance to locales, events, business establishments, or actual persons—living or dead—is entirely coincidental.

For the usual characters—Rob, Kimberly, Evans, et al.—and especially for Frank, who has become a character.

PROLOGUE

H is head is pounding. He reaches up to massage his temples, but his knuckles smack against something hard in front of him and scrape along it. The hollow thunk reminds him of a door knocker thudding into place. He runs his fingers along small cracks in the otherwise-smooth surface. Under his legs, he feels worn fabric and realizes his thighs are bare. His cheeks flush with warmth. Am I naked?

He blinks several times, but all he can see is darkness. He wonders if he's blind, and the thought causes his eyes to water. Why can't I see?

He listens, trying to make sense of his surroundings, why he's there, wherever "there" might be. The tick, tick, tick of the second hand of a clock. The hum of a radiator.

The stale odor of sweat fills the air like an aerosol spray too heavily applied. The sounds, feels, and smells form a picture in his mind, one of an empty carpeted room.

He hears heavy breathing, not his own. Not empty. His heart breaks rhythm with the second hand, racing as sweat drips from his armpits. Not alone.

Thump. Thump. Thump.

Each thump comes with dull, throbbing pain.

His legs are crossed beneath him, but they feel wrong—soft, flabby, and feeble. Shaking, his hands roam over them. What's happened to me? He tries to move them, but pins and needles course though his legs. Moaning, he gives up.

The thumping continues, and though his more rational side knows it isn't true, images of being buried alive race through his mind. The banging is so close, so internal, as if he's trapped in a coffin, pounding at a lid covered in dirt.

1

His fingers trace the grooves in the wood and lead his hands up to paper-thin edges peeled back and curling like rose petals dying without water or light.

Each thump derails his train of thought, frustrating his attempts to make sense of his situation. He sits up a little, taking care not to jostle his legs. His grogginess begins to dissipate as the pain in his head recedes. In its stead, fear seizes control. He gasps as he realizes something is holding him in place, something invisible, a force he is powerless to break. His body is his own, though it's entirely different and not his to manage. He shakes all over.

Why is this happening to me? *He tries to scream, but the words fall away from a thick, drooling tongue. He brings his hands up to his chest then plants them against the surface in front of him. With all his might, he pushes.*

He pleads with the force, to any god who will listen, but neither he nor the wall budges. Is this my hell? My penance for failing to stop Jimmy? For failing to help Tessa? *Tessa...*

He sways and feels nothing behind him, but when he tries to lie back, he's blocked by nothing but air. He could try to turn, but the cold voice of terror inside tells him that turning won't work. It tells him not to face that way, any way but that way—that somehow blindness is better than seeing.

He becomes aware of muffled voices behind him. One speaks in whispers, the other through sobs. They grow louder. Are they arguing?

"Hey!" His voice cracks, and what comes out is an incoherent wail. "Help," he whines, "please." But his heart tells him they will not help, that they can't see him any more than he can see them. He slams his forehead against the hard surface, and pain explodes through his head anew.

Gunfire.

He can't breathe, and he begins to hyperventilate. He pounds his head harder against the wall, faster. Not this way. Don't let me die this way.

"I'm sorry, Michael," the man who was sobbing says.

Michael?

The name sounds strange at first, then he realizes it's his own. He clings to that truth like an olive branch, but it's not enough to overcome the growing sense of hopelessness.

Another round of gunshots thunders, causing Michael to sway faster, his head hitting the wall over and over again. He closes his eyes and prays to be anywhere else. Like Dorothy in that old musical, he just wants to go home.

There's no place like home.

The internal voice answers, You are *home.*

Minutes pass in silence, save for the thudding of his head against plaster. He opens his eyes and catches a sparkle of light. Footsteps fall softly on the carpet.

"Michael?" a woman with a kind voice calls out.

He wants to answer but can't form any words.

"Michael, don't move, okay?"

He feels a cold hand against his leg, and he lurches forward, screaming.

MICHAEL BOLTED UPRIGHT with his faded blue blanket crumpled in his fists. The blanket was the only thing he possessed from his life before foster homes. He usually kept it folded and hidden in a wooden chest, not under lock and key but certainly not within easy reach. How he had obtained it in his sleep, he hadn't a clue.

The bed sheets were soaked, and so were his pajamas. He groaned at the thought of having to explain to Sam why he needed to wash his sheets but relaxed a little when he didn't smell urine. Feeling the dampness on his pillow, he was amazed at how much sweat had come out of him. "Must have been one hell of a nightmare."

Though he couldn't remember the details, the dream had left him with a feeling of dread, as it had the previous two nights. But this time, the dream was more vivid, as if his mind were trying to show him something it didn't know how.

It can't be happening again. It was just a dream. I haven't touched anyone.

That internal voice that had muttered to him in his dream followed him into the light. It warned him that the opposite was true.

The visions *were* happening again. The nightmare was only the beginning.

CHAPTER 1

The Frederick Watson Juvenile Detention Center was far worse than high school for a small teenager like Jimmy Rafferty. He'd gone from being the victim of one bully—a problem he had solved quite definitively when he sent a bullet through the other boy's face, which caused him no lost sleep at night—to sharing his living quarters, his meals, his showers, his every minute with an army of bullies. His new home was the worst parts of high school times infinity, and it lacked the pretty faces who had never given his ginger one a second look.

The boys at the center gave Jimmy plenty of looks, though. They thought him easy prey. On more occasions than he cared to remember, he'd proven them wrong. Unfortunately, just as many times, he'd proven them right.

"Hey, Gingerbread."

Jimmy didn't have to turn to see who it was. *Finn Fucking Doherty.* The older boy was a tall, wiry kid with bony shoulders, jagged elbows, and a meanness of spirit that surpassed that of all the other rotten people Jimmy had met in his life. The bully was feared by most and separated from the general population on an almost weekly basis. At five foot six, Jimmy was a few inches shorter and several pounds lighter than Finn's lackeys, Roger and a kid everyone called Jackal.

He must have been watching me, waiting for me to come in here. Jimmy sighed. *Here we go again.*

He studied his surroundings. A feeling of déjà vu came over him, leaving a pang of hollowness in his stomach. A row of stalls—complete with busted latches, crude graffiti, and rust spots that looked as if someone had doused the doors with an acid-filled squirt gun—lined the wall to his right. To his left several sinks were mounted beneath a large fake-glass wall mirror. The scene was too much like the one that had led him into the custody of the Commonwealth of Massachusetts in the first place. He glanced at the stalls, wondering if Michael was occupying one of them, even though he knew that wasn't possible.

"I'm talking to you, Gingerbread." Finn stepped closer and pushed him.

Jackal grinned. Roger, whose IQ might have legitimately been too low to warrant his placement at the center over a more nurturing environment, said nothing.

Jimmy slowly let out a breath. *Stay calm.* He headed the same way he had been going before he'd been interrupted, to the piss trough. He stretched out his elastic waistband, pulled down his pants, and with a satisfied moan, sent a steady stream spattering into the urinal. *Just let it play out however it will.*

Hot breath tingled the hairs on the back of his neck. Whoever was behind him hadn't been dumb enough to try to turn him mid-urination, and Jimmy felt a tinge of disappointment for the missed opportunity to piss all over one of them. But he wouldn't be the aggressor. That would make him no better than they were.

He shook off the final drops and tucked himself back in. His fingers curled around the newly made shank he had hidden in a pocket sliced into the band.

"Big, bad Jimmy Rafferty," Jackal said into his ear. "In for murder." He nudged Jimmy and laughed. "You don't look like no killer to me, Raff. You don't look like much of nothing to me."

Jimmy turned and looked at his fellow juvenile delinquent. The punk wore a large toothy grin. His eyes were nervous, darting everywhere. Jimmy stared at him without blinking. He wasn't the least bit scared of Jackal. He knew the difference between tough kids and those just pretending to be tough. But to be fair to Jackal, Jimmy wasn't scared of any of them. In the nine months he'd called the center home, he'd been in thirty-seven fights resulting in many black eyes, two chipped teeth, a twice-broken nose, and four broken ribs. Each time he fought, he felt the pain a little less, hit back a little more, and lost a bit more of the kid he used to be.

He couldn't remember when he stopped caring. He just knew that he no longer did—about anyone or anything, even his own life. At least, telling himself that made the days go by easier.

After the fourth fight, he barely noticed the pain anymore. Besides, pain was only temporary, but shame and cowardice were long-lasting and hurt far worse.

In school, when he'd been pushed around, he had never done anything about it, until he went overboard by blowing off Glenn Rodrigues's head. Since then, he'd learned to enjoy fighting back and that only fools fight fair. Win or lose, he'd walk away—when he *could* walk away—with his chin up and the respect of a few more of his peers.

If at all possible, though, Jimmy would walk out of that restroom and avoid a fight. He stepped around Jackal and swiveled between Finn and Roger to wash his hands in the sink.

A hand latched onto his shoulder and spun him around. "Did you hear me, Raff?" Jackal asked, his face reddening. "Don't you fucking walk away from me when I'm talking to you." He pushed hard enough to make Jimmy stagger back a few steps.

Jimmy clenched his fist tighter around the shank. He forced a smile, holding back his mounting anger. "I heard you. I don't look like a killer to you. The funny thing is, I don't really give two shits what I look like to half a shit like you." He glared at Jackal with a look that was meant to kill, if only it could. "But you really ought to reconsider. Take a good, hard look, Jack*ass*, and maybe think again about what I look like to you."

Jackal's nostrils flared, and he cocked back a fist. "I-I-I... I'll kill you, you little shit!"

Finn laughed and put a hand on his lackey's raised arm. "You've got a set on you, Gingerbread. I'll give you that. But running that mouth don't seem so smart, seeing as there are three of us and only one of you. And you ain't got a gun this time." He put his free arm around Jimmy's shoulders. "So why don't you apologize to Jackal here, and maybe, just maybe, we'll leave you with enough teeth to chew your food with."

Jimmy looked into the twinkling eyes of the maniac and knew the chance for peace had slipped through his fingers. *Oh well. So be it.* "Fuck you, Finn."

Finn straightened and let go of Jimmy. The look of stupid astonishment that came over his face made any pains he might deliver well worth it. Jimmy sniggered under his breath.

"Fuck me?" Finn asked as if he wanted Jimmy to sodomize him. "Fuck *me*?" He stepped up to Jimmy, toe to toe, their mouths close enough to kiss. Grinning, he slammed his fist into Jimmy's gut. "No, fuck *you*, Gingerbread. Fuck you very much."

Jimmy wheezed. *Game on,* he thought as he dropped to one knee, trying to catch his breath. Before Jimmy could rise, Jackal planted a sneaker between his shoulder blades and drove him forward onto his stomach.

Trying to get to his knees, Jimmy roared as Jackal stood on his calves. An arm snaked around Jimmy's neck.

Roger stood off to the side, clapping and laughing as if he were watching a slapstick comedy show. Jackal tightened the headlock as Finn stepped closer and dropped trou.

"I'm doing you a favor, really," Finn said. "A killer like you needs to be prepared for big-boy jail. You're gonna want to know how to make friends there."

Jimmy tried to scream, but the arm around his neck cut off most of his air supply. He thrashed, putting up a show of a fight, but he didn't struggle as much as his attackers might have expected from him. They had pushed him too far. They deserved what they got.

Jimmy let Jackal push his head toward Finn's flaccid penis. Jimmy slid the chewed and jagged point of the plastic spoon he'd stolen from the mess hall partway out of his fist.

"That's it," Finn said, licking his lips. "A little closer. And don't even think about biting, or we'll curb you against the sink."

Seething, Jimmy drove the point of his plastic utensil into Finn's inner thigh as deep as he could, aiming for an artery he believed was in that general vicinity. Finn let out a high-pitched cry. Jackal jerked Jimmy back, his chokehold intensifying. But as he wrenched Jimmy away, the shiv popped out of Finn's thigh, and blood arced through the air.

Jimmy turned and dragged the shiv's point down Jackal's arm. It sliced into the skin, not deep but enough to startle Jackal. He shrieked and released his hold on Jimmy.

As much as Jimmy wanted to finish off Jackal, Finn was the deadlier opponent, and Jimmy had a score to settle with the would-be mouth rapist. The older boy stood with pants clumped around his ankles, mouth agape, and hands pressed over his fresh wound. Blood seeped between his closed fingers.

"Get him, you idiot!" Jackal yelled at Roger, who was still laughing and clapping.

Jimmy shuffled toward Finn on his knees. Jackal grabbed Jimmy's ankle, but Jimmy easily kicked his hand away.

Jimmy latched onto Finn's pant leg and yanked it with all his might. The not-so-mighty Finn fell onto his bare ass. Jimmy hopped on top of him, his knee sliding onto Finn's left wrist. As he raised the spoon, he noticed the point had broken off. He aimed the jagged end at Finn's eyes.

The older boy tried to buck him off while defending his face with his free hand. Jimmy stabbed at Finn's face, reveling in the boy's anguished wails.

Stab. Stab. Stab. Jimmy pierced Finn's hand and face with short, quick jabs of the spoon handle. After ten seconds, Finn's hand fell away, and his eyes looked like meatballs with extra sauce. Jimmy kept stabbing the boy, over and over again.

Something hard collided with Jimmy's skull. He fell off Finn, his ears ringing with a dull tone that muffled all other sounds: a door slamming open, voices shouting, feet stomping. He had no idea what had hit him, not even when it struck him again. The gore-covered spoon fell from his hand. Drool slid over his lip as the restroom blurred.

Swaying, he tried to remember where he was and what he had been doing. Another blow hit his temple. The room changed from white to black over and over, as if the colors were two sides of a spinning coin.

Finally, the black side won.

CHAPTER 2

Michael yelped and fell back against his pillow. For a second, he thought he'd seen someone in a baggy black hoodie standing over him. But after he blinked, the figure was gone.

A leftover from my dream. The chill crept out of his body. He kicked off his blankets. His room was stuffy, unseasonably warm, even for early June. Or maybe he was sweating out the dream.

Michael groaned. *I really hope she doesn't wait until August to turn on the AC.* Living under another's roof always came with a unique set of rules. With Sam, touching the thermostat could get you shot.

The things you learn about people when you move in with them. He never would have pegged Sam for a hot-pink toothbrush. *Maybe a gun-colored one. Or a gun-shaped one.* He shook his head. *That doesn't even make sense.*

Wiping the sleep from his eyes, he jumped out of bed. He slept in nothing but his boxer shorts, which were covered in images of the cartoon dog Marmaduke. Where the underwear had come from, he couldn't recall.

He shuffled to the window and lifted the shade. "Damn," he muttered as he raised one hand to shield his eyes from the bright sun. "What time is it?" He lowered his arm and winced, the light causing temporary blindness. The day was beautiful, a fact he could tell despite his view of the neighbors' tenement apartments and the partial cover their eaves provided.

Michael dropped the shade. The funk he had carried with him from dreamland persisted, and simple tasks, like picking up a shirt off the floor, seemed almost not worth the effort. The shirt was one of several he could have chosen, all long-sleeved to cover as much skin as possible. The smell of detergent still lingered on its neckline. He winced again as he pushed one arm then the other through the sleeves. His body ached as though he'd spent his dreams powerlifting.

His spine crackled as he stretched. He grabbed a pair of wrinkled jeans he'd draped over his headboard, sniffed them, and put them on.

Now for the most important part. From the top drawer of his dresser, Michael removed a pair of black nylon gloves. Like any teenager, he was self-conscious about how he looked in just about everything he wore, but the weirded-out glances were worth the severe decrease in visions he'd experienced since he had decided to wear gloves and long sleeves even in the dead heat of summer. Kids looked at him as if he were a freak, but it wasn't much different from the way they looked at him before he started wearing them. Adults stuck their noses up at him as if he were diseased. Each time he had a seizure, Michael woke to constipated faces or, worse, expressions that cried out with false pity, as if he were an abandoned puppy just waiting for some do-gooder to champion his cause so that the do-gooder, not Michael, could feel good about himself.

People suck. I shouldn't give a shit what they think. As often as he told himself that, it didn't change the fact that he did care.

Still, he wasn't going anywhere without the gloves. *It's too sunny for black.* He reached back into the drawer and pulled out a light-gray pair. He rolled up his shirtsleeves, donned the gloves, their ends almost touching his elbows, then rolled his sleeves back down over the gloves.

Michael smiled. *I may not be the coolest kid in town, but hey, if they're good enough for Rogue...* He frowned. *But Rogue's a chick.* He scanned his brain for a male comic book hero who had to wear gloves. *Wildfire? No, he had to wear a whole suit.*

With a sigh and a shrug, he dug out some white tube socks and his black sneakers. He sniffed both and cringed, the socks falling way outside his cleanliness test. He put them on anyway, intending to give them a once-over with bathroom spray before heading out.

He walked through the sunlit living room with a hand over his eyes. The dining-study-hangout-reading-all-purpose-but-computer room separated the living room and Michael's room from the other two bedrooms, bathroom, and tiny kitchen.

He stopped in the doorway and thought of Tessa, as he did every morning. The thought of her coming to live with them seemed like a pipe dream. *If she ever gets out of that awful place.* So far, he hadn't seen any sign that she ever would.

Still, her circumstances had improved once she'd shown that she was no danger to others and had been transferred from Framingham to the less-intense Brentworth facility there in Fall River. Whether she was a danger to herself remained to be seen.

As he entered the kitchen, still only half awake, he nearly bumped into Sam. She was dressed in black pants and a stylish black button-down, like a waitress at a fancy restaurant or a metrosexual vampire. The rest might have been her work clothes, but Sam tended to dress more conservatively than that shirt suggested when she was heading into work. Her badge was pinned to her hip, but she wasn't wearing her gun.

He blinked a few times. "Oh. You're here?"

"Very observant." Sam laughed. "I'll make a detective out of you yet."

"I've seen enough crime, thanks. I don't need to go making a career out of it."

"Yeah, but with that unique skill of yours, you could be the best there ever was."

Michael stared at her solemnly. "You're the best detective there ever was."

"How nice of—"

"No, wait." Michael smirked. "The Question was the best there ever was."

Sam frowned. "What?"

"Nope, you're right. Sherlock Holmes was the best there ever was. No, sorry. Batman was the best detective there ever was. So, Batman, Sherlock Holmes, The Question... um, Agatha Christie..."

Sam had to cover her mouth to not spit out her coffee. "Agatha Christie! She was an author. Mysteries, true, but not a detective." She punched Michael softly in the arm. "You're a jerk. Those other three weren't even real people."

Michael rubbed his bicep. "Ouch! I'm calling DCF."

"Very funny," Sam said flatly. "And since when do you read Agatha Christie? There's no pictures of men in tights in her books."

"I am very learned." Michael kept a straight face for a good two seconds then sniggered. "Nah, I'm just kidding. I don't read that crap."

"Don't knock it 'til you try it."

Michael huffed. He slid past her and opened a cupboard. "We're out of Frosted Figments," he grumbled. "Guess it's Rice Crispers." He found a bowl and a spoon and carried them, the cereal, and a carton of milk from the fridge to the small table. There, he poured himself a heaping bowl of the crispy rice cereal. Michael checked the expiration date on the milk. Though it hadn't expired, he opened the carton and took a whiff. *Someone* liked to leave the milk sitting on the counter. He sighed. *It's her milk. She can do whatever she wants with it.* Smelling nothing off-putting, Michael decided to chance it. He drowned his crunchy rice flakes in the liquid and dug in.

"Don't eat too much," Sam said. "I figured we could get some lunch, maybe eat outside on such a gorgeous day. That was me betting you'd get up on time for once."

"Don't do that." Michael shifted in his seat then stirred the cereal with his spoon.

"Do what?"

"Sound like a mother. It doesn't suit you."

Sam looked as though someone had run over her dog, but she quickly composed herself.

Michael stared into his bowl, ashamed. He hadn't intended to hurt her feelings. He didn't even know he *could* hurt her feelings. "I'm just teasing." He laughed, the tone of it as hollow as his excuses.

Sam was the best friend he could ask for, surely the only one he ever really had. And she was great for advice, making sure he did the right thing, and generally just being there for him. But when she tried—sometimes too hard, he thought—to show she cared, things just got uncomfortable.

I know you care. He gave her a warm smile. *You don't have to try so hard.* Choking back the sentiment welling inside him, Michael changed the subject. "Not working today?"

"I'm always on call. I'll probably stop by the courthouse later to observe a hearing on one of my collars, a particularly nasty individual I'd like to see burn, but that's not until two. Other than that, my schedule is pretty much free."

"We need to find you a man... or a woman... or whichever. I'm cool either way."

"Are you being serious right now?" Sam huffed and placed her hands on her hips. "In the time you've known me, I've had *boy*friends, not that that's any of your business. Besides, who has the time?"

"I'm just saying, you should do something besides go after bad guys twenty-four, seven. Maybe try yoga."

"Thank you, Mr. Health Guru. When did you become a life coach?"

"Just saying."

"Crime's finally been down since... well, these last six months. I do have more time..." Sam crossed her arms. "Oh, why am I even discussing this with you?"

"Menopause?"

Sam laughed. "I bet you don't even know what that is. Anyway, crime's sure to be on the rise again real soon. Summer's basically here, and it's supposed to be a blistering-hot one. The heat always brings out the crazies, and this may be the warmest summer we've ever had."

Michael grunted. "Humph. And you don't believe in global warming."

"I don't *not* believe in it. I just remember how many times I had to shovel out my car last winter."

The coffee machine sputtered. Michael guessed it was her third cup of the morning. He had tried it once, black like she liked it, and found it so bitter that he couldn't understand how anyone could drink it. But to Sam, it seemed sweeter than sugar.

"Janet over at DCF is getting a lot of calls about you."

"Huh?" Michel froze mid-bite, processing Sam's interruption. He swallowed the half-chewed cereal in a gulp that scratched his throat. "Yeah, no doubt a bunch of freaks who want to adopt a freak." He shook his head. "I'll be eighteen in a couple of years. Can't I just stay here until then?" A pang of sadness caused his eyes to fill with tears. He blinked and looked away. "That is, if you still want me here?"

Sam came out from behind the counter and took a seat at the table. "Of course, Michael. This is your home." She started to reach for his hand.

He tensed but didn't pull away. To his relief, she did, instead using the hand to tuck her long brown hair behind her ear.

She chuckled. "You know, Janet did say a carnival called for you. They didn't even try to disguise who they were."

Michael groaned. "Great."

Sam's smile faded. "I'm sorry. I shouldn't have told you that." She slapped the table. "But cheer up! From what I understand, you're not going anywhere anytime soon."

"Good." Michael shoveled a heaping spoonful of cereal into his mouth. With the food still stuffing his cheeks, he said, "'Cause frankly, I don't know how you got by without me."

Sam laughed with real humor. He smiled. He had heard that more often lately. It made him think that maybe she really didn't mind having him around. He helped out where he could—doing dishes, vacuuming, and cleaning up after himself, and laundry, though he hated folding clothes—but he was kind of limited in what he could do, at fifteen and with no work experience or prospects.

Maybe I can get a paper route. He scratched his head. *With the internet, do people even still get the paper delivered?* He shivered. Delivering papers would probably bring him into contact with people. He doubted he could just whip rolled-up bundles at front porches like paperboys did in old movies.

Sam really needs to get Netflix, or at least HBO. He sighed. *I wonder if she'd let me watch half those shows, filled with F-bombs, sex, and gore, all the good stuff. Would she even try to stop me?* He sighed again. *I need a job.*

"You okay?" Sam asked.

"Yeah." For a moment, Michael considered broaching the subject with her then buried himself again in his cereal. Sam would just say what she'd said the last time he'd brought it up: "You worry about school. You'll have plenty of time to work later."

They sat in silence, Michael eating his cereal methodically and Sam sipping her coffee. Thoughts of his nightmare returned. He was pretty sure the woman's voice had belonged to Sam.

"What's wrong?"

Her words snapped him from his reverie. He blinked then raised his head. "I'm fine. It's nothing."

She raised an eyebrow. "You disappeared on me for a second there."

"Yeah, just daydreaming."

"Out with it. What's on your mind?"

"You knew my parents, right?" Michael was just as surprised by the question as Sam seemed to be.

She sat up straight then sighed and slouched back in her seat. "I wouldn't say I knew them, Michael."

"But you do know about them, don't you? How they died, I mean?"

Sam frowned and stared into her mug. "Where is this coming from all of a sudden?"

"I don't know. You sorry you asked what was on my mind?" Michael stirred the last bits of cereal with his spoon, watching as they spiraled in a whirlpool. "I just... I just wonder sometimes."

Sam leaned forward, resting her chin on her palm, one finger wrapping over her mouth. "About what, exactly?"

Michael sighed. "You know... if either of them was like me."

"You mean—"

"You know what I mean."

"That," Sam said, sitting up and folding her hands on the table, "I honestly don't know."

Michael leaned forward, huddling over his bowl. "I wonder other things too. Who they were, what they were like..." He raised an eyebrow, watching Sam closely as he said, "How they died."

"Michael—"

"I know, I know. Some kind of accident. Same old BS." He huffed and crossed his arms. "I'm not stupid, you know. I've looked into it online, but I can't find anything about any Turcottes dying and leaving behind a boy named Michael. So either I'm missing something obvious, or Michael Turcotte isn't even my real name."

"Your name was changed when you entered the foster system."

Michael rolled his eyes. "Duh? I figured that much. But it's not that simple, is it? I know what you do and how you must have met me. The last time I checked, you weren't getting called out to the scenes of accidents. Not now, not then."

Sam stared at him. Michael could almost see the gears winding in her head. She was going to try to avoid the issue again, to protect him, or so she would claim. *Not this time. I won't let her.* After all they'd been through together, he didn't need her protection. He was old enough to have answers. He deserved the truth.

"That was twelve years ago. I wasn't doing then what I'm doing—"

"Sam," Michael said softly. "Please, no lies."

Sam flinched as if she'd been struck and slumped in her seat. "These things you ask... they're complicated. I don't want to lie to you."

"Then don't."

Sam paused, and the corners of her mouth twitched. "You looked it up online, huh? Like I said, we'll make a detective out of you yet."

Michael set his jaw. "Sam?"

"Okay, okay." She took a deep breath and scraped a fingernail against her mug. "I guess I always knew you'd corner me with this sooner or later. But the truth may not be an easy pill to swallow. You have to believe me when I say I never told you before because I was looking out for your best interests. So was changing your name, your *last* name. Your parents did name you Michael, and I have no reason to suspect they didn't love you."

Michael almost choked up, but he suppressed the rising wave. "Go on."

Sam put her hand over his. "Let me think about this and how best to tell you about it. The time is as much for me as it is for you, so I can get my words right. No secrets. No lies. No spin. Just tact, I suppose, which is not one of my strong points. And I want to give you time to reconsider whether you really want to know and are ready to know the whole, ugly truth."

"I'm ready."

She nodded. "I'm sure you are. Just one day is all I ask. Sleep on it."

The idea of sleeping with the way his dreams had been lately made him sick to his stomach. He pulled his hand away. "Fine. One day."

"Fair enough. Thank you." Sam stood. "Now, if you're not too full of cereal, where would you like to go for lunch?"

CHAPTER 3

On her way to the courthouse, Sam tried to think of the best way to tell Michael how his parents had died. "Your dear old dad unloaded a full clip into your mom and her boyfriend when he found them in bed together" wasn't likely to have a positive impact on a growing boy's psyche.

And the brutal murder of his foster parents did?

She sighed. She could do nothing about the damage already done, but adding to it seemed a cardinal sin.

Still, she had to stop treating him like a child. In some ways, Michael was more adult than most adults. But in others, he was still just a kid. The thought of him, even when he was frustrated with her, brought a smile to her face. *How can I tell him about his parents after all he's been through? He's finally starting to heal.*

Leaving him in the dark about his past seemed equally wrong. *Should I even be the one to tell him?* She shook her head, scolding herself for her stupidity. *Who else is there?*

Pulling into the parking garage adjacent to the Fall River Judicial Complex, Sam was greeted by a morose-looking fellow in a gray shirt with a patch over the left breast pocket that read Mel. She had met the man a dozen times already, and although he was always pleasant, she never failed to have to read that name tag as he approached to avoid looking like a self-absorbed bitch.

Mel stepped out of a booth barely big enough for one. "Five dollars, please," he said, looking up from the ticket in his hand. His eyes lit up. "Oh, it's you, Detective! I'm sorry. I should have recognized the car. Just give me a minute, and I'll lift the bar."

"Thanks, Mel." Sam smiled back. "How are things?"

"Eh? Well, the back is aching, the hemorrhoids are burning, the wife is nagging, and the kids are... well, they're away at college, so at least there's some peace there. Unless you count the hell it's putting my wallet through. You got kids?"

Sam had to think about that one. "Yes and no."

Mel laughed. "Ha! I hear ya. Sometimes, I'd like to disown mine too." He hit a button, and the gate rose. "Have a great day, Detective."

"I'll catch you later, Mel." She drove into the garage and parked in a spot reserved for officers. After getting out, she clipped her badge onto her belt and straightened her holster. Then she headed to the courthouse.

Out front, a fire engine, an ambulance, and one of her precinct's squad cars sat in line with the curb, lights flashing. Officer Ronald Tagliamonte leaned against the police car, sipping from a Styrofoam coffee cup. He nodded at Sam after she made her way through the crowd in the courtyard. Lawyers in cheap suits stood talking with jittery clients, while court officers corralled everyone away from the front doors.

"What's going on?" Sam asked.

He swallowed and let out one of those annoying gasps of satisfaction jerks made after having a drink. Tagliamonte was not a jerk, though, so Sam mentally forgave the rudeness.

He wiped his mouth with his sleeve. "Someone called in a bomb threat. The fire department is finishing its sweep now. We should be all set shortly."

Bomb threat? Sam realized that she hadn't been listening to her scanner on her drive over. The courthouse, a gray stone monstrosity that looked as though someone had tipped a giant cinder block on its side and added another on top of it, was as cold and lifeless as the rest of the city, despite being the newest development on the block. "Another one, huh? Shit's getting old." The new courthouse, like the old one before it, received bomb threats on average once per week.

"I assumed that's what brought you here," Tagliamonte said.

"Nah, today's my day off. I'm just here to check on the status of one of my collars."

"Billings?"

"You got it."

"I hope you don't mind me saying so, but I wish someone would blow that son of a bitch up."

Sam glared at him. "Officially, I cannot condone that kind of talk." She kept her straight face a moment longer, watching Tagliamonte squirm, then punched him in the shoulder. "But since today's my day off, unofficially, I couldn't agree more."

The officer relaxed and laughed. He cleared his throat and turned his head toward the courthouse doors. "Well, here they come now. Looks like Billings will have his day in court after all."

"Well, I'm armed, so if he tries anything..."

"We can only hope. Make sure he fries."

"It's just a plea hearing today, but assuming he pleads guilty, sentencing is just around the corner. Every judge knows better than to go lenient on a cop killer like Billings, unless they want to see some good ol'-fashioned street justice."

Four firefighters exited the building and made their way to the truck parked behind Tagliamonte's cruiser. Their visors were all down. One of them was small, too small for the uniform he—*no, I think that's a she*—was wearing. The yellow coat hung down to her knees and the sleeves two inches past her wrists.

Having done her time as a beat cop, Sam knew most of the guys over at the FDFR and kept herself apprised of the new hires as best she could. None she knew matched the small-statured figure, and in full uniform with visors down, the rest were similarly unidentifiable.

But the oversized coat struck Sam as more than a mere peculiarity. She didn't doubt that Fall River's repetitive budget cuts might have created the need for hand-me-down uniforms, but the firefighter—the whole team of firefighters, actually—made her go on high alert. The way they carried themselves, their shaded faces, and something more that she couldn't quite put her finger on made her Spidey sense tingle.

"I can't stop thinking about what he did to those girls."

"Huh?" Sam turned back to Tagliamonte. "What was that?"

"The girls we found during the raid." Tagliamonte took a long swig from his coffee. "That man is a monster. He deserves the death penalty, if only Massachusetts had a death penalty. Think maybe the judge will make an exception?"

"If only it worked that way." Sam returned her gaze to the firefighters, who had just about finished boarding their truck. Even as the truck's taillights began to fade, her eyes followed. "Did something look off with those firefighters to you?"

"I didn't notice. But the truck is from the Third. I'd recognize it anywhere."

The court officers propped open the doors and called everyone back inside.

"Well," she said, "it looks like your job here is done. I'll be heading inside. Do me a favor, though, would you?"

"Of course, Detective." Tagliamonte straightened and stood at attention.

"Check in at the Third and make sure everything is order. Something's bothering me about that truck. It's probably nothing, but..."

"Sure," Officer Tagliamonte said. "I'll head straight there."

"Leave a message for me with dispatch if you even smell something not right."

As he turned to leave, a percussive boom split the air. The ground shook beneath her feet. Instinctively, Sam ducked and covered her head, half expecting the courthouse to topple down on top of her. Through the crossed arms over her face, she peered at the façade.

The courthouse was still standing and none the worse for wear. Shielding the sun from her eyes with one hand, Sam scanned the horizon. A few blocks to the north, thick black smoke billowed high into the air.

Tagliamonte hopped into his car and turned up the radio. Sam leaned in to listen.

The dispatcher said, "All units, we have a 4-8, Code Orange, in progress, 352 Pleasant Street. Fire department unresponsive. Neighboring jurisdictions being hailed." Pause. "Code Black in progress, 40 Stage Hill Road, St. Mary's Credit Union. All available units report in for immediate assignment."

"Armed robbery and arson?" Tagliamonte asked. "It looks like this bomb threat might have been a diversion."

Sam rubbed her chin. "Maybe." She tapped the gun at her hip. "But go. The fire department can wait. There may be civilians in immediate need." She backed out of the way.

"I'm on it." Tagliamonte slammed his door shut, hit the siren, and sped off.

Sam headed into the courthouse. In the foyer, metal detectors beeped as visitors removed belts and emptied change from their pockets.

"Probably just a gas main," Sherman, one of the older security guards at the metal detectors, announced. "Please form a line at each station, and we will get you all inside as soon as possible."

The queue had slowed to a crawl. Sam bypassed it by holding up her badge for the guards at the gate. A fairly new one named Corey waved her through without so much as a second glance. Guns weren't allowed in the courthouse, but her gut said she might need hers. She stuck close to a lawyer as she hurried past the court officers. The metal detector sounded, but she flashed her badge and ID, and no one paid her any attention.

Hordes of people waited at the elevators, so she took the stairs. The plea hearing for Billings was being held on the fourth floor. A ruthless drug dealer, Rex Billings had literally dismembered his competition, leaving a massive trail of evidence in his wake. Sam didn't hate the man too much for that, but she wanted to see him burn for the innocent bystanders he'd maimed or killed simply because they had unknowingly stepped into his warpath.

But the hearing would have to wait until she'd satisfied that creeping itch that told her something was amiss. The second-floor landing afforded her a view of much of the foyer. She stared over the railing at the shuffling line, a semblance of order returning as people were processed like groceries on a conveyor belt. Most of them seemed nervous and fidgety, their glances furtive and their hands fumbling in pockets to pull out identification, cell phones, and other paraphernalia. The charged air was to be expected, given the circumstances that had brought most to the building, so Sam focused on those trying extra hard to appear calm.

A man with a shaved head—at least where hair still grew, for his head was as much scar tissue as it was healthy skin—caught her eye. He stuck out like a dark cloud on a sunny day, and he must have known he would. His eyes were like those of a pit bull bred and beaten mean for the fights. One of them swirled a milky white, scarred over but still seemingly alive with sight. The entire left side of the man's face looked as if it had been held against a grill. He wore jeans and a T-shirt and had a spiderweb tattoo over his right elbow. A series of small red circles marred his left elbow crease as if someone had used him as a pincushion. She imagined him carrying a piece for no other reason than he looked like a criminal. But trying to get a weapon through security with a face like his was akin to madness, and he didn't look that stupid.

His eyes met hers, and he seemed to read her thoughts. She started then chuckled as he turned away.

Seeing criminals at a courthouse? Sam rolled her eyes. *No biggie there. Come on, Sam. You're just being paranoid. You've been on edge since Masterson almost got the jump on you. He's dead, and there's no such thing as ghosts, so stop spooking yourself.*

Sam's uneasiness began to fade, but her suspicion lingered. She decided to watch the man and find out what business he had at the courthouse that day. She leaned over the railing and spotted him again at the metal detectors. He held up his arms while Corey patted him down. The guard pulled an empty money clip off the man's pocket then passed the wand over him again. Corey was thorough to the point of intrusiveness but found nothing. The guards ushered the guy through, and he headed for the stairs.

Straight toward Sam.

Corey glared at the man as he walked up the stairs, perhaps sensing the same bad mojo Sam did. Sam tried not to stare at the man, glancing about to observe the scene, but when her gaze returned to him, she found him watching her. He saw her, not just as a person at the courthouse, not just as a cop, but as an enemy, taking her in with a cold and calculating mind.

The assumption chilled her to the bone. But fear had never halted her in her duty, and her gut had been right too many times to be discounted. He brushed by her so close she could smell his deodorant. She caught a whiff of something else, something like battery acid, as she turned to follow.

He made his way past a woman in a gray business suit. She was a young, pretty woman with fine black hair and a not-so-fine suit that hugged her curves a little too tightly as if it were an ill-fitting hand-me-down or she were trying to look a touch slutty. Her face wore the sour, almost-angry look of determination many lawyers with blue-collar beginnings carried through law school and into the profession. Still, Sam thought her too young to be an attorney. *Probably an intern, still in school.*

Sam noticed a subtle interaction between the woman and Scarface, a twitch at best, that hinted at recognition. The way the intern's grip tightened around her black briefcase as though he might steal it suggested fear, not familiarity. But her half nod as he passed her suggested something more. Scarface headed up the spiral staircase to the third floor.

"Hector?" A young boy, about four feet tall with spikey black hair, caterpillar eyebrows, and a guileless smile, hurried up to Scarface.

Sam got as good a look at the boy as she could as she continued past them to the announcement board outside the civil clerk's office. She flipped absently through the case list, her ears straining to filter their conversation out of the murmuring crowd.

"How many times I gotta tell you, kid?" Hector asked in a harsh whisper. "No. Fucking. Names."

The boy lowered his head as if scolded by a parent, but Hector didn't look old enough to be the kid's father. *A brother maybe?*

The boy brightened as he patted a stuffed manila folder under his arm. "Val already made the handoff. I have it. I'm ready."

Hector glared at him. "All right, already. Keep it down." He slapped the boy's cheek, not hard, but hard enough to hear. "As for being ready, you'd better be." His nostrils flared as he studied the boy. "Humph. We'll see soon enough. Go on up."

The boy grinned then bounded up the stairs. Hector followed, ascending at a much more relaxed pace.

Sam tailed him, but she kept her distance. Something was going down. *But what? And how many are involved?* She had no grounds to detain any of them. For all she knew, they could have been there for honest, legitimate reasons.

She thought about calling for backup, but she wasn't even on duty, and she hadn't witnessed anything criminal. Also, it would pull limited resources from the other crimes she had heard over Tagliamonte's radio. *Crimes conveniently happening in the city at this very moment, in broad daylight.*

She shook her head. The crimes, the courthouse, everything felt like a game board, and she was being played. But she needed something to act on. *If I keep following this Hector fellow, I'm guessing I'll have it soon enough. Hopefully, it won't be too late.* She smirked. *Damn it, Michael! Why couldn't I have been blessed with your ability?*

On the fourth floor, Hector nodded to another man sitting against the wall near Courtroom 12 with his nose in a book. The twenty-something-year-old was dressed in skinny jeans and a shirt with a monkey ninja on it. When he caught sight of his comrade, he nodded back.

That's at least four. Sam didn't like the odds stacking against her.

Hector didn't stop but headed straight toward a man wearing a gray maintenance uniform and black boots. The label over his broad chest read Earl. He was well close to seven feet tall and built like a lineman, his muscles having muscles of their own. He seemed older than the rest, maybe just shy of thirty. His smooth, dark skin fit him like latex on an Olympian.

Taking him down wouldn't be easy. *I bet he could bench-press eight of me.*

Hector extended his hand. Earl glanced around furtively, his eyes lingering on Sam a half second longer than anyone else. Sam fiddled with her phone, pretending not to be paying any attention to them. Earl took Hector's hand in his. They performed some kind of ridiculous, ritualistic handshake that foolishly drew attention to the transaction taking place.

Drugs? Sam knew a handoff when she saw one. Earl had given Hector something small enough to be a dime bag of whatever substance they liked to abuse. But to sneak drugs into a courthouse took a level of balls combined with a complete lack of mental functioning.

If not drugs, then what? She undid the snap on her holster, which protruded like a tumor from her hip, its only cover the end of her suit jacket. On the front of her opposite hip, her shield glimmered in the fluorescent lighting each time the pendulum swing of her jacket revealed it.

Hector leaned forward and whispered something into his friend's ear. Earl nodded, and the two parted and went off in opposite directions.

Not one to switch horses midstream, Sam stuck like a tick on Hector. He entered a small alcove with a supply closet at the end of it. There, he revealed the object that had been given to him: a key. He unlocked the door and disappeared inside the closet.

There's too many of them, and something big is going down right now. Deciding it was time to call for backup, she brought out her phone and punched in her passcode.

Before she could dial, a baseball-glove-sized hand snatched her phone away. With her other hand, she tried to draw her weapon. A hard metal object pressed into the small of her back.

"Don't do that," a man's deep voice commanded.

Sam froze. Slowly, she raised her hands.

"That's a good girl." The man behind her, who she guessed was Earl, moved closer, his body eclipsing the light and casting a shadow over Sam. She felt her gun slide from her holster. "Good." He pressed what had to be the barrel of a gun harder against her back. "Now move." He shoved her toward the supply closet door. "Open it."

She obeyed. The door swung open to reveal another gun trained on Sam.

"Looks like we've found our volunteer," Hector said, his sinister smile warping his face into something akin to a Halloween mask—burned clown meets freshly turned zombie. "Take off your jacket."

Sam did, making no sudden movements. She laid it on top on the shelf beside her.

Looking past her, Hector said, "Open her shirt."

Large, rough hands untucked her blouse. When those hands reached around her for her buttons, they felt like tree branches jabbing at her ribs.

"Easy," Hector told his partner in crime. "We'll need to close it back up. Good thing this bitch likes dark colors, no see-through shit."

The hands roamed over her breasts and stomach, working the buttons more gently. The sudden veering toward tenderness didn't make her feel any less violated. One by one, Earl undid each button until her shirt hung open, exposing her black bra and the large scar across her belly that had come from the last guy who'd torn off her shirt against her will, a guy who would never tear anyone's clothes off again.

Earl pinned Sam's arms behind her in a move called a double chicken wing, one she had learned at the academy. The hold jarred her shoulders, and she winced.

Hector tucked his gun into his pants and stepped closer. Clenching her teeth, unwilling to show the scumbag any fear, she met his gaze with all the will she could muster as he moved to stand inches from her face. His breath, hot and stale, reeked of garlic and banana peppers.

He squeezed her left breast as he slid his tongue up her cheek. His hand ventured toward her crotch. "Mmm," he moaned, sniffing her hair. "You're pretty tasty for an older bit—"

Sam drove her knee into his groin. He went down, coughing and groaning. Seizing her moment, Sam slammed her head back into the phony janitor's chin. As he lifted her an inch off the ground, she kicked wildly, her heels hammering his shins. She growled and thrashed and struggled with everything she had.

The huge man chuckled as he crushed the air from her lungs. She hadn't fazed him in the least. His grip relaxed long enough for him to shift her weight and slam her against a shelf lined with cleaning supplies. Blazing agony shot through her side. Earl was already reeling her back for another swing as her upper torso swept the shelf's contents onto the floor, some falling onto the still-downed Hector. Her fingers searched for anything she could use as a weapon.

"Help!" she shouted.

Earl smothered her in a bear hug that nearly broke her in two. Visions of her ribcage caving in and her spine snapping like a telephone pole in a lightning storm sent her into a frenzy. She tried to scream again, but his massive arms squeezed tighter. When Earl lifted her higher into the air, she arched her back, pressing her stomach against his arms in an effort to create space between them, but it didn't help. Her head began to swim in pool of hazy light and muffled sound.

Hector managed to get to his feet. "You bitch!" He threw a vicious haymaker across her jaw.

Her lip split open and rained blood. Hector followed the strike with a left to her stomach. Sam gasped for air then bent over, her upper body swaying like a child's inflatable punching bag in a breeze.

"Let up a bit," Hector said. "We need her awake. And grab her cuffs. They may come in handy."

Earl relaxed his hold, and Sam wheezed in a long breath. Her cheek throbbed, and her chest and stomach muscles felt as if they'd torn from overexertion. Her head swayed as if it were a thousand-pound weight on her toothpick neck, her chin sinking like an anchor. After a few seconds, her heart rate steadied, and her breathing eased.

When she was able to raise her head, Sam saw what Hector had planned for her. *My God!*

Three rectangular blocks of what looked like C-4 plastic explosives were affixed to some kind of mesh corset. Wires linked each block to a small metal box with copper wire spiraling from it.

Hector must have read her recognition in her expression. "Yes." He smiled in a way that made it seem as if his upper teeth curled over his lower lip. "Now be a good girl and keep your fucking bitch mouth shut, or I swear to God, I'll bring this whole fucking building down on top of everyone in it." He reached down and pulled a square device from an FDFR duffel bag.

"Why?" Sam asked between sporadic coughs. "What's this all about?"

"You'll see." Hector again flashed that ugly, wicked grin, all toothy and full of a sadist's zeal. "In fact, you're going to have a front-row seat."

CHAPTER 4

The Fall River Public Library was within a few miles of the YM-CA, the Boys and Girls Club, a police station, and an elementary school, but that seemed to have no impact on the number of drug deals negotiated on its back steps. And the front steps weren't much better. After stepping over a homeless man sleeping on the second stair and scooting past the mentally ill woman who spat curses at everyone, Michael made it to the heavy iron doors of the century-old building. Everything about the library was hard: hard doors, hard walls, hard steps, and all around them, hard lives.

Michael's visions had taught him that many of the city's unfortunates had likely been victims. And though he wished he could help them all, he was just a lonely and timid teenage boy. He had a "bleeding heart," Sam liked to say. If that meant he was some kind of wuss for caring about those who got the shitty end of the stick in life, he was fine with that.

He opened the door and jumped back, letting the door slam shut again. On the other side of it was the same figure he'd seen in his room that morning, the leftover from his dream. Only the person was real, and only a few inches of wood separated him from Michael.

I'm losing it. He shook out his anxiety, though some lingered as he reached for the door a second time.

The door flew open, nearly hitting Michael in the nose. He jumped out of the way.

"Excuse me," a tall, snooty-looking lady said without stopping. She hurried down the steps without a backward glance.

Michael laughed, beginning to feel foolish for his childish fear. He caught the door on its back swing and propped it open with his foot. Peering in, he saw no one. *There are no boogeymen in black hoodies haunting me.* Rolling away the tension in his shoulders and neck, he stepped into the library.

The air tasted stale, as if even that needed to be preserved, chronicled, and categorized for its historical value. The foyer, poorly lit by yellow bulbs that made everything glossy appear coated with urine, was a stark contrast to the bright, warm, cheery day outside.

Fall River made the best day bleak. Or maybe his thoughts were to blame for that. They always had a way of making things heavy and cold. His visions, which he took pride in having avoided entirely for the last two months, had shown him so much evil that it seemed to take form and lurk in shadows beside him, a monster creeping and toiling in the darkness, feeding on what was left of his soul.

But nightmares, not visions, were the malady *du jour*. He needed them to stop but couldn't shake the feeling they were trying to show him something. While his visions had always foretold the future, Michael wondered if his repeating dream served as a window to the past. *If so, why is it so dark? What is it I'm supposed to see?*

So far, he'd seen nothing but heard plenty enough to frighten him—sounds in a sea of endless black. Gunshots. Sobbing. People speaking incoherent blabber. A feeling of complete isolation despite all that. No one helping.

It's just a dream, he told himself. *It probably has nothing to do with me or my past, just some deep-seated fear of... of what? Being buried alive? Left all alone?* He sighed, wondering why his brain had to torment him even in his waking hours.

After moving past the disheveled circulation desk, Michael halted when he saw the artwork on the cover of the graphic novel in the librarian's hands. The Occultist! *He had to wear a glove... I think. I hadn't even thought to go into the Dark Horse guys.*

The librarian, an out-of-shape thirtysomething with bad hair plugs and so much back fat that it made him appear hunchbacked, looked up from the book and stared at Michael, apparently annoyed at being interrupted. "Can I help you?" he asked.

"Uh, sorry," Michael said, chuckling uneasily. He scratched the back of his neck. "Just noticing the graphic novel you've got there. *The Occultist.* I haven't read much with him in it."

The librarian raised an eyebrow. "Are you a fan of Dr. Strange?"

"I wouldn't say he's my favorite, but I like him well enough."

"This guy's way better."

"Cool. Maybe I'll check it out when you're done with it."

"You should." The librarian grunted and went back to his reading.

Michael turned and headed through the maze of oddly placed magazine stands, card catalogs, and podiums highlighting staff selections. Sitting behind the reference desk of the research area, a thin, plain-looking lady about Sam's age was marking index cards at the backs of thick volumes.

As Michael approached, she looked up at him through round bifocals that magnified her eyes. Her brow furrowed, and her nose crinkled as if she'd smelled something unpleasant. "May I help you?" she asked, not quite pleasantly. Her sharp features—pointed chin, high cheekbones, thin nose, and straw hair that curved to a point like falcon wings along her jaw line—reminded him of the Wicked Witch from *The Wizard of Oz.* But she had a kindly smile that matched the gleam in her eyes.

"Hi," Michael said then drew a blank. He hadn't really thought out how he'd ask for what he wanted. "I'm doing some research... um, I'd like to do some research into Fall River crime."

She nodded. "God knows there's enough of it. Any particular crime? Timeframe? Lizzie Borden is a popular topic among students for school proj—"

"No, I mean real crime. I mean, not real crime... well, I mean, I want real crime, and Lizzie Borden was *real* crime, but I want to look into more modern stuff. Major crimes mostly."

"Ah. I see." Her eyes rolled toward the ceiling.

Michael tilted his head. He wondered if she thought the answer was scrawled somewhere in the water-stained tiles. He forced himself not to look up then cleared his throat to regain her attention. He was beginning to think all librarians lacked people skills, not that he was one to judge. "I just want to, you know... I just want to learn more about crime in the city during my lifetime."

"Do I know you?" the librarian asked.

Michael rubbed the back of his neck. "I don't think so." *Maybe it's me. Why am I always so awkward with strangers? And adults? And just about everybody?*

"Well, uh, Mister..."

"Michael," he offered.

The librarian smiled and nodded. "Well, Michael, we can certainly help you with your research." She turned toward a college-aged blonde, who was returning a book to a high shelf nearby. "Katie, could you please help Michael here? He's researching recent crime in Fall River. Probably best to start with the Newsbank database."

Michael's stared at the younger woman's long neck, which was exposed on the sides where her ponytail didn't cover. His gaze went down over her hourglass figure to the most perfect ass he'd ever seen. When he realized what he was doing, he turned away, blushing.

"Certainly," Katie said, bouncing over to them. She thrust out her hand. "I'm Katie."

Michael gave it a feeble shake. "Michael," he squeaked.

"Nice to meet you, Michael. Follow me." With that same bounce in her step, Katie led him to a computer.

Michael followed, casting a final glance back at the older librarian. He could have sworn she'd been watching him with that narrow gaze and had looked away just when he had turned to face her, but the view of Katie's ass in front of him was all he needed to forget the suspicious old coot.

Katie pulled out the chair in front of the computer. "Have a seat."

Michael sat and scooted forward. On the screen was the library's homepage. Katie leaned close and pointed at the screen, one of her breasts brushing his shoulder. He could feel the heat rise in his cheeks. *She is so hot!*

She jabbed her finger at the screen. "Click right here."

"Wh-Wh-Where?" He had enough trouble talking to girls at all, never mind one so unbelievably beautiful.

"Did I lose you for a moment there?" Katie asked. "Here, silly." She tapped the screen again. Her smile faded just a little, and Michael detected a hint of impatience.

"S-Sorry." Michael moved the mouse over the words Fall River Herald Newsbank and clicked. A search screen appeared.

"What kind of crimes are you looking into?"

"Just the big ones, where people may have died... I think. To start anyway."

"Oh, juicy!" She smiled again. "But aren't you on summer break?"

Michael thought fast then said, "Extra credit," though his voice rose as if it had been a question.

She nodded. "Well, are you looking for any specific timeframe? Like a range of years or anything?"

"Just since I've been alive."

"And how old are you?"

"Sixteen," Michael blurted, the lie coming out before he could stop it. He didn't know why he'd lied. But when she smiled at him, he sort of knew why.

"Well, Fall River and the county as a whole have seen some pretty messed up sh—*stuff*, even in your lifetime. You were probably just a baby around the time, but when I was a kid, there was a religious cult going around cutting out people's hearts and eating them."

"Gross! Why the heck would anyone think that's a good idea?"

"I know, right? They killed a whole lot of people too. I'm not sure what your assignment is, but that's a morbidly interesting topic. I don't even think they caught all the guys responsible."

Michael shivered, thankful nothing like that had made it into his visions. "Thanks, but I'll pass on that for now."

"Well, then we had some other famous cases going back before then, like the whole Father Porter sex-abuse thing. I don't think anyone was killed there, but *he* should have been. Heck, our records can take you all the way back to Lizzie Borden. If you want to do her, we have loads of material—"

"I'm looking into the more normal kinds of major crimes... murder, I think... starting when I was, uh, four." *Murder?* No one had told him his parents had been murdered, but for some reason, that felt right. All he knew for sure was that they weren't around anymore. They could have been in prison. They could have just abandoned him at the police station. *So why am I so stuck on murder?*

Katie straightened and smoothed out her shirt. "Well, if it's murder you want, then murder you shall have. The library has an index for the *Fall River Herald News*, and anything pre-2000 can be found on microfilm."

"Is that like a film projector or something?"

Katie rolled her eyes. "You don't even want to know. The good news is, for the timeframe you're working with, we have this online database called *Newsbank*, which is what you're looking at right now." She patted him on the shoulder. "Good luck." She turned to walk away.

"Wait. I don't—"

She spun back around. "Just kidding!"

Michael laughed.

"But it's actually pretty simple. You'll probably learn it better through trial and error." Katie put her hand over his on the mouse and moved it until the cursor was over to the search box.

He trembled, but he forced himself to pay attention. She showed him how to maneuver through the database, which was just like surfing the internet.

"Call me over if you need help," she said, straightening.

After watching her walk away, which was a mesmerizing sight, he turned back to the computer. *Now, how to find me?* He stared at the screen, momentarily blanking on all that Katie had just shown him. Sam popped into his head. He wondered if he was betraying her wishes. She had promised to tell him tomorrow. *Am I really so desperate to know that I can't even wait a day?*

He thought about *how* Sam would tell him, how she might sugarcoat it or spin it for his protection. *Yes, I am.* He wanted the facts and nothing but the cold, hard facts, and he wanted them immediately. *I'm not a kid anymore. After all we've been through together, she has no right to treat me like one.*

He typed "murder" into the search box and waited as hundreds of entries came up. A series of explosions in Bristol County several years back and that cult Katie had mentioned topped the list. He read the dates, the former occurring after he met Sam and the latter happening a few years before.

As he thought about how to limit his search, absently scrolling down the page, he felt a tickle on the back of his hand. "Gyahh!" He jerked his wrist to fling off the cream-colored spider. It scurried down the back of the desk and was gone.

Michael sighed. *Fucking spiders. No wonder no one goes to the library anymore.* His heartbeat returned to normal. He typed, "Michael Turcotte murders 2002-2006."

His search revealed a few murders in which the killer or victim had been named Michael and even a couple in which the victims had been named Turcotte. *Even my fake name is unlucky. Probably shouldn't have included it in the search.* But it was a shorter list, so he read through them. Only two concerned the deaths of couples, and neither mentioned a child named Michael.

"Stupid," he muttered. *They wouldn't have put a kid's name in the paper.*

He adjusted his search term to "murder, Samantha Reilly, Fall River, 2002-2006, child." The list came back long again, but only the top hits incorporated all the terms he used. He scanned the articles for his highlighted terms. One jumped out: "Murder-Suicide in the Flint." He swallowed hard. *This is it. I just know it is.* He opened the link, leaned in closer to the monitor, and began to read.

> *September 3, 2005 – Fall River Police responded to reports of shots fired at a duplex at 181 Spruce St. Arriving on scene, Detective Samantha Reilly discovered the bodies of husband and wife, Mark Florentine (age 42) and Alice Florentine (age 29), as well as the body of commercial real estate salesman James Whittaker (age 34). All three individuals died of apparent gunshot wounds inflicted by Mark Florentine. Authorities believe that, upon finding his wife and Whittaker together, Mark Florentine opened fire, killing both individuals, before turning the gun upon himself.*
>
> *No other suspects are being sought in relation to this crime. The Florentines are survived by a son (age 3), who has been taken into the custody of Child Services.*

Oh my god! This is it! This is really it! Michael's knee bounced like a jackhammer. He read the article a second time, making sure not to miss any detail. His excitement began to waver. *Something so important to me... barely even a footnote in the grand scheme of things.*

"Michael Florentine," he muttered, trying out the name. He didn't know how he knew, but he was certain that was his name.

The fact that the news wasn't making him fall apart stunned him more than anything else. His father had killed his mother and that Whittaker guy too. He had left Michael an orphan. And though any strong feelings that might have inspired had died long ago, Michael still needed to know why.

"That's screwed up, Dad." He had found what he'd been looking for, but it left him unfulfilled. He wasn't sad, and he wasn't happy. He was just sort of empty.

So now you know. The knowledge irked him. It raised new questions, and... something else, something not quite right. He felt he was missing an important detail.

He sent a screenshot to the printer then folded the article and stuffed it into his back pocket. After thanking Katie for her help, he walked to the front door. He barely noticed the stacks of books he maneuvered around or the less-fortunate people who crowded around outside as he headed to the sidewalk, where he had chained his red-and-black Schwinn to a lamppost.

While he was unlocking the chain, three police cars whizzed past, lights flashing and sirens blaring. He snorted. *Good thing Sam's got the day off.*

CHAPTER 5

J immy closed his eyes and smiled, raising his face to soak in the warm sun. *Funny. I had to kill someone to get a vacation.*

"Move it, shithead." The overgrown douchebag from the Bristol County Sheriff's Office shoved him.

Jimmy stumbled forward and fell to his hands and knees when the short chain linking his legs together went taut. Gravel scraped into his palms. He staggered to his feet and wiped his hands, chained at the wrists, on the front of his jeans, the very pair he'd been wearing the day he'd entered the juvenile justice system. They were two inches too short but still fine around the waistline. He turned and glared at the officer. *Just another bully.*

The officer laughed. "You got something to say, shithead?"

Jimmy smiled with clenched teeth. "Why don't you unlock these chains? You're real tough against a kid who can't defend himself, aren't you? Big, brave officer of the law, only picks on those who can't fight back." He noticed the deputy's wedding ring and went for a bigger insult. "Your wife and kids must think you're a real treat to have around. You bully them too?"

The deputy's smile vanished. He shoved Jimmy in the shoulder, nearly spinning him into the ambulance parked beside the patrol car. The deputy yanked him back then pushed him again to make him walk. "You've got a mouth on you, boy," he snarled. "We'll have time to play later, I promise. I'll even give you first punch. But after that, you're going to find it hard to talk back when your jaw's wired shut."

The officer pushed Jimmy every third step as they walked toward the back entrance of the Fall River Judicial Complex. They descended a short stairwell with an intercom and a reinforced door in an alcove

43

surrounded by concrete. The deputy hit the intercom button and faced the camera over the door. A loud buzz was followed by a series of clicks as the door unlocked.

The deputy pushed Jimmy inside. The fluorescent lights in the hallway flickered and hummed, making the white linoleum floor appear grimy. They stopped in front of a wooden door that was ajar.

"Move," the deputy said, shoving Jimmy through it.

A court officer stood with his back to them, filing documents in the cabinets along the wall. "Yes?" he asked without turning around.

"I've got another one for you, Dale. James Rafferty, two o'clock in Courtroom 12. He's in from Juvie, but he's got a date with the big boys today." The deputy nudged Jimmy. "Ain't that right, boy? Killed another kid in lockup. Seems like a double win for me. One less of you scum I gotta deal with 'cause he's dead and one less 'cause you're about to graduate."

Dale grunted and continued his filing. "You know the drill." He pulled a set of keys from a door and tossed them across the desk.

The deputy grabbed the keys with one hand and Jimmy's elbow with the other. He hurried down a hallway to the right so quickly that Jimmy had trouble maintaining his balance. The hall opened into a large room divided into holding cells, three to the left and three to the right. Only the first two on the left were occupied, three in the first and two in the second. Like Jimmy, the cell-dwellers wore civilian clothes, trying to look presentable in worn jeans, stringless hoodies, and ragged tennis shoes. In the back, two officers stood near an elevator.

"Look at Fortnoy bringing in a mad dog," said a mustached, barrel-shaped man clad in the forest-green uniform of the sheriff's office.

The deputy beside Officer Mustache was a wiry guy with a scar running across his cheek. His hair was cropped close, military-style. He slipped something into his pocket as Fortnoy walked Jimmy toward them.

"Robertson." Fortnoy nodded to Officer Mustache then to Officer Scarface. "Bautista."

"Whatcha need them leg cuffs for?" Bautista said. "That boy looks maybe a hundred pounds soaking wet."

"This boy's killed two people," Fortnoy replied. "Plus, I'm by myself today. Spinx called in sick, but he's probably just hungover after last night. But if you want to know the real reason for the leg cuffs, I just don't like this prick."

Fortnoy hauled Jimmy past the first cell, where a brooding man with curly gray-black hair and rabid-dog eyes stared as they passed. Jimmy tried to meet the man's eyes and show no fear, but he couldn't. The skill he'd picked up in Juvie to tell the truly hard criminals from the wannabes and pretenders told him he should look away. Assuming his skill translated to the adult population, Mr. Short Fro was no one to mess with. Even the other two prisoners in his cell kept a wide berth.

Calling him Short Fro would probably get me beaten to death too. With the mental note taken, he suppressed a smile as he shambled toward the second cell.

"Step back," Fortnoy ordered the two prisoners in that cell, neither of which had been standing anywhere near the door. They each took a step back anyway. The deputy unlocked the cell door and slid it open.

"You know you aren't supposed to be putting a minor in with the adult population," Robertson said, stroking his caterpillar mustache. He looked like the guy on the Pringles canister.

"Watch me," Fortnoy answered.

"You should lock up your gun while you're in here too," Bautista added. Jimmy noted that although they were stating the rules, neither deputy was lifting a hand to enforce them.

"Fuck that," Fortnoy said. "I ain't staying long enough for that shit. This little prick is your problem now." Laughing, he booted Jimmy into the cell.

The force of the kick sent Jimmy sprawling.

Fortnoy slammed the door shut and turned to leave. "We'll finish our talk later, Jimmy," he said. "I'm looking forward to it." He laughed some more, and Short Fro laughed with him, which had the effect of cutting short the deputy's laughter. The other two deputies shared a look then went back to their hushed conversation as Fortnoy left the room.

Prison-issue sneakers appeared in front of Jimmy's face as he pushed himself up to his knees. Smiling, the prisoner who wore them offered his hand.

Jimmy took it and stood. "Thanks. That guy's a real asshole."

"Seems it." The man chuckled. He had piercing brown eyes speckled with green. His teeth were as straight as his posture, and he was tall and toned, with perfect olive skin and slicked-back hair. He made his blue button-down shirt and black pants look dapper, *GQ* even. In his late twenties, he didn't look as if he'd lived a hard day in his life, the present day being the possible exception.

Jimmy might have thought the man would be easy prey in prison if not for the steel he saw behind those smiling eyes. He didn't read wannabe or pretender in them. But the incessant smile, as if being jailed at a courthouse was the best thing on earth, hinted at madness. *What could he possibly have to be so damn cheery about?*

"The name's Victor, with a V," the man said, as if there were other ways to spell it. "And you are?"

If Jimmy had closed his eyes, he might have been able to pretend he was meeting the man at a fancy dinner party, his tone all prim and swagger. "Jimmy."

"And what brings you to this fine establishment on this beautiful, sunny day?"

Jimmy shrugged. "They say I killed someone."

"But you didn't?"

"I say it was self-defense."

Victor grinned and slapped Jimmy on the back. "Of course it was!" He glanced over at their cellmate, a short, pudgy bald man chewing his fingernails. "You hear that, Ernie? Self-defense! Nobody's guilty here!"

Small in stature and clearly out of his element, Jimmy knew better than to ask what anyone else was in for. That sort of questioning could have been interpreted as a challenge. Short Fro looked as though he had a laundry list of offenses, but everyone else was a complete mystery. Jimmy was fine not knowing. And as friendly as Victor seemed, Jimmy found the man's cheerfulness weird. The hint of an edge gleamed off every word.

Victor took a long breath while massaging Jimmy's shoulders. "Well, my new friend, today is your lucky day."

"Oh yeah?" Jimmy asked, shrugging off the man's touch. "Why's that?" He glanced over at Ernie, who was pretending not to be listening.

"You'll see, my friend. You'll see."

Jimmy didn't like the sound of that. He was just there to plead not guilty and be assigned an attorney, hopefully not still in diapers, though he wasn't placing much faith in it. In fact, he was pretty sure an attorney should have already been appointed. He took a seat at the far side of a bench from Ernie. The man seemed harmless enough, despite giving Jimmy a scowl before returning to his avoidance of eye contact.

The two remaining guards sat at the table in the corner and started playing cards. Jimmy thought Ernie's policy was sound. He buried his face in his hands and waited for someone to take him to a judge.

About an hour later, Jimmy heard the soft ding of a doorbell followed by the sliding of a partition on rollers. Two more sheriff's deputies appeared, each carrying a long length of chain. Affixed to the chain by what looked like D rings but sturdier were three pairs of handcuffs bolted around half-inch-thick links, one at the beginning, one in the middle, and one at the end.

"Which one of you morons put a minor in with the rest of these guys?" asked the tall, silver-haired one with gold-rimmed glasses and a potbelly.

"Don't look at us, Wentworth," Bautista said, slapping a card on the table. "We weren't on Juvie."

"Fortnoy again?" The new deputy whistled. "You guys being lazy, sorry excuses for deputies is one thing, but that guy should be in one of these cells himself."

The older deputy sighed and turned to face the cell. "Ernie, that you? Back so soon?"

"Hey, Matt," Ernie said sullenly, studying his shoes as if ashamed.

"How's the wife?" Matt asked.

"You know," Ernie said with a shrug. "She says she's gonna leave me this time."

"Doesn't she say that every time?"

"Yeah, but this time... I don't know."

"I'm really sorry to hear that, Ernie."

Jimmy listened for sarcasm in the court officer's voice but was surprised to hear none. The other one with him, a broad-shouldered, baby-faced man with spikey-designer bedhead, didn't seem the least bit interested in Ernie's marital woes. Jimmy pegged him for another meathead, like Fortnoy.

"Sobriety's a son of a bitch, Ernie," Matt said. "Believe me, I know. But you can't give up on rehab and keep violating your probation by running off to get high. Maybe another stint locked up will be good for you, help get you clean."

"Yeah, I know," Ernie said, his voice sadder than a funeral. He looked up with watery eyes. "It's hard."

"Listen to this fucking pussy!" Short Fro called from the adjacent cell.

Ernie cringed. His eyes returned to the floor.

"You shut the hell up, Rex," Matt said. "I'm not surprised to see you back here. Cages are meant for animals like you. Maybe this time your charges will stick, huh?"

"Oh, you know how it is, white boy." Rex gave the deputy a shark-toothed grin. "People are always bearing false witness, even with it being a sin and all." He shook his head. "Usually, they come around to the truth before trial, something having put the fear of God back in them."

Matt scowled. "Or they disappear."

"Well, yeah. There's that." Rex laughed and raised his hands, palms out. "Can't blame me for their wanting to hide away with their sins."

Matt grimaced as if he'd swallowed vomit. He turned back to Ernie. "Don't pay that one any attention, Ernie. Some people make mistakes. That one, he makes those mistakes on purpose and never regrets them."

"Damn right, old man!" Rex laughed.

Matt sighed. "Why don't you take the lead, Ernie? Show some of these new guys the ropes, seeing as you know the drill. Everyone, turn around and kneel in front of the bench."

He opened the cell and stepped inside, his partner hanging back. Ernie got off the bench, knelt in front of it, raised his arms, and waited patiently for Matt to cuff him to the chain.

Matt paused. "The minor is wearing leg cuffs? Isn't that a bit much?"

"Again," Robertson said, "not us."

"Well, do you have the key?"

"Nope."

"Damn Fortnoy," Matt muttered.

"We're assigned to the cell block," Bautista said. "You want we should take them up?"

"No," Matt said. He jerked a thumb over his shoulder at the other deputy. "Gordo here is still new to the job. We'll do it. It'll be good experience for him."

"Suit yourself," Bautista said, returning to his card game.

"Stand up, Ernie," Matt said. "I have to search you first."

Robertson slapped a palm on the table. His face had gone beet red. "Search them? We already searched them, Wentworth. Your comments are trying my patience. How incompetent do you think we are?"

"Okay, okay," Matt said. "Just making sure. You can kneel again, Ernie. For those of you who don't know, we call this a stacker three." He held up the thick chain. "This will keep three of you connected to each other at all times."

I haven't been searched. Jimmy assumed the deputy had been referring to the five others, but why he wouldn't mention Jimmy seemed odd. *I guess he just doesn't see me as a threat.* Matt stepped up behind him, and Jimmy raised his hands. "How many chains do we need? I'm not David fucking Copperfield."

"Sorry, kid," Matt said, "but it's the rules. Normally, we'd take you up separately, but since you're already mixed in with the general population..." He huffed. "Just follow Ernie's lead." The deputy clicked the cuff around Jimmy's chain rather than cuffing him a second time. "This'll give you a little more breathing room."

When Matt finished joining the three of them like train cars, the other officer tugged on each loop and double-checked all binds. Jimmy had a vague memory of preschool when the class would go outside for walks, strung together like popcorn garland on yarn.

"Now, no funny stuff," Matt said as he chained up the three in the first cell. "That goes double for you, Rex." He led the trio out of the cell to stand alongside Jimmy's group.

"No, suh, massa," Rex said in his best mock Uncle Tom. "I's a good little nigga, I am. Wouldn't try nothin'. No, suh." Rex threw his head back and cackled.

Gordo's hand flittered over his gun. "You're a fucking nigger all right," he said, not as softly as he probably intended.

Rex lurched at Gordo. With eyes like ice and teeth coated in saliva, the prisoner truly looked like a dog gone rabid. The young deputy jumped back and yelped. He drew his gun, hand trembling. Rex let out a mocking chuckle and returned to his spot at the end of the line.

"Enough!" Matt waved his partner back. "What the hell is wrong with you, Gordo? I have half a mind to unleash that son of a bitch on you. If I ever, and I mean *ever*, hear you say something like that to a prisoner—no, to *anyone*—ever again, I'll have you shit-canned before you even have the chance to remove my boot from your ass. You got that?"

Gordo stuck out his chest. "You're not my boss."

Matt grabbed the front of the man's shirt. "This is your first, last, and only warning. Do. You. Copy?"

Gordo's face flushed a deep red, but he nodded and kept his mouth shut.

"Good." Matt let go of his shirt. "Lock up your gun and take up the first three. I'll take the rear so Rex doesn't try to bite a chunk out of your throat. I swear. Where the hell does the state keep finding ignorant inbreds like you?"

Gordo hurried over to a cabinet and locked up his weapon. He returned and took his place in front of Ernie. He yanked the man forward as if Ernie had been the cause of his berating. Ernie began to march like a horse pulling a carriage out of mud, Jimmy and Victor in tow.

Jimmy took a deep breath. *This is it.*

CHAPTER 6

Sam hurt just about everywhere, but her anger kept her focused, kept her breathing. Her captors maneuvered her through the hall. She hoped someone would notice her severely battered body and the two men rough handling her—Earl had discarded his fake janitor uniform in the closet, so he no longer looked as though he worked there—but if anyone did, they didn't do anything about it. *Fall River: home of the willfully ignorant and the conveniently blind.*

Hector and Fake Earl shuffled her straight toward Courtroom 12. She prayed it wasn't crowded. With the exception of the madness occurring all over the city that day, crime had been way down lately. Other than Rex Billings...

Sam gasped. *No, no, no. Not Rex. Don't let this be Rex's doing.* Rex's hearing was in Courtroom 12. If that bomb had to blow while she was wearing it, she swore she'd be giving Rex a huge hug when it did.

After opening the doors, Hector patted his pocket where he'd slid the remote. *Idiot could have set it off just by doing that. Just what kind of assholes am I dealing with here?*

"One wrong move," Earl whispered into her ear, "and everyone dies."

Sam believed him. She stood still, biting her lip while awaiting instructions. Hector took a seat in the back row to her left.

"Slide onto the bench to your right, second from the back," Fake Earl said. "You do as you're told, and nobody has to die today, not even you. I'll be right behind you." He shuffled sideways into the back row, always keeping his eyes on her. He wore a piece stuck in the back of his jeans. It bulged beneath his fitted Polo.

As she slid down the pew-like bench in front of him, Earl slowed to escort her the rest of the way. When she felt a slight tug at her belt loop, she stopped and sat. Each bench ended at the wall, so the only means of escape would be to scoot back over to the center aisle. The benches were five rows deep. The guy in the monkey-ninja T-shirt plopped into the seat at the aisle end of her row, slightly behind an elderly couple. The woman Sam had suspected was a legal intern sat in the front row, next to a string of overweight middle-aged white men in cheap suits and yellow ties, most likely lawyers. Sam rose just enough to appear to have been adjusting to a more comfortable position. She could just make out the corner of the intern's black briefcase on her lap.

She looked around for anyone else who appeared to be part of Hector's clan. She found the kid Hector had scolded earlier sitting on the left-hand side, diagonally behind a frumpy, puffy-faced woman, who seemed to have been crying all over her best Sunday clothes.

Some others sat whispering with lawyers, and a few more sat alone and away from everyone else. Sam saw no contact between those individuals and the suspects she had identified, but she couldn't discount the involvement of any one of them. Whether they were there for themselves or for someone else, they all looked guilty. She'd been in enough courtrooms to know they were like churches in that everyone in them felt shame and judgment. Sam wondered how it would judge her if she let people die that day.

And how am I supposed to stop it? She counted five guns in the room minimum, one directly behind her. Her blouse was buttoned over a bomb-laced girdle. Everything about her, from the sloppy clothes to the bulbous, bruising tender spots, screamed hot mess. Her nose bloodied, her lip split, and her hair a tangled bird's nest, Sam looked as bad as she felt. *Can't these people see what's happening right in front of them?*

Her gaze fell upon Old Stanley, a court officer more ancient than the earth itself, standing behind the podium beside the jury box. With a shaky hand, he was picking his nose and trying to make it look like a scratch. *Is he the best ally I can hope for?*

Stanley's coworker, Rhonda Banks, leaned against the railing separating the actors from the spectators. She called out to Sam, "Hey, Detective. Did you get caught in a tornado?" She laughed then sobered. "Seriously, what in the hell happened to you?"

Their best chance for survival is for me to play along. Sam grinned. "You had it right on the first try. Tornado."

"Gawd, you look like you went over Niagara Falls in a barrel only to get hit by a cement truck at the bottom."

"I'm guessing there aren't a lot of cement trucks at the bottom of Niagara Falls."

"Aw, hell. You look like—"

"I think I got it." Sam faked a laugh. "I nabbed a perp just before coming here. He nabbed me a few times back. I thought I had straightened up in the car well enough, but no sooner than I get out and take ten steps, a kid on a skateboard mows me over."

Rhonda nodded. "I've told the guys at the door a hundred times that those skateboarders have got to go. The sign's right there. It says No Skateboarding. I hope you arrested the little creep."

Sam shook her head. "He got one look at my face and the day I've been having and ran."

Rhonda pursed her lips. She gave Sam another once-over then shook her head and whistled again. "Damn shame."

Two sheriff's deputies—a new guy Sam had never seen before and good ol' Matt Wentworth, who had been a fixture in the old courthouse well before the Commonwealth had broken ground on the new one—marched in with sausage-linked scumbags in tow. Oddly, there was a teenage boy grouped in with them.

Rhonda nodded to Matt, and he smiled back. Matt was smart, reliable, and moral. If he could be alerted to what was happening—*I don't even know what's happening*—he wouldn't do anything rash or foolish. He'd find a way to sound the alarm without alerting Hector and his crew.

Sam raised her eyebrows and rolled her eyes up and to the left, trying to point out Earl without Earl knowing. Matt squinted at her, a quizzical look on his face, obviously put off by her appearance.

She considered trying Morse code through a series of blinks. All she knew was SOS, but that would do the trick, since Matt, with his navy background, was sure to pick up on it.

Too risky. He'd have to stare at me long enough to notice, and they'd notice him staring first. Before she could think of anything else to try, Matt turned back to his task of getting his charges seated in the corral. She understood why he could give her so little attention, given the monster who occupied the caboose position in his human train: Rex Billings, scumbag of all scumbags. Again, she found herself praying Hector's party wasn't there for him.

Rex spotted her and smiled. He grabbed his crotch and blew her a kiss.

Think, damn it! How do I stop this... whatever this is? Terrorism?

"All rise," Rhonda announced as a door at the back of the room opened.

Sam got to her feet, along with everyone else in the courtroom. A grave-looking middle-aged woman dressed in a long black robe entered the room. With the poise of a marine, she walked to the bench and placed several files on top of it.

"The Honorable Justine Baker presiding," Rhonda announced. After the judge took her seat, Rhonda said, "You may be seated."

Everyone sat down simultaneously, even the chain gang, but not without a lot of clanging. Rhonda took her spot to the right end of the rail. She seemed to have forgotten about Sam and all her injuries.

"Remember," Earl whispered into her ear. "Just do as we say, and no one gets hurt."

Sam doubted that, but she had to believe that cooperating might get fewer people hurt. She was in no position to fight anyone, never mind an entire group, and though she had allies in the courtroom, they were no match for armed assailants who had the drop on them. Compounding the issue, she didn't know the first thing about defusing a bomb.

Ninja Monkey got up as if to leave, but out of the corner of her eye, Sam saw him lock the door and kick down the doorstops. Rhonda was watching him too, and she moved toward him as he retook his seat.

"Why don't we jump right into it," Judge Baker said, her face buried in a file. "Who do we have first, Marty?"

The clerk, an older man in a drab brown suit with a matching tie, sat on the dais below the judge in front of a computer that looked as outdated as the man's attire. He cleared his throat. "In the matter of the Commonwealth versus Ernest Juniper—"

Hector shot to his feet. "Actually, Your Honor, I'd like to go first, if it's all the same to you. You can save your sham justice, your false bureaucracy loaded with hypocrisy, for the rich benefactors pulling your puppet strings. We'll have none of your lies. Not today."

As Judge Baker reached for her gavel, Rhonda approached the gate to the center aisle.

The intern drew a pistol from her briefcase, jammed it under the chin of the lawyer next to her, and forced him to his feet. "Nobody fucking move!" she shouted.

After the initial gasps and shrieks, the courtroom fell eerily silent. Rhonda stopped and faced the woman, her hand drifting toward her radio.

"I wouldn't do that," the intern said, indenting the lawyer's chin with the snub nose of her weapon. "Toss it to me."

Rhonda bent over and slid her radio across the floor. The intern kicked it under her seat. She then ordered Stanley to give his to Ninja Monkey, who took it, turned it off, and returned to his position.

Ninja Monkey pressed a gun to the back of the head of the old man sitting in front of him. The young boy, who was a few years younger than Michael, wrapped a prepubescent arm around the neck of the frumpy woman in front of him and buried a pistol into her temple with his other hand.

A short, chubby, middle-aged prisoner jumped up. "Leave her alone!"

Matt threw out a steadying hand. Chained to other prisoners and stuck in what resembled a hockey penalty box, the man wasn't going anywhere.

Sam watched the judge closely as the woman slid a hand under the bench. A panic button was there, and Judge Baker had triggered it.

Sam smiled. *Good girl.*

Her smile was choked off her face when Earl yanked her up by her neck. She gasped for air, struggling instinctively before logic trumped her inclination toward self-preservation. A new round of gasps and shrieks emitted from the gallery as Earl tore open her shirt. The stenographer fainted and fell to the floor.

Hector laughed. "Good. Now that I have all you assholes' attention, that woman"—he pointed at Sam—"is rigged with enough explosives to blow up this courtroom and all you fine people in it."

Rex cheered. "Yeah! Kill that bitch! That fucking whore put me in these chains." He sneered at Sam. "If they don't kill you, Reilly, I'm gonna. Nice and slow." He rubbed his crotch as he said the last part.

Hector glared at Rex. "Do you mind shutting the fuck up when I'm talking?"

Rex snarled and glowered at the scarred bomb-wielder. But to Sam's surprise, he did shut up.

Hector cleared his throat. "Now, we're all short on time, and some of us more so than others." He nodded toward the bench. "And yes, Judge, we know all about that alarm you hit, but I think you'll find the cavalry won't be arriving quite as soon as you might like. Anyway, let's get right to the point. Release those prisoners, and no one dies. Don't, and we start shooting. If, by some cruel twist of fate, the police arrive before we're gone, then we'll all be heading to hell together." He raised the remote, his finger over the trigger.

The young deputy who had accompanied Matt crept slowly backward so that he was only a foot away from the side door. With one hand, he reached behind him for the knob.

Matt mouthed, "Don't."

The female intern reeled her arm toward them with blurring speed.

Matt jumped in front of the deputy. "Don't!" he yelled.

The woman fired twice. One bullet pierced Matt's chest. The other went into the side of his neck. Arterial spray spattered over the young deputy. Instantly, alarms blared throughout the building.

As Matt fell, Rhonda charged the intern, tucking her head like a running back squeaking out an extra yard. But the intern wheeled around and slammed the butt of her gun into Rhonda's jaw. The court officer fell against the rail then slumped onto the floor.

"Stay down," the intern said, holding her gun on Rhonda.

"Any other heroes?" Hector groaned melodramatically, raising his arms high then letting them fall to his sides. "No? Perhaps now you assholes are ready to listen?"

A scream burst from the prisoner closest to Rex. The psychopath had grabbed his neighbor's hand and was smashing it against the wooden railing.

"Be quiet, you pussy," Rex said. "I'm helping you out of those cuffs."

"Enough!" Hector shouted.

Rex released the prisoner's wrist. "What?"

Hector huffed. "That pig should have the keys, you moron. You"—he waved his pistol at the new deputy—"get those cuffs off them." He turned to the boy in his crew. "Kid, give Victor your gun. If that pig deputy tries anything, shoot off his balls."

Kid let go of his hostage and leaped over the rail. He handed the third prisoner—Victor, Sam assumed—his gun. Victor thanked the boy and ruffled his hair before sending him back to his spot behind the plain-dressed woman.

Victor pointed the gun at the deputy. "The keys, if you'd be so kind?"

The deputy raised his hands. "H-H-He has them," he sputtered, pointing at Matt, who was bleeding out on the carpet. The injured man's heart was evidently still pumping, though Sam doubted that would be the case for much longer.

"Back up," Victor said. When the deputy complied, the prisoner pointed his gun at the short guy at the head of his chain, the one who had told Kid to leave the woman alone. "Get the keys."

The short prisoner shook his head. "I don't want any part of—"

The blast that tore apart his face stopped him mid-sentence.

"No!" the frumpy woman shouted. She was over the rail and running toward the fallen man when Victor shot her in the stomach. She collapsed to the floor, clasping her hands over the wound, but the blood coming out was thick and dark.

"I-I-I didn't mean to let her go," Kid stuttered, his face ashen. "I couldn't grab her in time. I didn't mean to..."

The situation is rapidly deteriorating. Sam thought about making a move, but every action she considered ended with someone dead. A man who could bench-press a car had her arms pinned behind her. That alone might have been the beginning and end to all plans, unless those plans included broken bones or her own death.

Victor sighed. "This isn't open for discussion." He pointed his gun at the teenage prisoner.

For the first time, Sam took a good look at the boy. *Is that Jimmy Rafferty?* Her heart skipped a beat. *Poor Jimmy.* She stiffened. *Poor Jimmy? Might as well say poor murderer. Damn, Michael, you're making me go soft.*

Jimmy scrambled over the wooden railing but only managed to get his shackled feet a few inches from the floor on the other side before the chain pulled taut. When Victor heaved the dead prisoner over and leaned over it himself, Jimmy had enough slack to reach Matt and pull his key ring from his belt. He found the key and unlocked the chain from his cuffs before handing the key to Victor.

"Good," Victor said, smiling.

Sam suddenly noticed that Victor looked remarkably like an unscarred version of Hector. *Brothers?*

"I don't think any of those keys will work on my cuffs," Jimmy said.

"No worries, friend," Victor said. "I have people inside and out, and I try to prepare for all contingencies." He jammed his index finger down his throat. After four or five dry heaves, he threw up some liquid. Dangling from his mouth on a strand of dental floss tied around a tooth was a small key. Victor pulled it loose and handed it to Jimmy. "This baby is like a skeleton key for most handcuffs. It should work on yours. When you're done, I want it back."

Victor passed Matt's key ring to the prisoner behind him. The blond man with the rotten teeth undid his cuffs and handed the keys to Rex, skipping the prisoner who sat sobbing and cradling his injured hand.

Jimmy went to work on his cuffs. After straining with the skeleton key for a few moments more, Jimmy groaned and slapped his thighs in frustration.

"No luck?" Victor asked.

Jimmy shook his head.

Victor chuckled and took back his key. "Works on all but yours, I guess." He shrugged. "Sorry, kid. I guess it isn't your lucky day after all."

Rex looked as though he was feeling pretty lucky. He beamed as he uncuffed himself. Three of the prisoners were free, and two of them were certainly dangerous. Circumstances had gone from bad to worse to abysmally dismal.

Rex held out his hand. "Give me that gun." Without waiting, he snatched it from Victor's hand, turned, and shot the young deputy in the head.

The shot brought further cries of terror from the gallery. Some were quietly weeping. Victor gave Rex a sharp look.

"What?" Rex shrugged. "He called me a nigger. Now, if you need me, I'll be having some fun with that detective bitch over there." He grinned at Sam.

As Rex threw his leg over the side of the box, Sam swallowed hard. She could think of a thousand better ways to go out than by the hands of that monster. With the number of civilians in the room dwindling, she was beginning to think setting off the bomb could be worth it. She saw no other way to stop the criminals from winning. *A tie seems the best I can hope for.*

"Wait," Victor said, grabbing Rex's arm.

Rex snarled and raised the pistol. All the other guns in the courtroom turned on him.

"Maurice has that one under control," Victor said, motioning to Fake Earl. "And in case you didn't notice, she's our guarantee out of here."

"My hand... he ruined my hand," the still-cuffed prisoner moaned.

Victor rolled his eyes. "Will somebody shut this guy up?" He sighed melodramatically.

Rex turned and fired. The whining prisoner whined no more. He slumped back on the bench then fell sideways, dead.

Victor frowned. "Will you stop shooting people?"

He shrugged. "You asked if someone would shut him up. I did. Problem solved."

Three free. Two dead. Five more in the crowd. Sam's odds were a person better than they had been a moment earlier, and she supposed she had Rex to thank for that. At the least, the dead man had been an unknown. *Just like Jimmy.* She glanced at the boy, still cuffed and trembling. *Which side will you choose, Jimmy?*

One of the lawyers in the front row jumped up and bolted for the door. Ninja Monkey stuck out his foot and tripped the man as he passed. While the lawyer lay sprawled on the floor, Ninja Monkey shot him twice in the back. The lawyer did not get up.

Hector pointed at the new corpse. "Anyone else want to try that?" No one said a word. "Good." He waved toward Sam and her captor. "Bring her up."

Maurice shoved her into the aisle then down it. He stopped when her thighs thumped into the gate.

Victor unlocked the dead prisoner from Rex's chain and handed it to Jimmy. "Cuff her to the rail. Her and as many others as you can fit. Your choice who, kid."

Jimmy took the cuff chain and hustled over to Sam. "Hold out your hand."

"You don't have to do this, Jimmy," Sam said.

"The hell I don't." Jimmy laughed nervously. "Look around you. If I don't, I'm dead, and your fate seems pretty much sealed."

The kid has a point. After a deep breath, Sam held out one arm.

Without making eye contact, Jimmy clicked the cuff around her wrist. She noticed he left the cuff loose. Sam was confident she could squirm out of it. She lowered her hand so he could attach the other end to the rail.

The intern in the front row kicked out her hostage's leg, sending him crashing down into his seat. She sauntered over and grabbed Sam's wrist. "You have to make sure these are nice and tight," she said, smiling and squeezing the metal cuff until it bit into Sam's skin. When she let go, she ran a finger down Sam's cheek, down her arm, then around her, where she pinched her butt. "Such a waste."

"We're all cooperating," Judge Baker said. "You're all free now, but this place will be surrounded soon, if it isn't already. If you need a hostage, take me. No one else needs to get hurt."

"We're getting to that, Your Honor," Victor said. "But for now, shut the fuck up." He looked over at Jimmy. "Five more, kid. And time's short. Who's it going to be?"

Jimmy glanced at the old woman in the second pew. He beckoned her with a curled finger.

The old man beside her got up instead. "I'll do it, kid. Just leave my wife alone, please."

"No, Jack," the old woman muttered, touching his arm. "Your heart."

"It's okay, dear," the old man said. He smiled wanly, but his hands were shaking. He walked slowly through the gate and over to the rail.

Jimmy's eyes shimmered as he watched the man approach. Sam was glad to see the boy had some compassion left. He swallowed then cuffed Jack beside Sam.

"Me too," Rhonda said, stepping toward Jimmy.

Jimmy nodded and cuffed Rhonda to the rail.

"Yo, boss," Ninja Monkey said. "The clerk's missing. I think the dude's hiding under his desk." He laughed.

"I got this." Rex stormed behind the clerk's desk and dragged him out.

"Looks like we have another volunteer," Victor said. "They're making your job easy for you, Jimmy." He looked at Rex. "Please bring that coward over to the rail."

Rex complied, leading the clerk by his ear. When he got to the rail, he tore the clerk's ear off and laughed. Screaming, the clerk collapsed to the floor. Blood trickled down his jawbone. Piss stained the front of his pants.

"You're sick, Rex." Sam scowled.

Rex smirked. "Your turn will come, Reilly. I'll show you sick then." He punched the clerk just once, but it was enough to send him into la-la land. Jimmy picked up the man's limp wrist and cuffed him to the rail.

Judge Baker's face reddened, and she shot to her feet. "You have me. You don't need these people." She slammed her palm against the bench. "Take me and let them go!"

"Should I cuff her too?" Jimmy asked.

"No," Victor said. "She's coming with us. Hector, grab her. It's time to leave."

Hector headed toward the judge like a lion stalking a gazelle.

Victor turned to Jimmy. "You have a choice, kid. Cuff one more and come with us—that is, if you can keep up—or cuff yourself, spare one of the others, and die with the rest."

"Don't you want to cuff a couple of lawyers?" Maurice asked. "We still have two spots left."

"Those spineless sacks?" Victor shook his head. "Nah. No one would miss them."

Rex laughed. Jimmy slid a cuff around his wrist, and Rex stopped laughing. He backhanded Jimmy so hard that the boy went airborne and crashed down flat onto his back. The kid's lip was a swollen blob.

Maurice and Baby Intern had their guns on Rex before he could stomp out the boy's life.

Victor chuckled. "You've got balls, kid."

Jimmy was slow to get to his feet, the chains around his ankles and wrists making the move more difficult. "You told me I could choose."

"And so I did." Victor guffawed. "So I did. Maurice?"

Maurice grabbed Rex and slammed him into the rail. Jimmy crept closer. Rex flinched, and Jimmy jumped, but the boy moved in again when he saw the gang's guns holding the madman at bay. He clamped Rex's wrist and slapped the other cuff around the rail.

"You're gonna pay for this," Rex said, glaring at Jimmy. "I'm going to eat you alive, boy."

"Slev, give us a head start," Hector said to the young man in the ninja-monkey T-shirt. "Shoot anyone that moves." He pointed at Rex. "Even him."

Victor hurried to the door the sheriff's deputies had used and opened it while Baby Intern covered him. They disappeared out the door, Rotted Teeth close on their heels.

Pushing Judge Baker through the door at gunpoint, Hector called back, "Bring another hostage. We may need one if Bautista betrayed us."

Maurice grabbed Old Stanley, who had been standing against the wall. Sam had all but forgotten he was there. The old man put up no struggle as the man-beast dragged him out the door.

The young kid seemed to have been in some sort of a trance, but he snapped out of it when his gang had all but left him behind. He sprinted for the door and was soon out of sight.

Before Sam could formulate a plan, Jimmy tackled Slev. He fell on top of the twentysomething's back, and the gun slid across the floor. With lightning speed, he threw his arms over Slev's head and snagged his cuff's chains under the gang member's chin. Sitting on Slev's back, Jimmy pulled Slev's neck up and in a camel clutch, a move Sam recalled WWF's Iron Sheik having made famous. The hold was supposed to put pressure on its unfortunate victim's spine.

Slev grimaced as his eyes bulged. His spine looked as if it could snap, but the worst stress was on his neck. Jimmy's chain sawed into the skin there, at the same time choking him on his own Adam's apple. Slev's face turned dark red, venturing toward purple.

After a few more seconds of flopping, wheezing, and clawing at the chain, Slev fell limp. Jimmy held him a moment longer before letting gravity send Slev's face slamming into the floor.

Rex tugged at the chain linking him to the rail. When it wouldn't budge, he began kicking at the wood. Even with his awkward angle, the rail began to splinter.

Jimmy stood and ran back to the corral, moving surprisingly well for a kid bound at the ankles. He picked up Matt's key ring and tossed it at Sam's feet. "I'm sorry, but I can't go back." He bolted for the door.

Sam lunged for the keys as Rex began to beat his way toward her. She ducked a right hook as she scrambled to jam the key in the lock. The old man and Rhonda attempted to slow his progress, but Rex batted them away as if they were gnats. The court officer lay atop the clerk, neither attempting to rise. The old man was on hands and knees, coughing up blood. Rex dragged each of them, all tangled up, closer to Sam.

"I'm gonna kill you, bitch." Sweat glistened on Rex's forehead. "That's a given. But if you don't hand over that motherfucking key, I'm gonna take my time doing it."

Sam's hand shook as she twisted the key in the lock. The click might have been the most beautiful sound in the world. "Yes!"

She unclasped her wrist and rolled away, only to be yanked back by her hair. Tugging against the pull, she shrieked as she heard a rip. But after the initial burst of pain in her scalp, she was able to scramble out of his reach. When she turned back around, Rex was staring down at a clump of her hair between his fingers. He tossed it aside with an expression that was a mixture of disgust and hatred.

Sam's head stung, but she supposed the sensation was just one more injury to add to a growing list. Had she had a moment to gloat, she might have taken it, but the bomb strapped to her chest required immediate action.

"You leave me, bitch, and I'll kill them!" Rex waved his unchained arm at the three captives sprawled at his feet like supplicants then raised his foot over Rhonda's head. "You know I will."

"Damn it, Rex! Don't you get it? If I don't get out of here *now*, you, me, *all of us*, are as good as dead."

"Throw me the key, and I'll let them live."

Sam couldn't trust him, but she could trust that he'd kill the others if she didn't do what he asked. She had no time to argue. "This isn't over, Rex." She bowled Matt's key ring at his feet and ran for the door Hector and Jimmy had used.

Rex's laughter followed her into the back hall, which led to an elevator and a stairwell. She figured the prisoners had gone down, looking for an escape, but she couldn't worry about them. The safety of everyone else still in the building came first. The blaring fire alarm suggested that the building was being evacuated, but she couldn't count on that.

As she entered the stairwell, the alarm was so loud that she put her fingers in her ears to muffle it. She raced for the roof. On the top landing, she reached for the access door, praying it wasn't locked. It opened easily, and Sam thanked whoever liked to sneak up there for a smoke or a moment of peace in the workday.

The mesh material of the bomb belt had some give to it, so she didn't bother fiddling with the straps in back. She stretched the thing over her hips then shimmied the explosive garment down her legs.

Now how do I dispose of the damn thing?

She ran to the nearest ledge and peered out, down, left, and right, analyzing every option and discounting each with split-second rulings. After another second, her heart already exploding against her ribcage, she ran to the middle of the roof and dropped it. She figured the people on the street would be safer that way. *Please, please, please let everyone have gotten out safely.*

Tires screeched on the street below as she sprinted toward the stairwell.

CHAPTER 7

"Where's Slev?" Victor asked, holding the elevator door open as Jimmy ambled toward it.

"Rex grabbed him," Jimmy lied. "Got his gun too. I ran before the fucker could shoot me."

Victor eyeballed him suspiciously, and Hector looked as if he might open fire, but something in Jimmy's appearance—his sweat-stained shirt, his stunned expression—must have convinced the gang's apparent leader that Jimmy was telling the truth.

"Come on," Victor said, pulling Jimmy into the elevator. The door closed, and they began to descend to the basement.

"Everyone, hug the sides," Hector said. "When those doors open, we should be in the clear. If not, though, they'll have to shoot through the judge and this old guy if they want to hit me and Maurice. We'll take them out." He pushed Judge Baker forward until her nose was almost touching the door. Jimmy could see her reflection in its shiny surface, and though she didn't make a sound, he could see she was crying.

Please don't let anyone be waiting. Jimmy hugged the left wall of the elevator, fitting snugly between Baby and Victor. Across from them was Maurice, the little boy, the blond prisoner, and the old court officer who had remained quiet through the whole ordeal.

Ding. The doors creaked open. Shots came in. Hector and Maurice fired back. The old officer slumped, and Judge Baker crouched and put her arms over her head.

"Did Bautista screw us?" the woman asked, raising her gun.

"No," Hector said. "I think we're clear. Just one guy."

"Well, this guy's useless," Maurice said, shoving the dead body of the court officer forward.

"Get up!" Hector shouted at the judge. He pulled her back up by her hair and pushed her out the door. "Let's move!"

When Jimmy stepped out of the elevator, he saw the court officer who had been reading when he'd arrived at the courthouse. Sitting against the far wall, the officer was filled with bullet holes. His eyes stared blankly at the ceiling.

"Grab his gun," Victor said, tapping Jimmy on the arm. "You may need it."

Jimmy pulled the gun from the court officer's grip. He half expected the man to grab his wrist or sputter alive like supposedly dead people always seemed to do in horror movies. But the dead man stayed dead.

As the grip of the pistol pressed into his palm, Jimmy thought of the last time he'd held a gun, the day that had changed his life forever. Setting his jaw, he hobbled forward. *There's no going back to the way things were. Things are bad now, but were they really any better then?*

They passed the holding cells, rounded the corner, and exited the courthouse, prepared for resistance but receiving none. The others scaled the stairs easily, but Jimmy had to hop because of his chains. Halfway up, Maurice grabbed him and slung him over his shoulder. Jimmy's cheeks flushed with warmth, but the big man put him down again once they had reached the top.

The blond prisoner raced toward the front of the building.

"Not that way!" Hector shouted, but the prisoner kept running. "Eh, fuck him."

Jimmy heard a car screech and a loud thud and guessed the blond guy had run out into the street. He shook his head and followed the rest of the group toward the back of the building, where Deputy Fortnoy had parked.

As they rounded the corner, Fortnoy was leaning against the patrol car. The cigarette hanging fell to the ground. "What the fuck?"

Baby put three bullets into his chest. She clapped as if she'd just won a prize in some twisted carnival game then threw her arms around Victor's neck. She shoved her tongue into his mouth. Victor seemed happy to receive it.

"We gotta move," Hector said, opening the rear door of the ambulance. "Get in! We don't have much time!" He tossed the judge into the back then rounded the vehicle for the driver's side. Victor, Baby, and Kid hopped into the back, while Maurice headed for the passenger seat.

Jimmy walked over to Fortnoy. "Not so tough now, are you?" He crouched beside the man.

Fortnoy's hands were pressed over his wounds as he desperately tried to plug the leaks. Dark blood cascaded between his fingers. "Help... help me..."

"No." Jimmy fumbled through the deputy's pockets until he found the man's key ring. He took them and shuffled over to the ambulance.

"Let's go! Let's go!" Victor shouted. He pulled Jimmy into the vehicle and slammed the door behind him.

Hector floored the accelerator. The ambulance lurched into motion, and Jimmy fell on his ass.

As they sped away, Hector pulled what looked like a remote control from his pocket, the same one he'd held up in the courtroom. "This should keep them occupied for a while." He pressed a button.

Jimmy crawled to the back windows as a blast reverberated through the air. The courthouse lit up like a candle, its rooftop a ball of flames.

CHAPTER 8

As Michael stepped inside the stairwell and began to climb, a cool breeze chilled the beads of sweat on his neck. About halfway up the staircase, sunlight beamed in through a window, illuminating swarms of dust motes that swirled in the air like sand in a sandstorm. But the hallway at the top was as black as a starless night, an unnatural pitch black that made Michael's skin crawl.

Is the light off? He stared up at the hall, an inner voice telling him to beware, to stay away from the darkness, that there was something evil about it. *The hall just shouldn't be that dark.*

And something else was wrong. The hall wasn't just dark. The whole stairwell was colorless. Michael rubbed his eyes and blinked out the dust. Everything remained as black and white and grainy as the picture on a 1950s television set.

He rubbed his eyes again. When he looked up, he shrieked, so startled that he would have fallen had his hand not landed on the rail and instinctively clenched. On the second-floor landing, standing in front of Sam's apartment was a boy with shaggy hair, dark eyes, and a playful smile. The kid's toes hung over the top step, and he swayed.

Michael caught his breath. "God, kid, you scared the crap out of me." When the child didn't respond, Michael asked, "Who are you? Where is your mom?"

The boy started to blur. Michael pressed his eyes shut then opened them, trying to clear his vision. Everything else came in clear enough. The boy seemed ethereal, a glowing apparition against a field of darkness.

The ghost boy's rocking intensified, and he giggled as his eyes rolled back into his head, revealing blank, white sheets. His body wavered dangerously over the lip of the stair.

"Stay where you are," Michael said. He didn't want to be anywhere near that kid, but he couldn't just let the boy fall down the stairs. He wiped his sweaty palms on his jeans, grabbed the railing, and started up the stairs.

When he was halfway up, the boy's mouth creaked open like a marionette's with a loose hinge. A low guttural sound emerged from somewhere deep inside the boy. The sound, which grew louder, wasn't human, or at least Michael didn't think it was. It chilled him to the bone.

He raised a hand. "Careful. You're going to fall."

A figure emerged from the darkness behind the boy—not *out of* the darkness, but rather formed by the darkness itself. Dressed in black from head to toe, the person standing behind the boy had a hood drawn low over his eyes and nose. Michael couldn't make out more than the individual's chin, glowing white like the boy. His instincts screamed at him to run, but he couldn't leave the boy in danger. His gut told him he knew the boy, but how or from where remained a mystery. His brain told him he didn't want to know.

"Who are you?" he asked, his voice quivering. "What do you want from me?"

"I see you," the hooded figure whispered. He grabbed the boy by the back of his neck and threw him off the landing. The child squealed with delight.

"No!" Michael scrambled up the steps, reaching out to catch the boy.

The kid fell straight into his arms, but Michael felt no impact, held nothing in his hands. The child had simply vanished, leaving behind the echo of a giggle and a tornado of dust motes with Michael at its eye.

Blackness closed around him.

*HE IS SURROUNDED BY darkness. His head feels like it's been bat-
ted around by a couple of Major League sluggers. He reaches out and
smacks his hand against wood.*

Not this again.

*He tries to blink away the darkness, even though he knows in his
heart that it's no use. He wants to scream, but his voice won't cooperate.*
What do you want me to see? And why won't you let me see it?

*The sounds from his dream return: the clock's tick, the radiator's
hum, the muffled voices. The smells of sweat and sex fill the air.*

Thump. Thump. Thump. *Michael concentrates. The thumping
stops, and he can hear the voices.*

"Do it," one voice whispers.

*"I... I can't," an adult male answers. His voice is shaky, and he's
breathing so loud and fast that Michael can almost hear the lungs working inside him. The man sniffles.*

Is he crying? *Michael tries to turn, but like all the other times, he
can't.* But this isn't exactly like the other times, is it? I can hear their
words! *Michael lies still and focuses on listening, on hearing whatever
the invisible force doesn't want him to know.*

Michael grimaces. To know the truth.

*His thoughts come as if dialed in. They are not his, yet they are his,
his from another time. He feels his legs. They are short and pudgy.*

*"You can, and you will," the whisperer says. "Unless you prefer four
bodies to two?"*

*"I can't!" the man shouts. His voice, even in distress, is somehow
comforting, the voice of lullabies.*

*"Now!" The other voice sounds demonic, as if the person is speaking
in slow motion.*

Michael cowers, sure the voice really does belong to a demon. The sobbing man roars in agony as a series of sharp, succinct blasts assaults Michael's ears.

"See?" *the demon whispers.* "You can. Now the other."

Click. *Something falls to the floor.* Click.

"No. Don't... please..." *This plea comes from a third person, someone to the left, where the musky scent seems strongest.*

Michael also smells something metallic from that direction. The air somehow tastes like pennies. He turns his head in that direction and is shocked that he can see something. It's not much, just a shadow in the shadows, a table leg maybe.

Another scream shatters the calm, followed by a second barrage of blasts. The person to Michael's left falls silent.

"You've done well, Mark," *the demon whispers.* "And they... well, they got what they deserved."

Michael can hear the slithery smile in the demon's tone. Footsteps trail away. A door opens, and someone exits. Michael hears the crying man and breathes a sigh of relief. The demon is gone.

"I'm sorry, Michael," *the man says through his sobs.*

Michael's gut clenches. A dazed stupor comes over him, and tears stream from his eyes. His mind goes blank. He begins to rock.

A garbled voice that sounds as if the person is underwater calls out his name.

CHAPTER 9

Sam bounded down the stairs, taking three at a time. As her foot touched the next landing, the roof exploded. The shock wave came with a deafening rumble. The blast blew out the door and most of the ceiling and sent Sam airborne when she lost her grip on the rail.

The far wall retained its integrity. It was unforgiving when Sam smashed into it. Her shoulder took the brunt of the impact, but her momentum carried the side of her head into the stone and plaster like the crack-snap of a whip. She ricocheted off the wall and crashed onto concrete steps, knees and elbows first.

Her head spun, and a dull ringing in her ears drowned out all other sound. She stood, happy to be able to, and tried to find her balance, but she couldn't remain standing without the assistance of the rail. Smoke, clouds of plaster, and debris filled the air. It coated her and everything around her. The smell of ash assaulted her nose. Her vision blurred and almost went dark.

No. Sam slapped her face and fought off unconsciousness. The ringing in her ears lessened, and she heard muted screams from somewhere below. She stumbled down the stairs, stepping over or around chunks of the building that dotted her way out. Retracing her steps, she made her way back to Courtroom 12.

"Help!" a voice shouted as soon as she entered.

She slapped her face again, trying to shake off her disorientation, but she could only manage a sort of absent alertness. She bent over and hurled.

Wiping her mouth, she raised and saw eight—*no, four*—people at the railing: the old couple, Jack and his wife, the woman having stayed with her husband even though she wasn't cuffed; the clerk, a mutilated mess where his ear had been; and the court officer, Rhonda, who was waving at Sam, apparently trying to tell her something.

Sam couldn't make out what the court officer was saying over the jackhammer breaking through her skull. "What... what is it?" She heard the slur in her voice, but couldn't seem to get rid of it.

"Stop!" Rhonda shouted.

The word registered just as Sam put her foot down on uneven ground. Metal clinked underfoot. The clerk moaned, and Sam could see that he wasn't just bleeding from his ear, but from his nose and teeth, as well. Their white enamel looked as though they'd been smeared with pink lip gloss. She blinked away some of the fogginess and almost wished she hadn't. She could see better, which was good, but her other senses returned with a vengeance. And she felt everything, all her bruised and broken bits.

"He thought it would be funny to put the keys just out of reach," Rhonda said.

Sam raised her foot and saw the key ring. She bent over to pick them up and fell. After grabbing the keys, she took a deep breath and focused on them. They came in fuzzy, but that was an improvement over double. She slid the keys over to Rhonda, who quickly removed her handcuffs then took off the clerk's.

"Billings?" Sam asked. "Which way?"

"That asshole? Out the main doors." The clerk pointed behind them. "I hope you kill the bastard."

Sam started to nod, but the pain made her keep her head in place. "How long?"

"Not too long. Maybe three or four minutes. Long enough, I suppose."

"Follow me, and be quick."

Rhonda finished freeing Jack. "What about her?" she asked, pointing at the woman who had been shot in the stomach and lay in a wide pool of her own blood.

Sam stood on wobbly legs, walked over, and grabbed the woman's wrist. After finding no pulse, she held the glass face of her watch over the woman's lips. Not a hint of fog appeared. Shaking her head, she said, "Too late. We need to go. We're heading out the front doors. It may be safe now, but I can't be sure. Let's go."

Sam led the small group out of the courtroom and down the stairs as fast as she could manage. The clerk ran ahead, but Rhonda took the rear to make sure everyone got out safely. Jack and his wife—Edith, he called her—not only kept up, but might have lapped Sam had she not been in their way.

At the bottom of the stairs, Sam could see out the glass doors lining the front of the building. She didn't see any cops, but she spotted seven or eight court officers trying to keep everyone away from the building and another four watching the roof with the rest of the gawkers.

The majority of the court officers looked like they pissed protein. Some of them were enormous, and a few were bigger than that. All wore white button-downs, navy slacks, black shoes, and shoulder radios. They stuck out like sore thumbs. Rex wouldn't be stupid enough to try to mingle with that crowd. *He wouldn't have gone out this way.*

"Where are the other exits?" Sam asked Rhonda.

"There are two in the back, but you need a scan card and ID badge to get to them. The other is in the rear of the library, but it's an emergency exit. An alarm will go off... oh... I can't remember exactly when the alarm went off, but it was way before Rex escaped."

Sam nodded. "Okay. Get these people out safely, but first, point me toward the library."

Rhonda shook her head. "I think maybe I should take you to a hospital. You're in no condition—"

"I look worse than I feel," Sam lied. "All superficial injuries, thankfully."

"I don't know..."

"Please, Rhonda. Billings is an animal. As long as he's loose, no one is safe."

Frowning, Rhonda pointed at the hall behind Sam. "The library is that way."

Sam shoved all her hurt into a small closet in the back of her mind and hurried after her prey. Out of instinct, she reached for the gun that should have been at her hip. She groaned when she remembered it wasn't there. *I can't just let him go free. Anyone else he hurts would be my fault.*

Rex would hurt many. Of that, Sam was certain. She and a SWAT team had brought him down the first time, and she had needed every one of them. *The things he had done to his competition... those women he kept chained...* The man was capable of unspeakable horrors. No, she would not let him escape.

Sam entered the library and, keeping her back to the wall, carefully walked around the perimeter until she spotted the red letters that spelled EXIT. She shoved the push bar and barreled outside. Skidding to a stop on the sandy walkway, she looked left and right. She saw no sign of her criminal. *The trail's gone cold. I'm too late.*

"Fuck!" a gruff voice cursed. Sam could just make out Rex's black-and-gray curls around the front of a Bristol County Sheriff's Office transport vehicle. "Where are your motherfucking keys?" He was down on one knee. With each word, his body jerked.

Two legs clad in the forest-green slacks of a deputy jutted out from the opposite side of the van. *Christ, he's already killed another one?* She crouched and peered under the vehicle, hoping the deputy's gun was somewhere within reach. The pistol was still holstered at the deputy's hip.

She stood and shouted, "Freeze!" She wanted Rex's back to her. With no gun and no cuffs, her only chance to take him down was to bluff her way to the gun before Rex could grab it. "Turn around and step out from behind the vehicle with your hands over your head where I can see them."

"Is that you, bitch?" Rex stood with his hands raised above his head.

She took a step toward him. He slowly turned, hands still in the air. When he looked at her, he smiled and winked, then he took off at a sprint.

Sam ran to the fallen deputy and checked his pulse, not expecting to feel anything given the man's gunshot wounds. After confirming that the man was dead, she grabbed his radio. "Sheriff's deputy down behind courthouse. Officer in need of immediate backup. Chasing murder suspect on foot, east on Spring Street." She picked up the deputy's gun and cuffs and headed after Rex, ready to shoot to kill if need be.

He had nearly four hundred yards on her, and she saw him turn a corner. But in the busy downtown district, Sam didn't need to see the sadistic monster to follow him. All she had to do was follow the screams.

"Watch it, asshole!" someone yelled.

Sam booked it in that direction. She ran at a diagonal where she could, anticipating his path and shortening the distance between them. Even with her bruised ribs making every inhalation painful and her shoulder burning with every swing of her arm, she could catch up to Rex. He was stronger than an ox but built like a pro wrestler, too top-heavy to be fleet of foot.

She tore her badge off her belt and flashed it at the first pedestrian she saw—a woman with a stroller—when she rounded the Government Center. "Where? Where?"

The woman gasped and backed away, so Sam didn't bother stopping. When she reached a café where a table had been knocked over on the patio and patrons were standing and watching her approach, she received several more dumb looks but also a few pointing fingers.

She went where the fingers pointed. After a few more yards, she heard Rex's harsh breathing and turned down an alley. He was attempting to climb a fence, but its crossbeams were on the opposite side.

"Freeze!" Sam shouted again. The pistol's weight in her hand was like holding a Bible for the religious man. She raised it and awaited Rex's move as she stalked toward him.

The length of the alley, maybe eighty yards, separated them. Sam smiled. *Who's the bitch now, bitch?*

A door opened a few feet in front of Rex. A chubby teenager in a white T-shirt and a black apron came out, carrying a garbage bag. Rex leaped forward, grabbed the kid, threw him aside, and dashed through the open doorway.

Sam hurried over and checked on the kid. After verifying that he was okay, she said, "Stay out here and call 911."

She put her back against the door and examined the interior: a poorly lit storage area with shelving lined with dry goods, the back of a market or restaurant. Leading with her gun, she stepped into the room.

Rex charged out of the shadows to her right. Before she could turn and fire, he seized her wrist and bashed it against the wall. She shrieked and dropped the gun. Rex's huge hand closed around her throat and squeezed.

"Killing you will be worth getting caught," he said.

Using her elbow, Sam chopped down on his bicep, breaking his grip. She followed with a knee meant for his groin, but the blow was blocked by his thigh. The combo created some breathing room but not much.

Rex laughed as he grabbed her hair and slammed her head against the doorframe. Flashes of bright light crisscrossed her vision, and she barely saw his next strike coming toward her in time to duck. His knuckles scraped across her scalp as she shot under the punch, pushing into him with all she had.

Rex stumbled backward and collided with a shelf, knocking several cans to the floor. But he stayed on his feet.

A woman stormed into the storage area. Sam assumed she was a manager of some sort but couldn't exactly read the name tag pinned to her chest.

"Get everyone out and call—shit!" Sam cut herself off as Rex threw another haymaker. She had managed to create a couple feet of space between them and some room to maneuver. Though Rex had her with power and reach, she had him in speed and, she hoped, training.

In an instant, she confirmed her hope. Rex's eyes telegraphed his every attack, aligning his aim with his body's movements. Sam's father hadn't known much, but he had the talent of a Golden Gloves boxer and the fiery Boston Irish temperament to use it in the ring and out when challenged. He had imparted his knowledge—and his temperament—to Sam.

She weaved low under Rex's jab and lunged forward, closing the gap between them with ballerina grace. Putting all the strength in her legs behind her punch, she blasted her body upward, releasing an uppercut that would have made her father proud. Her fist collided squarely with his chin.

Rex cried out in anguish. Blood sprayed from his mouth. "You... you... biffthh! You... nnng... you made me bitthh mytthhongue." His eyes were red with rage. His knuckles jutted like craggy mountains from his clenched fists.

Here he comes. Sam's father had taught her boxing, but her first love, judo, gave her the means to react when Rex charged. When facing a larger opponent, leverage and momentum were everything. And timing was everything else.

Rex was a bull and she the wary matador. She waited until he was right on top of her before grabbing his shirt and pulling it into her chest as she dropped to her knees and spun completely around in one fluid motion. The move was called drop *seoi nage*, and when done right, the attacker's own momentum sent him flipping forward over the counterattacker. Sam nailed it perfectly.

Except for the landing.

As Rex rolled head under feet over her, Sam didn't pull him into her so that he landed flat on his back. Instead, she dropped him on his head.

Rex's skull collided with the floor with a sickening crunch, but the damage seemed to have affected the floor more than him. He sat up quickly, but he swayed, most likely from dizziness.

Sam locked her arm under his chin and her legs around his waist then fell backward, pulling him on top of her. Arching upward, she stretched him out while clamping down on his neck.

Rex clawed at her arm, but she had the choke so tight that he couldn't dig his fingers under the hold. He was like a turtle on its shell, weakened and quickly losing steam. His clawing turned to pawing then to nothing more than a slight twitch. Eventually, his arms fell to his sides.

Sam held the choke a few seconds longer in case he was faking. When she was satisfied he was out cold, she slid out from under him and cuffed him to the shelving.

CHAPTER 10

"He sees me," Ryan said, cleaning the barrel of the M24 Sniper Weapons System, the military-grade version of a Remington 700 rifle. "He knows."

Of course he knows, the Voice—always present, always watching—answered. *You should never have let him live. And to reach out to him now? It's unwise, to say the least. To think, he turned out just like you.*

"You don't know that." Ryan squinted at the barrel. "How can you know that?"

The Voice laughed. *You know it as well as I do. I saw him at the library as clear as if I had been there myself, so I know you recognized him too.* He tsked. *Loose ends, Ryan. What did I always tell you about loose ends?*

"He was just a little boy. He couldn't have understood back then. He couldn't have remembered it."

He's remembering now.

"What did you want me to do, huh? Really? I'm a professional. I don't just kill little boys for no good reason." Ryan scoffed. "Besides, he wasn't part of the contract."

Neither were his parents.

Pounding a fist on the table, Ryan said, "He was still innocent. They were not, and they were necessary for the setup. You know that. You helped me plan the job. You never said anything about killing the boy then. Why are we discussing it now?"

Because now, he matters. The Voice let out a long sigh. *So many successes, never getting caught, never so much as leaving behind any shred of evidence that could be traced back to you or reason to doubt the story you crafted, and it'll be a three-year-old boy who will be your undoing.*

Ryan jammed five rounds into the magazine. "He's not three anymore."

And he still hasn't told anyone what he's beginning to suspect. You know what you have to do, while there's still time to do it.

"What? Kill him?" Ryan wasn't ready to even entertain that possibility. "I don't need to do that. I *won't* do that."

You do. You will.

"No one would even believe him."

That detective might.

Ryan sighed. "Let me talk to him first. If he's like us, maybe he'll understand."

Sounds like a hard sell.

"He'll at least have questions. Maybe I can talk to him. The world has not been kind to him. He'll understand. I'll *make* him understand."

The Voice sighed again. *Have it your way. In the end, you'll agree. Little Michael Florentine should have died years ago.*

CHAPTER 11

B andaged and hurting so badly that the slightest movement made her wince, Sam shambled up the walkway to her apartment building. She would need to sleep for a week, but at least she hadn't been permanently damaged. She turned to wave at Tagliamonte, but that meant lifting her just-relocated shoulder, so she let her hand drop by her side. The officer had been kind enough to give her a ride home from the hospital. Sam—with a concussion, a ruptured septum, undetermined auditory damage, a chipped tooth, and a shoulder that had been slipping in and out of the socket—was in no condition to drive. Beyond the recorded injuries, she wore enough purple to make her more plum than peach. Dr. Kilpatrick had given her a dose of Percocet, but it was already wearing off.

"You saved some lives today, Detective," Tagliamonte called out the cruiser window. "We're lucky to have you."

"Thanks, Ron." Sam might have smiled if that, too, didn't hurt so much... and if her thoughts didn't drift toward the seven or eight lives she had failed to save. "I'll see you tomorrow."

"I hope you don't." He laughed. "That would mean you would be at the precinct."

She held in a breath and walked toward the door, one excruciating step after another. Not until the cruiser was long out of sight did she realize she had called Tagliamonte by his first name.

She dropped her keys. "Shit!" It took her a full minute to bend over and pick them up, every second of which was an exercise in agony. Her hip flared, and her knees started to buckle. She thought about curling up there on the walk, not moving until someone made her. But stopping would have meant stopping for good, so she propped her good shoulder against the door while she shimmied the key into the lock.

As she pushed the door open, it hit against something heavy. Sam heard a soft moan. Instinctively, her hand went to her hip, though no gun was holstered there. She supposed the deputy's gun had already made it to an evidence locker, and she had no idea where hers was.

The moaning grew louder. Sam squeezed her head and shoulder into the space between the door and the frame. Two legs dressed in blue jeans lay across the foyer. One leg ended with a heel propped on the second step.

"Michael?" She wriggled through the opening, her elbow, shoulder, back, and head all exploding in cyclic bursts of mind-splitting hurt. "Michael!"

The boy lay on the floor, his eyelids fluttering like butterfly wings. He didn't appear to be injured until Sam lifted his head and found a crab-apple-sized lump on the back of it. She was happy to feel nothing wet or sticky.

She cradled him in her arms, meaning to carry him up the stairs, but then she realized she couldn't in her condition. "Michael?" She brushed his hair off his forehead. "Michael, what happened?"

The events of the day were weighing heavy on her, and to end it with Michael hurt was just too much. Stifling the tears that threatened to fall took all the resolve she could muster.

Michael's eyes opened, and he squinted up at her. "Sam?" He shifted his head left then right. "Where am I? Why are you holding me?"

Sam moved her arm so he could sit up. "I think you fell down the stairs."

"I fell?" He winced as he rubbed the back of his head. "What the heck happened to you?"

Sam tried but couldn't choke down the fit of laughter that rose in her throat. Michael had fallen down the stairs and had been lying on the floor, unconscious, and he was criticizing *her* injuries. Michael watched her with a frown that slowly flattened out. Soon, he was giggling with her.

"I look like shit, don't I?" She chuckled. "Are you hurt?" She reached into her pocket for her phone, then she remembered that had been taken too. "Where's your phone? I'll call an ambulance. I don't think I could drive us to the hospital. I'm loaded up on painkillers."

"Ugh." Michael stood and dusted himself off. "I'm okay. Just a bump on my head. No biggie. Besides, didn't you just come from the hospital? With all those bandages, I'm guessing you were just at one."

"No biggie?" Sam frowned. "You fell down the stairs. That's nothing to laugh about."

Michael rubbed his head. "At least I don't look like I got hit by a bus then run over by a steamroller, only to be mauled by a bear after that." He smirked. "You look almost as bad as when I kick your butt in judo."

"You wish!" Sam had been teaching Michael a little self-defense. He'd shown a gift for balance, which made his fall that much more peculiar. She eyed him suspiciously. "I guess we've both seen better days."

Michael's grin widened. "Just don't tell me I should see the other guy." Michael looked away, and his smile shriveled. "What happened, Sam? Are you okay? Really?"

"You first. Why were you lying at the bottom of the stairs? Was it a vision? Did someone touch you?"

Michael's face darkened. "It's... it's nothing."

He didn't lie often, but Sam could always tell when he did. "Michael—"

"Let's just go inside, okay? You promised me you'd tell me about my parents, remember? I want you to tell me. No, I *need* you to tell me."

Need? Sam didn't like the sound of that. "Michael, it's getting late, and we've both obviously been through a lot for one day."

"You promised."

"I promised that I would tell you *tomorrow*, that is, if you still want to know then."

Michael's chin lifted. In his eyes, she could read his anger, but she also saw something else there: fear.

"Please, Sam." His shoulders drooped, and he suddenly looked twenty years older. His eyes shimmered. "I need to know."

There's that word again. Sam studied her charge for a moment then sighed before hobbling over to the stairs. On every fourth step, she paused to catch her breath, her adrenaline spent, and the exhaustion of the day having caught up to her and then some. Not all of her plodding was due to her injuries. Though she usually hid her battle scars from Michael, she hoped that letting him see her every ache and pain would convince him to give up the fight and let her sleep.

But Michael was as stubborn as a sticky door when he got an idea in his head. Sam grinned, her back to Michael. *He's like me in that way, I suppose.*

He ran up beside her before she could get her keys back out of her pocket. "Here, let me." He put his own key into the knob and opened the door.

Sam half smiled and followed him into the apartment. In the dining room, she rested against the back of a chair, feeling over a hundred years old.

Michael hit the lights and went to the kitchen. "Sit down," he said, opening a cupboard. He retrieved a can of instant coffee. "I'll make you a cup of coffee, and you can start talking. Tell me everything you know about what happened to them."

Sam tucked her hair behind her ears, wincing as her fingers found yet another bruise. "Are you sure you want to know this?" She already knew the answer but felt she had to try to dissuade him one more time. *The duty of a mother.* She rubbed her forehead. *But you're not his mother. And he wants to hear about the real one. What good can come from this?*

Michael rolled his eyes. "You're stalling. I'm never going to stop asking. Please, Sam. Enough already. This is really important to me."

Sam pursed her lips. "All right. But no coffee. I'm going to have enough trouble sleeping tonight as it is. Decaf tea is fine. Thank you. I'm going to the bathroom. I'll be right back."

Michael nodded. He lit the burner beneath the kettle on the stove.

In the bathroom, Sam splashed some water on her face. She tried to avoid the mirror, but she caught a glimpse anyway. *I really do look like hell.* She tried to gather her thoughts and figure out what she was going to tell him, but exhaustion won out. She would just have to tell him the truth, as she'd promised. Having stalled as long as she could, she headed back to the kitchen.

Gingerly sitting down, she said, "I don't know too much about them, really."

Michael leaned over the counter, glaring at her.

Before he could open his mouth, she added, "But yes, I know how they died and why and some other basic facts. Everything else I learned about them came later. I found out all I could many years after the fact, in case... you know, in case you ever asked about them."

The kettle whistled, and Michael poured hot water into a mug that read World's Greatest Detective. He'd given it to her after the whole Masterson ordeal.

Yeah, some detective you turned out to be. So many dead... Matt and others today, Michael's foster parents yesterday, and before that... She studied her fingers, feeling smothered by the veil of sadness and death that followed her through life. *So many killers responsible for so many deaths, my missteps responsible for more. They're like fucking weeds. Pluck one, and another sprouts in its place.*

"Well?" Michael nudged, startling her from her thoughts. He placed the mug in front of her and plopped into the opposite chair.

"Your father's name was—"

"Mark Florentine?"

Sam gaped at him. "Yes. How did you know that?"

"I did a little research. You can relax. I know how they died. I just want to hear it from you, the whole story, or at least what you know that the papers left out."

In a way, Sam was thankful he already knew. That made telling him so much easier. *But how long has he been carrying this burden alone?* She searched his face for any sign of how the news of his father's murder-suicide had impacted him. But Michael's expression was as flat as the tabletop. He seemed dead to it. *Why shouldn't he be? They died when he was too young to remember them.*

"I wasn't that young," he said as if he'd read her thoughts. "I don't remember them... not exactly. I can't see their faces. But I remember how my father used to pick me up and throw me on the couch, and I would get up laughing and begging for him to do it again. I remember my mother would always plant a wet kiss on my forehead, and I would wipe it off with the back of my hand and tell her no, but she would keep doing it anyway. I remember how her hair smelled..." He seemed to drift away into some long-lost memory.

Sam wasn't equipped with the skills to comfort him, didn't know how to reach him, to let him know she was there for him. She put her hand on his.

He snapped back into the present and shrugged. "I think we had a cat." He stiffened. "Anyway, I've been dreaming about it, I think."

Sam's heart swelled. While part of her was happy to have him opening up to her, that happiness made her feel guilty and sadder for his sorrow. "Oh, Michael, that's—"

"Please, just keep going."

Sam shifted in her seat, hissing as her shoulder cried out and her hip flared with refreshed agony. She knew it was all going to feel a whole lot worse in the morning. "I wasn't the first on the scene. And I hadn't been a detective long, which is probably why seeing you there had such an impact on me. A couple of officers had responded to a report of shots fired at your former residence."

Sam realized she was shifting into cop mode—she always did when talking about her cases—but it was the easiest way for her to say what Michael needed to hear. "By the time the responding officers had arrived, your mother and father were already dead. If it's any consolation, they did not appear to have suffered." She studied Michael again, but his face remained closed. Her own mask felt as if it might crumble to dust in the slightest wind.

He waved his hand. "Go on. I'm fine."

Sam cleared her throat. "Simply put, your father shot your mother before turning the gun on himself."

Michael rolled his fingers against the tabletop. "And?"

"And what? That's really all there is to it."

"I know that's what he did, Sam. *Why* did he do it?"

Sam took a sip of her tea. "Your father found your mother in bed with another man. You see, they were separated at the time, and—"

"Where was the Whisperer?"

Sam frowned. "What?"

"I mean, uh, who else was there?"

"What do you mean?"

"I mean, who else was there?"

Sam shook her head. "No one."

Michael raised one eyebrow. "Well, I was there, wasn't I?"

Sam bit her lip. "Yes, you were there, but I don't know how much of it you saw. We found you sitting in front of a wall with the murder weapon between your legs. How it got there has always troubled me. But prints on the gun, powder residue, blood spattering, bullet trajectory analysis, and a host of other evidence confirmed my initial theory that your father, upon entering and seeing your mother in bed with another man, shot and killed her and her lover before turning the gun on himself."

Sam gasped and covered her mouth. She chided herself for forgetting the fact she was talking about the poor orphaned boy's only kin.

Michael seemed unfazed. "And you're sure no one else was there?"

"Yes. No one was there, except you."

"You're absolutely sure of it?"

"If someone else had been there, he or she left no evidence behind." She frowned. "Just because the case had, at initial blush, seemed pretty much open-and-shut doesn't mean we shirked our responsibilities. We combed that place for any evidence that would either prove or *disprove* my assessment."

"Then who's whispering?" Michael muttered, looking off into space.

"Huh?" Sam had heard him, but she didn't understand. "I don't hear anything."

"It's nothing." He shrugged. "Sorry." He tapped the table. "What did my father do, like for work?"

Sam leaned back in her seat. "He was some kind of technician down at the power plant."

"Did he own a gun?"

"The one he had wasn't registered."

"So where did he get it?"

Sam grinned. "You sure you don't want to be a detective? You ask a lot of good questions. Anyway, I don't know, but believe me, in this city, you can get a gun pretty much anywhere."

"And you're sure no one else was there?"

"Yes, I'm sure." She leaned forward. "Why do you keep asking me that?"

Michael sighed and looked away. "I don't know. Maybe I just don't want to believe my father was responsible. Maybe I want someone else to blame for screwing up my life."

"Michael—"

"Never mind. I'm sorry. I didn't mean that. And I'm sorry I made you tell me all that. I know it wasn't easy for you."

He smiled, but Sam saw straight through it. "Talk to me, Michael."

"Really, I'm okay. Let's just drop it. Anyway, you look like you have one heck of a story to tell. What happened to you today?"

Sam wasn't thrilled about it, but she let whatever dogs were sleeping in that head of Michael's lie right where they were lying. With as much detail as she could, preparing herself for the mountainous report she would have to write in the morning, she recounted the events of the day. He listened with apparent interest, particularly when she told of how she was injured and of Jimmy Rafferty's actions. As the conversation progressed, Michael's muscles wound tighter, his agitation so obvious in his white-knuckled fists and clenching jaw that Sam stopped often to see if he was okay and still wanted her to continue.

Each time, he nodded and gestured for her to proceed. By the time she finished, Michael was on the verge of tears.

"But I'm okay now," Sam said, reaching across the table to give his gloved hand a squeeze. "Billings is back where he belongs. The others will be caught sooner or later, I promise you. We have a pretty tight net around the city and roadblocks at every way out of it. We're going to catch these guys."

Michael's lower lip trembled. His tears began to fall. He sniffled and tried to hide his eyes.

"If you're worried about Jimmy—"

"The hell with Jimmy!" He tore off the glove over his right hand and came around the table. "I've been so selfish." He was crying hard, no longer trying to stifle it. "You've been here for me all this time. You've done everything for me, and all I do is sit here and take it for granted. You risk your life every day, and I do nothing."

"Michael, it's okay. I'm okay, really. This has nothing to do with you. And I don't want you involved. I was wrong to have ever included you in my work." She thought back to John Crotty, the man she'd used Michael to catch, and felt the shame all over again.

"I could have helped you today. I maybe could have helped those people who died too. I'm not going to sit here quietly anymore, not when I can do something about it."

Before she could pull away, Michael had her by the hand. A moment later, his eyes rolled back in their sockets, and he fell to the floor in the throes of a seizure.

CHAPTER 12

Michael is walking. A double door with an exit sign above appears to be his destination. He is alone, and a pang in his gut insists that he always will be. He slaps the bi-colored wall, white wood on top and blue tile on the bottom, a wall he has seen before, though he can't immediately place it. When he feels the sting in his palm, he knows the vision is his future, and he is able to interact with his environment. These visions are better than the other kind, where he is barely more than a ghost forced to watch unspeakable evil. In visions of his own future, he isn't quite so powerless.

The flip side is that he feels everything. He can be hurt.

Or worse.

Come on, Michael. Get a grip. This is someone else's fate, not yours. No one is going to hurt you. *He takes a deep breath.* You hope.

He knows he's there for a reason, though the explanation of that reason has never been revealed to him. Still, he brought this on himself. Didn't I? What triggered this? *He can never remember. But he does remember sitting at the table with Sam and wanting to help her.*

I must have touched her, which means I'm here to see Sam get hurt. *That's the last thing he wants to see.* Move your ass, Michael. Her life may depend on this.

"Okay, okay," he says aloud. "Get a good look at the scene." His surroundings are old and dull, like a high school that was built a century ago, but clean and still in use. The floors are waxed linoleum and reek of Pine-Sol. Machinery thunders to life behind him, and he jumps, but it's only a janitor starting an industrial-sized buffer. The man is wearing earplugs and seems oblivious to Michael's presence. Michael studies the guy, though he doubts the janitor is the threat.

I was heading out those doors. Whatever I'm supposed to see has got to be out there. *He stares at the ominous letters of the exit sign, so covered in dust and grime that their red is dampened and darker—like blood. On the door, a sign reads Emergency Exit Only. Alarm will sound when opened.*

To his right, a fire alarm is affixed to the wall. Michael takes note of it and of the axe in a locked glass case beside it. Those may be useful if I find myself here again. Sam's job brings her into contact with so many crazies.

The words painted on the axe box read Break glass in case of emergency. Michael silently vows to do just that. He is tempted to do so at that very moment, but it may prevent him from seeing what will become of Sam if that's what he's truly there to see.

Please be just some small accident.

He places his hand on the push bar. Holding his breath, he presses it and opens the door. The heat of the sun beats against his skin, a pleasant contrast to the over-air-conditioned hallway. But the bright light is blinding.

When his eyes adjust, he steps into a big parking lot. Its surface is cracked and broken, and Michael nearly stumbles over a divot. Humid, sticky heat radiates off the pavement, creating a rippling haze. The smell of mulch fills the air.

A forest sits at the edge of the lot a hundred yards or so away. There, tree roots bulge and bust through the cement, their owner a giant elm offering the lot's only shade.

Sam's Toyota Camry sits beneath its outstretched branches. She is leaning against the side of the car. "Michael," she calls, smiling and waving.

Michael's suspicions are confirmed. He touched Sam. And in spite of what that probably meant for her, he can't help but feel a smidgen of happiness to see her.

Until the guilt sinks in.

The pang in his stomach persists, seizes his insides, and turns them weak. Soon, it spreads through him like a disease, infecting his muscles and his brain, turning him into a frightened, useless little boy.

The déjà vu makes things considerably worse. He has been in a similar situation before, running toward Sam while she waits beside her car. History seems to be repeating itself. Like in one of those Final Destination *movies, Death is getting another chance to take the soul that got away.*

He can't stop his mind from conjuring images of Tessa's father, Christopher Masterson, just as the man himself steps from the shadows.

"It can't be," Michael mutters. "He's dead."

The man steps into the light. He brandishes the very knife Tessa used to kill him.

Michael screams a warning, but the words come out wrong. "Can't be you! Dead! You are!"

Sam's smile falls away. She turns to face the masked man—Michael sees the mask now, the cheap plastic face of an Indian warrior—just as the man plunges the knife into her stomach.

The man is taller and beefier than Masterson. He uses his strength to press Sam against the car. When he steps back, she jerks and falls against the side mirror before crashing down to the pavement.

Michael's fear and panicking heart keep him planted. He stares at Sam, trying to detect the rise and fall of her chest, but she's still. "No!" he screams, and his shaky legs jerk into motion. He is running, weaponless and terrified, into the heart of danger. Anger has overpowered his other emotions, fueling his muscles. He charges to his friend's side.

"Yes, Michael. Come and get me," the masked man says. Michael doesn't recognize the voice. It's calm and smooth, tinged with what sounds like pleasure.

Michael covers the distance in seconds, not sure what he will do when he reaches his destination, only knowing Sam needs him. Every fiber of his being wants to hurt this man who attacked his friend, hurt him worse than what he's done to Sam.

If he's killed her... Michael roars, adrenalin feeding his hatred. He lowers his shoulder to drive it into the man's midsection, conscious of the weapon in the man's hand but not caring about it.

The masked man sidesteps as gracefully as a dancer, simultaneously cupping the back of Michael's head and continuing its momentum into the side panel of Sam's car.

Michael slumps to the ground. His head spins, and he thinks he might vomit.

"I see you, Michael," another voice says. It belongs to the Whisperer.

As his grogginess clears, he sees the masked man's legs in front of him. To the right, he spots the figure in the black hoodie, face hidden under cloth.

"You can't be here," Michael mumbles. "You can't be responsible for all this too."

"I see you," the Whisperer repeats. "I'm coming."

The masked man never turns. He seems completely unaware of the other's presence. "You're mine now, Michael." He thrusts his weapon into Michael's side.

Michael's skin burns like fire at the point of contact. A jolt of pain runs through his body so fiercely that his mind fails him. Darkness swallows him once again.

WITH HER REMAINING strength, Sam hauled the seizing Michael out of the kitchen. The only way she could manage it was to lay him across her forearms as if she were carrying a hundred-plus-pound box, and even that didn't work for long. Pain crippled her, spurting from every joint and tenderized muscle in her body. By the time she was outside his room, she had to scoop him beneath the armpits and pull him the rest of the way, his heels dragging across the carpet.

After heaving him onto the bed, she pulled a blanket over him. After a few minutes, the seizure stopped, and his breathing regulated. He began to snore softly, but his eyes danced behind their lids.

I hope your dreams are sweeter than whatever vision you were forced to endure this time. Sam kneeled beside his bed, kissed her fingers, and pressed them against his forehead. *Let me into that head of yours, will you?*

She stood and went to the doorway, where she paused and looked up at the ceiling. *If you're up there, let this boy rest.* She turned and headed for her own bedroom in search of much-needed rest of her own.

WHEN SAM AWOKE THE next morning, her every injury screamed at her to stay in bed. She couldn't believe how much worse she felt, as if she'd been trampled under the biggest stampede in Texas. Craning her neck, she checked her nightstand, hoping she'd had the forethought to put her Percocets and maybe even a bottle of water there before going to bed.

No such luck. She groaned and crashed back down into her pillows. She listened for any signs that Michael was up and about but heard nothing. With another long, strained groan, she climbed out of the bed, stood, and tossed some life into her hair. She was still wearing the clothes she'd had on the day before, as bloody and ravaged as they were, but she didn't want to take the time to change.

She stumbled down the hall to Michael's room. His bed was empty.

"Michael?"

No answer.

"Michael?" she called louder. *Maybe he's in the shower. I don't hear the water running, but—* A folded piece of paper was propped against a pillow on the bed.

"Oh God..." She hobbled over and fell onto the bed. The paper could have been anything, said anything, but her mind immediately conjured images of Michael running away. *Is this what it means to be a parent? Always afraid?*

"Has it been *that* bad for him?" Sam muttered. "Have I been so blind? How could I not have seen this?"

She snatched up the folded paper, which had her name on the outside in big bold letters. On the inside, it read:

I'm sorry. I have to leave. If my stupid visions are good for anything, it's that they tell me that as long as I'm in your life, you're in danger. Someone is after me. He's coming for me. I won't let him get you too.

"Someone's after you?" Sam had learned months ago to trust Michael's visions, and for that reason alone, she needed to find him immediately. Her pain was nothing. She grabbed her keys and headed for the door.

CHAPTER 13

Michael peered into the water. He couldn't pierce its chocolate-brown surface. Out deeper, where the waves crashed into the pillars of the skeletal remains of a decommissioned bridge, the salt water fizzled like cola and looked like it too. But at the Taunton River's rocky and garbage-strewn shoreline, the poison water sloshed up the putrid gray mud from the river basin. The mud smelled worse than the garbage and salt combined, and it turned the water to sludge.

And this is my happy place. What does that say about me?

Michael liked the spot under the old bridge because, at least in the daytime, he could be alone there. A soft-shell crab scuttled sideways then darted into the water as Michael leaned over to pick up a rock. *Well, not entirely alone.* His find was smooth and oval and good for skipping, he assumed, if he could ever figure out how to skip rocks. He threw it side-armed and watched as it hit the water and continued through it, plunking down into the depths.

And it was never seen again. He sighed and wiped his hands on his jeans. *I wish I was that stupid rock.*

Of all the times he kept to himself, when he had carried on alone, swearing he was invisible and that no one anywhere gave a damn, the times spent at his hideaway under the bridge were the only moments he liked being alone, especially at high tide when the odor was more bearable. He had heard his old guidance counselor had washed up somewhere upstream, not that Sam would confirm it. He guessed many other bodies had been claimed by the river.

Room for one more?

If he were to wade into the river and just keep walking deeper and deeper, weighted down by rocks, he wondered if anyone would even notice. And if someone did, would he or she even care? No one had ever bothered Michael when he was there. He had only seen an amateur fisherman, once on the old bridge and once at the shoreline, but the man had kept to himself just as Michael had, a sort of understanding among those lost and forgotten. The man would throw his line into that primordial soup, hoping to catch only he knew what. It turned Michael's stomach to think the man would eat anything pulled from that river, and he guessed—or hoped—the man would throw it back.

He glanced up at the bridge and saw no fisherman. The only eyes on him were those of the skittish seagulls who pecked at the garbage that had washed up there. They watched him furtively, as though he might steal their meal, moving in for a peck at the waste or grabbing pieces and carrying them off.

The sounds soothed him: the waves crashing against the columns of the old bridge, their smaller brethren lapping near his feet, the occasional honk of a goose or the cry of a seagull, and the whistle of the wind. He loved the feel of the salty breeze, the tingle as it kissed his skin. It reminded him that he was part of something bigger, even if no one else seemed to think so.

His shoulders drooped. *What am I doing?* A skiff rolled past, and its captain tipped his hat. Michael nodded back at him.

It would be better for everyone if I just disappeared. Sam would be a thousand times better off. Sam... she's probably worried about me.

"Still coming here, I see."

Michael jumped. He'd been so lost in thought that he hadn't noticed the boy standing beside him. He didn't recognize the kid right away. The other boy's red hair was buzzed close to the scalp, and he had a couple of new scars. But when he did recognize Jimmy Rafferty, Michael forgot everything and was filled with excitement.

"Jimmy!" Michael stepped toward Jimmy with his arms out. He stopped when his mind caught up with his emotions. "What are you doing here, man? The police are looking everywhere for you."

Jimmy smiled, but Michael saw no warmth in it. He was clean and wore a sweatshirt and jeans.

Someone's helping him. Or he had some money stored away somewhere. He needs to get out of this city. Maybe I can go with him.

Michael was surprised that he found the thought appealing. He was about to suggest they escape Fall River together when he noticed Jimmy was fidgeting. The other boy seemed nervous, and his eyes were wild, looking everywhere but at Michael. *Is he afraid the cops might show?*

Whatever was troubling Jimmy, Michael could see that the past nine months had changed his friend. He wasn't the same Jimmy with whom Michael had formed a brief but undeniable bond, united by their comparable circumstances and their shared hatred for a school bully named Glenn Rodrigues, whom Jimmy had taken care of permanently.

"Are you okay, Jimmy?"

"Yeah, I'm okay, you know, aside from the whole 'wanted' thing. You know how it is."

Michael raised an eyebrow. "Not really."

"Well, anyway, I came here looking for you." Jimmy tried his smile again, but the strain behind it was obvious.

"Me? For what? If you need help, Jimmy, you know I'll do what I can."

"I was hoping you'd say that."

"How did you know how to find me?"

"You told me all about this place. You said you came here all the time when you needed to clear your head. Of course, while you were telling me that, I was plotting how to kill Glenn, but hey, this proves I listened." He shrugged. "But the past's the past, right? How's Robbie Wilkins? I heard you're actually friends with that d-bag."

"For a kid who's been locked up, you sure know a whole lot about me." Michael shrugged. "Robbie's okay now. He's changed. Feels real bad about what he did to you."

Jimmy balled up his fists. "What he did to *us*." He looked down at his hands then relaxed them. "Are you still having those visions?"

Michael scowled. "Okay. How do you know about them?"

"Everyone knows about them. Do you really think I wouldn't know everything about my own case?"

"I... I tried to stop you. I wanted to stop you."

"Don't sweat it." Jimmy nodded at Michael's hands. "Nice lady gloves. Those essential to your superpowers?" He chuckled. "But seriously, how does it work? You just gotta touch somebody?" He moved closer.

Michael frowned and stepped back. "What do you want, Jimmy?"

"You should know something, Mikey. I don't hold it against you for not stopping me from killing that dumbass, Glenn. That prick deserved what he got. Not a day goes by that I regret killing him. Not even a little bit. I only regret where it's left me and how it's brought me here today." The whole time he spoke, Jimmy kept trying to get closer to Michael, but Michael continued to back away, maintaining some distance between them.

"What are you saying, Jimmy?" Michael raised his hands. "You're my friend, aren't you? What is this? Why are you here?"

"Yeah, we're friends. I stopped Glenn from drowning you, from hurting or bullying any kids ever again. They only slapped him on the wrist before, didn't even kick the jerk out of school. I saw to it that justice was done."

"What you did was vengeance."

"Ha! You have been reading too many of those comic books. I got news for you, Batman. Justice and vengeance are the same damn thing, except maybe for one difference—vengeance is justice you can feel good about. There's a reason people cheer for the Punisher, Ghost Rider, Rorschach, Wolverine... the freaking Red Hood. They want to hurt people just as badly as they've been hurt by them if not worse. They crave it like a nympho craves dick. What I did to Glenn, I'm not the least bit sorry about. Hell, I wish I could exterminate every damn Glenn on this planet."

"Why are you telling me all this?" Michael didn't like the look in Jimmy's eyes, something manic bordering on madness. He continued to backpedal, his feet unsteady as he stepped blindly over the rocky shore. Until he hit a wall. He tried to turn, but biceps as big as his head curled around him. "Jimmy! What is this?" He pushed at the arms while kicking his feet. "Help me!"

"Quit squirming, you little shit," the man who held Michael snapped.

The voice spawned another wave of terror. Michael wriggled like a slippery eel. He found a gap in the hold and popped out beneath the man's arms, smooshing his nose in the process. Michael's eyes watered, but he was free. Before he could dash away, a firm hand grabbed his shirt and yanked him off his feet.

"We're not here to hurt you, Mike," Jimmy said.

Michael's shirt, torn and stretched, hung loose over his shoulders. As he tried to get to his feet, he looked around for a means of escape, but before he could even stand, he was being lifted off the ground. The man held him so tight he couldn't breathe.

Jimmy sighed. "I'm sorry about this, Mike. I really am." His voice cracked, and Michael was almost inclined to believe him until Jimmy's face went deadpan. "But we need you," he added.

Jimmy extended a hand to Michael's cheek. Michael craned his neck to avoid the touch, but in his captor's grip, he had nowhere to go.

CHAPTER 14

After searching for Michael at all his usual hangouts, at least all
those she knew, Sam drove back home, hoping he was already
there waiting on her. But the apartment was empty. She popped a
couple of painkillers, showered, and dressed in clean clothes.

She couldn't just sit there, so she went to the precinct, where a
wealth of resources would be at her fingertips.

He's all right, she kept telling herself. *He's going to be all right.*

As soon as she arrived, she issued a BOLO for a boy matching his
description. Most of the officers at the precinct at least knew what he
looked like, so that was easy enough. At her desk, she reclined in her
chair, trying to figure out where he might go, but she couldn't stop
dwelling on how Michael must have been feeling at that moment and
how she had failed to help him. Her cell phone sat silent beside her.
She picked it up every so often to check it anyway. *If only I'd seen it
sooner.*

A knock at her door broke into her reverie. Officer Paltrow stood
in the doorway, her mouth curled in an uncertain smile. "Sorry to
disturb you, Detective Reilly. But you have a visitor."

Sam spotted Agent Franklin Theodore Spinney standing behind
Paltrow. Dressed in a black sports coat, blue jeans, and a white Polo,
the tall, gaunt man had a look and air of experience and shrewdness.
Ten years her elder, he had already been a skilled sleuth when she'd
last seen him, while she'd been barely off her training wheels.

"Frank!" She leaped to her feet and immediately regretted doing
so. She pursed her lips and sucked in a harsh breath, hoping Frank
hadn't noticed her pain.

He put out his hand as she strode over, and she slapped it away, breaking away from her usual professionalism to hug him. As he hugged her back, she saw Officer Paltrow walking away.

Sam ushered Frank into her office and closed the door behind him. "It's been so long, Frank! How have you been?"

"Good, good. It's good to see you again, Samantha." Frank pulled out a chair. "May I?"

Sam nodded. "Of course. Have a seat."

He sat down and leaned back in the chair. "How long has it been?" He stroked his short beard. "You look as fantastic as always."

Sam blushed. "And you're still a terrible liar." Though she was an attractive woman, her often-stern expression and cool demeanor deterred many a male advance. Add to that the fact that she was bruised and busted, and she knew he was laying it on thick. Still, she wasn't used to flattery, false or otherwise. "The whole damn force is out looking for Judge Baker. I've had a rough yesterday and a rough today, so I'm a little beat up at the moment."

"Still as beautiful as ever."

Sam lowered her eyes. That flattery had just moved from awkward to uncomfortable, yet strangely exciting. She couldn't deny a certain attraction to the man, even back when she'd found him more pomp than substance. The ten years since she'd last seen him had done little to lessen that feeling. Frank had aged like fine wine... or George Clooney. His smiling eyes belied a harder nature. It drew her in. She glanced at his ring finger. The skin was a bit lighter where a band had been.

He caught her looking. "Yep, married and divorced since the last time we saw each other. You?"

"Never even close."

"Really? I bet it wasn't for lack of men trying."

"Never the right men. I might as well start dating my collars." She thought of Rex and shuddered.

"Or your colleagues." Frank raised an eyebrow and offered a wry smile. "Anyway, I've been following your career. The young amateur has blossomed into a damn fine detective. I hear you even have a serial killer or two under your belt."

Sam smirked. "I was never an amateur."

Frank's gaze narrowed, and they both started laughing.

A memory turned Sam sober again. "Well, I had a good teacher."

Frank nodded solemnly. He pressed his fingertips into each other, bending his fingers back. "Your partner, yes. He and I butted heads at times, but I never had anything but respect for him. His was a truly excellent mind. Law enforcement lost one of its heroes when he fell."

"Thank you for saying so." She went to sit behind her desk and surreptitiously checked her cell phone. "You'll have to forgive my appearance and if I have to run out. I've got a bit of a personal crisis on my hands right now."

"Oh." He started to get up. "I'm sorry. If you'd like, I can come back at some other time when—"

"No, no. Don't be silly. I'm not sure there's a whole lot I can do about it right now, which makes it that much more frustrating, if you know what I mean."

"I do."

"So, what brings the FBI to my office? This business at the courthouse?"

"In part." Frank sat back again. "What do you know of the people behind it?"

"Not much beyond what Victor Suarez was facing. Felony assault on a senator in Brockton, which is Bristol County, but I'm not sure why Fall River got him. A serious-enough crime for sure, but worth the murder and terrorism charges six people now face?"

"Six? Was the boy there too?"

"Yeah, he put a gun to a woman's head."

"Luther Suarez." Frank shook his head. "Christ, he's only ten years old."

Michael's only fifteen... She tucked her hair behind her ears. "Tell me everything."

Frank slapped his thighs. "We call them the Suarez gang because three of them are named Suarez, though Luther is Victor and Hector's half brother." Frank shook his head. "He does so try to meet their expectations."

"You're not going soft on me, are you, Frank?" Sam snickered but quickly felt guilty for her comment, remembering her own situation. "Sorry. I know how hard it is to keep a boy on the right path."

He cleared his throat. "Victor, you know. We think he runs the show, but his brother Hector is probably the more dangerous of the two."

"The evil son of a bitch who looks like somebody held his face to a grill?"

He nodded. "I see you've met him. We haven't been able to pin him on anything yet, but he's a suspect in several bombings in and out of New England, now that we have firsthand knowledge of his MO."

"He's the one who grabbed me and is largely responsible for my injuries, him and his *American Gladiator* friend, a Maurice something-or-other."

"A six-foot-something monster of a man with arms like cannons? That would be Maurice Thibeault."

Sam scoffed then winced, remembering how easily the man had manhandled her. "His shirt said 'Earl,'" she muttered absently.

"Maurice is the muscle of the group, but don't let that fool you. He's smarter than the lot of them, save for maybe Sleven Berkowitz, the one they call Sleven Eleven. That kid has a genius-level IQ. He and Maurice could have done anything they wanted in life and even had financially stable upbringings to support them. How they ended up with the Suarez brothers is beyond me. I hear you've got Sleven penned up in the back. I would very much like to talk to him."

"Yeah, when the boys got back into the courthouse, Berkowitz was still there, snoring away despite the blaring alarm. Another prisoner, a juvie, had choked him out." She laughed. "Easiest arrest we've ever made. So you'll pardon my disbelief when it comes to his mental acumen. If you ask me, I'd say he'd have to be pretty damn stupid to be associated with the rest of them. Plus, I saw him shoot a man point-blank without so much as a second thought. The man's a cold-blooded killer. Maybe he just wanted some muscle to back his deviant pastimes." Sam shrugged. "Anyway, you're welcome to him, but so far, he's not talking."

"Everyone talks eventually if we can find the right incentive."

"You FBI folk with your ominous talk. I like it!" She laughed, and Frank gave her a wink. She could instantly feel her face turning red. "Anyway," she said, regaining her poise, "what about the girl?"

"Valeria Perez. She gives new meaning to the term 'hot-blooded Latina.' Her rap sheet is a mile long, all violent crimes. She once bit the nose off a guard who had her in cuffs and leg restraints. Add in her history of violence, theft, drugs, you name it, and she's a ticking time bomb."

Sam cringed.

"Sorry for the analogy."

"No worries. But if she's done all that, why isn't she behind bars?"

"Good question. Most of what she's done happened when she was still a juvenile. She's managed to make herself appear more presentable in her old age, and she has a soft spot for Victor, who keeps her on a leash. But if you ask me, these low-level thugs have a friend or two in high places."

Sam stroked her chin. "Who are they really, Frank? What's their end game?"

"Damned if I know. They've been on our radar for a while, but up until last year, they've been low-level players. They used to hand out fliers at colleges with liberal propaganda like 'Release Mandela' and shit like that."

"Mandela was released and died years ago."

"You get my point. Victor, Maurice, and Sleven were the educated-hippie types, always out to change the world, one petition at a time. I doubt any of the three had even seen a gun before. Then a few years back, without rhyme or reason, they turn into some sort of militia, with Hector and Valeria and all their nastiness added to their ranks. From then on, they really stepped up their game, and they've had access to weapons and explosives typical local gangs can't procure."

"C-4 and handguns aren't all that uncommon."

"And all the equipment and planning needed to orchestrate the bank heist and each explosion?" He raised a finger. "And let's not forget they also stole an ambulance and a fire truck, neither of which has been accounted for, and set off a bomb in a courthouse that had been swept for explosives."

"You're preaching to the choir here. Some of those connections were the reasons I entered the courthouse in the first place. Anyway, they gave us a hundred threads to follow. We have personnel working the more-promising leads as we speak."

"You won't find them easily, unless the one you have caged gives them up. I'm telling you, these guys are connected. If our suspicions are correct, the gang is linked to several anti-government, antiestablishment crimes: the bombing of an empty post office and several of their trucks in a coordinated scheme of vandalism across Boston, the bludgeoning and mutilation of various regional politicians, the murder of a governor's aide, the bombing of a crowded MBTA line under the financial district, and now, the concerted effort to divert police to the scenes of other felonies while perpetrating several of their own at the Fall River Judicial Complex."

She leaned forward. "Divert police? I had suspected that, but are you saying the bank robbers and arsonists were part of their crew?"

"Yes and no. The fires were set through timed contraptions. The arsonists were long gone before the fires even started. As for the robbery, the suspects were surrounded in Brockton soon after. I stopped by the Brockton PD on my way down here. Two of the criminals died in a shootout, and the third got away. Before one of them bled out, he gave up the whole gig. The courthouse was meant to be a distraction so that they could pull off the robbery. He described a deal they made with a man matching Hector Suarez's description."

"So you're saying the robbers were in with the Suarez gang?"

"I'm saying they were puppets of the Suarez gang, who, in turn, is a puppet of some greater malevolent force."

Sam hung her head. "This again! You tried to convince me of this ten years ago, and here we are discussing it now. Most of the mafias are shells of their former selves. There is no Moriarty behind the nation's crimes, at least none that you or I could ever prove."

"The circumstantial evidence—"

"The circumstantial evidence is the same now as it was then." She slammed a palm onto her desk. The references to the case that saw her severely wounded and her partner dead, all while her worry for Michael lingered on her mind, were taking their toll. She rubbed her temples. "I'm sorry, Frank. I just have a lot on my mind." She sat back. "I do believe you that there are bigger fish out there, pulling strings, but it's never been about what we believe or what we know. It's about what we can *prove*."

Frank sighed. "That's true. I'm hoping Sleven back there can help put some more links in the chain. I would have preferred Hector or Victor, but beggars can't be choosers."

"I want to help you on this, Frank. I *will* help you on this, for both personal and professional reasons. You'll have full access to my prisoner and any evidence we dredge up in the case."

"Thank you, Samantha."

She smiled. "Sam. You've earned that right."

Frank smiled back and nodded. "Sam, then. Thank you."

"You're welcome." She marveled at how far they'd come. The red tape and office politics had vanished. They had become two cops working together to close a case, *sans* egos or the need for credit.

We all had a lot of growing up to do. Before she could dwell on whether things might have been different had they grown up sooner, she forced her mind away from the subject. "Now, you said this Suarez gang was only part of the reason you're here. What's the other part?"

"Can't a guy just visit an old friend?"

Sam arched an eyebrow. "Really?"

"No use trying to fool you." He slapped his thighs and stood. "I really am happy to see you again, you know?" When she didn't respond, he shook his head. "The truth? I'm looking into another case."

He said it matter-of-factly, and though she knew the agent had crossed paths with several Fall River detectives in his distinguished career, her heart told her that only one case would fit the bill. "Oh yeah?" she asked. "What case would that be? Maybe I can help."

"I'd rather not say just yet." He smiled. "Can I buy you lunch? Maybe we can discuss it then. That is, after I question your prisoner, if that's all right with you."

Sam rose, her body weary and her smile wary. "Sure." She led him out of her office just as an officer was walking by with a red-and-black Schwinn. She stepped in front of the officer and, snapping more harshly than she intended, asked, "Where did you get that?"

The officer—*Nolan,* his tag read—looked ready to piss himself. "A man dropped it off a couple of minutes ago. I was bringing it to the back, where, um... do we have a lost-and-found department?"

"What man?" Sam shot back. "Where is he? Point him out." She scanned the precinct for anyone not employed there.

"Some old guy, real old and hunched over. He gave us his information in case there was any reward for it. He just left, though. If you hurry, you should be able to catch him."

Sam sprinted for the door.

CHAPTER 15

To Michael's left, broken pallets line the floor in stacks as tall as he is. A rusty forklift sits alone on the concrete-slab floor like the last of a great race of machines fallen into ancient history. Tall shelves stand empty to his right, those at the ends of the rows leaning against each other like falling dominoes. Pigeons coo high above in the rafters, while the light of a setting sun twinkles in through fractured windows. As if sensing his ghostlike presence, one of the birds relieves itself, raining excrement down on the spattered floor only a few feet in front of him.

He hears a screech and a loud banging like a car being crushed in a trash compactor. He turns toward the sound, but the stacks of pallets block his view. He moves closer to them. More light is pouring in through what looks like a misshapen garage door. The heavy clamor of boots moving surrounds him.

With her gun turning toward his face, Sam rounds the stack of pallets then passes right through Michael as if he's made of air. He shudders as he considers whether in that half second, he'd caught a subliminal glimpse of her insides. Another officer, an older man in plain clothes, comes around the corner, and Michael steps out of his way then turns to follow. A squadron of blue-uniformed soldiers carrying assault rifles appears next. They all fan out. Everyone, including Sam, is wearing a bulletproof vest.

Michael is on high alert, but as far as visions go, this one is turning out to be kind of cool, like a virtual-reality video game playing out all around him. He tempers his enthusiasm, knowing that, like video games, his visions often end when lives are lost.

"I've got one!" an officer yells from beside an ambulance parked in front of the damaged garage door. "He's been shot. There's no pulse."

"Got one over here too!" someone else calls out. "He's DOA."

"Either of them Michael?" Sam asks, her voice cracking.

"Negative," one officer says.

"Negative," the other repeats.

"Freeze!" Sam shouts, snapping her gun up to eye level and taking aim. She raises her free hand, signaling her team. "Nobody shoot!"

Michael hustles over to see what she's seeing. Sam's gun is trained on Jimmy.

"Why couldn't you have just run away, Jimmy?" Michael asks, even though he knows no one can hear him. "Why did you have to come after me?"

Jimmy is holding a gun. It hangs in a loose grip by his side.

"Jimmy?" Sam asks. "Are you alone? Where's Michael?"

"He's gone," Jimmy says, staggering forward. "They're all gone." Blood trickles down over his hand and drips onto the floor. His shirt is saturated with blood.

"Gone?" Michael shouts. "What do you mean I'm gone? Come on, Sam. Ask him what he means."

"Put the gun down, Jimmy," Sam says, softening her tone a little. "Lower your weapon, and we'll help you. You have my word."

"I'm not going back there." Jimmy's voice trembles. He begins to cry. "What I did to Glenn... that was a good thing! I don't deserve that place. I don't belong there!"

"You helped me at the courthouse, remember?" Sam says. "We can put in a good word for you, commute your sentence."

"You don't understand. That place... even juvie turns screwed-up kids into career criminals, or... something worse. I never wanted that kind of life. I never wanted this. I just wanted to do my time in school, maybe work with animals when I got older. That place, that fucking place! They're the animals!"

His arm twitches. Michael hears several clicks all around them.

"Hold your fire!" Sam orders. "Don't do it, Jimmy. Don't make me shoot you."

But Jimmy's arm, quivering, is slowly rising. "Maybe I'm just an animal too." He jerks the gun up.

"Don't!" Sam yells, but even as she's saying the word, her finger compresses the trigger on her own weapon.

"Aim low, Sam!" Michael shouts. "Aim low!"

Her bullet tears through Jimmy's chest. He jerks back then falls to the ground.

The figure in the black hoodie appears and stands in Jimmy's place. "I've found you!"

"JIMMY... NO... JIMMY... you! Stay back! Stay back!" Michael was barely conscious of what he was saying as he awoke in the darkness.

He sat up and cracked his head against something. For a moment, he thought he was back in that nightmare. When he felt a rumbling, he realized he was in the trunk of a car.

Don't these things have levers or something to prevent people from locking themselves in? He wasn't bound in any way, so he rolled-scooted toward where the taillights were glowing. He felt around for a latch but didn't find one.

Why, Jimmy? What do you want from me? Fucking dumbass. What are you thinking, Jimmy?

He checked his pocket for his cell phone. Gone. Seeing no reason why Jimmy or his meathead friend would want him dead, Michael rested his head on the carpet and tried to remain calm.

About fifteen minutes later, the brakes squealed, and the car came to a stop. The engine shut down. Doors opened then slammed, and someone approached the rear of the car. The trunk lid popped open, sending bright light into his eyes.

CHAPTER 16

Thank God for busybodies. At least, Sam hoped that was all the bent old man was. She scratched her head. *Why does this guy look so familiar?*

The man, Mac Gilmore, had been walking his dog in the park across from the old bridge when he noticed three suspicious "fellers" sitting in a beat-up old Honda in the parking lot of the adjacent church. The car had been idling there when he entered the park, and it hadn't left the lot for the entire time good old Mac was walking his dog, maybe half an hour. He hadn't thought too much of it and was heading home to his apartment a few blocks over when a kid on a bike rode past him, going in the opposite direction.

"So as this kid passes the Honda," Mac said, "the three of them fellers inside, well, they got out. One was this colored feller... I mean, a Negro... he wasn't green or nothing." Mac laughed.

"Can you hurry this along?" Sam asked. Mac had her undivided attention, but every second wasted with him was a second Michael might have been spending in danger. She'd stomach the witness's racism and his halitosis for as long as necessary if it would lead her to her charge but not a second longer.

Mac stopped laughing. "Ahem, of course, Officer. Where was I?" He rubbed his chin. "Oh yeah. Well, the Negro was as big as an ox, bigger even. And boy, did he look like trouble, he did. That poor sweet boy on the bike, well, he was just a scrawny white boy, barely even a man yet. He goes under the bridge, and the Negro follows. Another scrawny white boy was with him."

"The third person in the car? What did he look like?"

"Ah, that feller was shifty, I tell you. He was trying to hide his face with a hat pulled low, like right over his eyes, but I could see that it was scarred on one side. Burned like."

"Did you see them leave? Which way did they go? Was the kid on the bike with them?" Sam fired one question right after the other, so revved up that she couldn't wait for the answers. Michael was in danger. *Her* Michael. And she was pretty sure she'd kill anyone who laid a finger on him.

"I'm sorry, ma'am." Mac shrugged. "You see, I decided I didn't want to be stepping in no shit, so I went on back home. But the worry was just eating away at me. I got to thinking, what if the boy's hurt? What if that gigantic Negro means him harm? I couldn't sleep at night with that on my conscience. No sirree, Bob. So I did right by the boy and Jesus. I dropped off Plum Dog—that's my gal—and headed back there. But by the time I showed up, those fellers, their car, and the boy were long gone. I seen no sign of a struggle, though, just this nice bike laying on its side, waiting to be stolen by less God-fearing folks than myself. Mm-hmm."

"Thank you, Mr.... Gilmore was it?"

"Mm-hmm. That's the name my pappy give me." He nodded and smiled, showing a mouth so full of yellow, brown, and black teeth. He looked as if he were eating Indian corn. "It's a pleasure, ma'am. I didn't realize they let girls be detectives now. Ain't it a wonderful world we live in?" He leaned in close, and his rank breath hung over Sam like a heavy fog. "I don't suppose I get some kind of reward for returning this bike here," he whispered.

Sam turned and pointed toward the entrance. "The sergeant at the front desk will take down your info." She snarled when she realized where she knew him from. Mac's picture was pinned to the bulletin board beside the door, the one that held photos of local registered sex offenders. Sam grabbed him by the front of his shirt. She wanted to claw his eyes out. "If I find out you touched so much as a hair on that boy, I'm going to rip your damn dick off and feed it to Plum Dog. Then after I torture you, I'm going to kill you."

Mac jerked free, spun around, and took off. For a dirty, misshapen old man, he could run fast.

"Officers!" Sam shouted. "Detain that racist, sexist, pedophile piece of shit for questioning."

Sam believed the pedophile's story, but she wasn't about to risk letting him go on the off chance she was wrong. She figured the "scrawny white boy" was Jimmy. It made sense that Jimmy would try to reach out to Michael, his only friend, but she didn't know about the others. They didn't have any reason to—

Sam gasped. *Unless Jimmy told them what Michael can do and they plan on exploiting him somehow.* "Shit!"

When she entered her office, Frank was waiting. She had completely forgotten the FBI agent.

"What, Sam?" He stood. "What is it?"

Sam placed her hands on her hips and looked him straight in the eye. "How badly do you want to catch this Suarez gang?"

"Violence? Terrorism? Mass murder? Badly enough, I'd say."

"I might have a good way to find them, but it isn't exactly legal—"

Frank raised a hand, cutting her off. "Will it poison the validity of our arrest? I can't risk these guys getting off on a technicality. They'll be ghosts by the time we make a proper case against them."

It'll be his word against mine, Sam thought. "I don't think so." *The fucking hell with procedure. Michael's life is at stake.* She rifled through her desk until she found a stun gun, which she clipped to her belt. Returning a calculating eye on Frank, she took a chance that he might understand. "They have Michael."

"Michael?" The wrinkles in Frank's forehead relaxed with the emergence of understanding. "The boy in your care, the *psychic* boy alleged to have helped you with the Crotty and Masterson cases?"

"You really do do your homework. Just don't believe everything you read. I'm his guardian... sort of."

"But how?"

"Never mind that now. He's really important to me, and I... I..." She covered her mouth with her hand then pulled herself together. Breaking down would do Michael no good.

"Say no more," Frank said. "What do you need me to do?"

"Come with me. Help me save my... Michael. You can have all the credit for the arrests, and if there's any backlash, I'll make sure it all lands squarely on me."

"I don't care about that. Not anymore."

Their eyes met, and she could see the sincerity in his. Had he tried to put his arms around her then, she might have let him.

"But don't keep me in the dark," he added. "What's your plan for finding them?"

"When we get to the cells, I'll need you to distract the officer stationed outside the general population. We're holding two killers, one being Berkowitz, each in his own cell in what we call 'solitary.' Just two more cells where we put those who might be a threat to others." She headed out the door. "Follow me."

Without thinking, she took his hand and led him toward the holding cells. When his fingers tightened around hers, she let go, ashamed and afraid to let him see the embarrassment flushing her cheeks. "The cells are up ahead. That's Officer—"

"Reynolds," Frank finished. "Yeah, I remember the man. Took a bullet in the Jefferson matter. Lucky to be alive." He blinked and took another look at Reynolds. "Wow, he really let himself go. How does the man pass the annual physical?"

Outside the door to the cells, Officer Peyton Reynolds sat reading a newspaper at a small desk barely wider than he was. Peyton's rotund belly rested on top of it, the buttons of his shirt straining.

He looked up and smiled as they approached. "Here to talk to Rex, I assume? Or is it that pedo who was just thrown into the drunk tank? I know it ain't Berkowitz. He's already invoked his right to counsel. But that Rex! He sure does love to brag, doesn't he? And always a new crime to chat about."

"He sure does." Sam forced a laugh. "How are you, Peyton?" she asked in a best-of-chums way that she knew probably needed work.

"Good," he answered, the response sounding more like a question, as if he couldn't be sure he was good until he heard what Sam really wanted.

"You remember Agent Spinney, don't you?"

"I sure do." Peyton smiled and began to rise, the attempt a slow and arduous one.

"No need to stand on my account," Frank said, flashing a toothy grin that oozed charm.

Peyton settled back again. "Thanks," he groaned. "My back hasn't been the same since I took that bullet. Just light duty for me now."

"I'll just be a sec," Sam said, opening the door.

As she stepped into the holding area, she could hear Frank laying on the flattery, thanking the officer for his sacrifice in a case long gone cold. Peyton was guffawing, eating up every word. She hoped Frank meant at least some of it. Peyton *had* sacrificed. *That should never be forgotten.*

She hurried through the holding area. None of the usual suspects paid her any attention except Gilmore, who sat with arms crossed and glared at her as if she'd shat on his rug. Usually, the area was good for a catcall or two, but the afternoon crowd was quiet. *Maybe I'm losing it,* she wondered, half in jest.

She moved into the back area, hugging the inner wall. Rex was taunting the prisoner in the cell next to his, the young man Sam would never call "Sleven Eleven." *That's okay. Sound is okay. I just can't be seen.*

She slid along the wall, keeping out of view of the camera mounted in the corner. She knew where the blind spots were. Once she was under the camera, she pushed it up so that all it was recording was ceiling tile. The sound was never on unless there was a specific reason, and Peyton hadn't had it playing.

When Rex spotted her, he let loose with a slew of insults, foul language, and threats. Sleven just sat there, brooding. A retractable wall of bars separated the two cells. In times of overflow, prisoners could be shifted from one cell to the other to allow police access to one or two prisoners at a time without having to worry about a mob.

As Sam passed Rex's cell, he simulated masturbating while leering at her. She grimaced when she realized he wasn't *simulating* anything.

"Better get used to that," she jeered. She stopped and planted her feet outside Sleven's cell. "I don't have a lot of time, so I'm going to make this quick. You need to tell me where your friends are, right now."

"What's the matter, little piglet?" Sleven asked, rising from the metal bunk. Even in his bad situation, he adopted a cocky swagger. "You lost?"

Fast forward a couple of years, and we'll see who's swaggering. "You're facing life in prison, and I hold the key to a commuted sentence. You've got one chance to do this the easy way. Tell me where your friends are, and I'll tell the DA you cooperated."

Sleven laughed. She grinned at him through clenched teeth, thinking how nice it would be to put her fist through his face.

Sleven stopped laughing and leaned toward her. "I have nothing to say to *cunts* like you." He spat between the bars, but Sam was able to dodge the thicker parts of it.

That hateful word sent Sam over the edge. The spit was just icing on the cake. In a low, quiet rage, her body shaking with anger, she growled, "I thought you'd say that. Have it your way, asshole." She took two steps to the left. "Hey, Rex. Do you want to have a little fun?"

"With you, Reilly?" Rex chuckled. "I'm just dying for the chance."

"Sorry, but not today. Not with me, anyway." She glared at Sleven. "But this asshole's gang, didn't they handcuff you to the railing at the courthouse?"

Rex squinted at her. For once, he was silent.

"Wait a minute," Sam continued. "Didn't they leave you cuffed to that railing in a building rigged to explode while they made their sweet getaway? They left you to die, Rex. Do you remember that?"

Rex snarled. She had cast her bait and was easily reeling in the big one. Rex glared at Sam, then at Sleven, then back at Sam, a feral sadism twinkling in his eyes.

Though separated from Rex by bars and well out of reach, Sleven backed away from the more dangerous caged animal. "Don't listen to her, man. She's the pig that put you in here."

Rex stepped toward the bars separating the two cells. "You're damn straight I remember!" he snapped. Then as if realizing he'd been played, he said lower, "He'll get his, Reilly, just like you'll get yours. Don't you worry your pretty little head about it."

But Sam could see the rage boiling over inside him. Rex wrapped his hands around the bars separating him from Sleven, squeezing until his knuckles turned white.

Sam turned to the panel on the wall behind her. The panel had three buttons, each labelled according to its function. She put her thumb over the green button. "All I have to do is push this, and those bars separating you two disappear."

Sleven laughed, but it sounded tinny, lacking his earlier swagger. "You wouldn't," he said.

Sam sneered. "Last chance, asshole. Tell me what I want to know, or Rex here is going to fuck you like it's prom night and beat you like it's fight night. Then he'll hurt you in ways you never thought possible. See, Rex here loves to cause pain. He gets off on it. Hell, the man is a certified expert on hurting people. And if I know Rex, and I believe I do, I can safely guarantee you that it won't be quick."

Rex cracked his knuckles. He was smiling and staring at Sleven with something akin to lust but mutated and all wrong. "I have a long memory and a longer dick, boy." He sucked back an errant trail of drool. "No, it won't be quick."

Sleven faked a yawn. "Your bluff might work on idiots like this guy—"

"Oh," Sam said. "You probably shouldn't have said that."

Sleven raised his voice. "Your bluff might work on morons like this stupid shit, but I'm not just some uneducated monkey."

"Oh, I know you didn't just call me a monkey," Rex said. "Let me at him, Reilly, and when your time comes, I'll make it quick."

"You sure you won't reconsider?" Sam asked Sleven.

"Fuck you, cunt." He returned to his seat on the bench. "You won't open shit. You do that, and you'll be in here with us soon enough."

That word again. Sam blew her top. "Last chance!" She set her jaw.

Sleven flipped her the finger.

"Suit yourself." She pushed the button. A single buzz sounded, like the noise when the tweezers touched the sides in a game of Operation, and the wall separating the two prisoners began to retract.

Rex let go of the bars, his eyes widening like a child's on Christmas morning. He snickered, low at first, but the sound soon grew into bellowing laughter. She could see from the front of his pants that Rex was aroused, and he hadn't been boasting about his size.

"What the hell?" Sleven jumped off the bunk and backed up against the bars farthest away from Rex. "What are you doing? You can't do this!"

"Who's the cunt now, Berkowitz?" Sam smirked. "Looks like Rex is going to fuck you like one."

"Stop!" he shrieked as he flattened his body against the wall.

"Where are they?" Sam shouted back.

"I-I-I don't know!" Sleven was pushing his back so hard against the bars that he might have been trying to push his way through them. His face went the color of spoiled milk, his mouth curdling into a grotesque gape stricken with horror.

"Liar!" Sam made the proclamation so full of spite and contempt that she almost wanted Rex to have him. No, not almost. She would love to see the trash take out the trash, but as tempting as vigilantism was, she had to find Michael. "Tell me where they are, and I'll make him stop."

"Oh no," Rex said, rubbing his hands together. "That boy's mine, now." Rex was apparently savoring the anticipation by waiting for the bars to pass in front of him instead of squeezing through the opening that was already there. A second later, and he didn't even have to squeeze through. Yet he still waited with a patience she was surprised he possessed.

She had another second or two before—

"243 Walnut Street!" Sleven blurted.

"If you're lying—"

"I'm not lying! Shut the gate!"

Sam had no time to close it and, in fact, couldn't close it once the sequence was set in motion. She would have to wait for the partition to open fully before she could push the button and close it again.

Rex stepped forward, his huge erection comical, sinister, and painfully distracting all at the same time, something so wrong about it and about Rex in general. He was oblivious to Sam, his eyes never wavering from his prize.

Still, Sam felt no pity for "Sleven Eleven," the nickname alone enough to draw her ire at that moment. Nevertheless, she drew the stun gun, aimed it through the bars, and pulled the trigger. Rex jerked as two prongs attached to long wires sent pulsing waves of electricity through his body. But he didn't go down. Instead, he reached for the leads.

My god... Sam kept the juice flowing, praying Rex would fall before he could rip out the prongs. Rex's hand closed around one wire. He fell to his knees then onto his side. His hand vibrated over the cable, his legs twitching like a dog running in its sleep.

"Get in the other cell," Sam barked at Sleven.

Sleven stayed pressed against the far wall, trembling with fear. Urine began pooling around his right foot.

"Now!" Sam shouted. "He won't be out forever."

Sleven escaped whatever terror had hold of his mind and, giving Rex's spastic body a wide berth, ran into the opposite cell. Sam retracted the prongs and hit the button on the wall. With that same buzzing sound, the partition began to move.

"I hope they kill you," Sleven whispered. He was crying.

"You pissed yourself," Sam said matter-of-factly.

Without a smidgen of guilt, she adjusted the camera and exited the room. She briefly considered how she might explain the cell swap that had occurred but decided she didn't care. *Sometimes, the ends justify the means.* Her old partner had taught her that.

Outside, she rendezvoused with her new, albeit temporary, partner. Frank was sitting on top of Peyton's vacated desk.

"Where's Officer Reynolds?" Sam asked.

"Bathroom break," Frank said. "I'm pretty sure he knew what you were up to in there. Plausible deniability and all." He shrugged. "As for me, don't tell me. I don't want to know."

"Consider it my dirty little secret."

"Did you get what you need?"

"I did. Let's go."

CHAPTER 17

Jimmy hated bringing Michael into his mess, but he hadn't been given a whole lot of choice in the matter. Escaping from the criminal justice system had indebted him to the Suarez gang. Still, ever since he'd seen the courthouse roof blow up, he'd been looking for a chance to flee. But they were always watching him, especially the ugly one.

The whole thing had happened so fast. One minute, he was being pushed into the courthouse, and the next, he was running from it. *Did I kill that guy?* Jimmy hoped he had, because if the gang found out what he had done to its missing member, he would be missing soon too. The short ride in the ambulance had done little to settle his nerves. A night spent in a warehouse full of strangers didn't help, either.

The ambulance was parked by the row of garage doors lining the front of the huge, loft-like building. All the windows were blacked out or boarded over. Each door was chained and locked to the floor, the keys to them residing in Hector's pocket. Jimmy had tested the single-door side entrance during the night, but something blocked it on the outside. In the back, loading bays with giant conveyor belts and heavy metal shutters offered another way out if he could restore the power to them. *I guess this gang isn't too up on fire safety.* If not for all the pigeon poop and broken windows, the warehouse seemed in decent shape and useful for just about anything. Jimmy wondered why it went unused and how the gang had come by it.

The Honda they had boosted sat near the ambulance. They had risked exposure once by going out to get Michael and some supplies, which mostly consisted of junk food and soda, and they weren't willing to do it again unless absolutely necessary.

Victor has the keys to the Honda. Jimmy had seen Hector toss them to his brother when they had returned. He assumed Hector still had the keys to the ambulance.

"Any word?" Victor asked his brother. The two stood several yards away from where Jimmy sat on a forklift. Victor had his girlfriend, Valeria, tucked under his arm.

"None," Hector grunted. "I don't like it." He peered over his shoulder at Jimmy, who kicked at the dirt floor, pretending not to listen.

"Relax," Victor said, flashing his easy smile as he massaged his brother's shoulders and led him away from Valeria. "We never needed anyone but ourselves."

"You really think this kid can help us?" Hector asked.

"I wouldn't have had you risk nabbing him if I didn't." Victor pulled Hector close by the nape of his neck so that they rested forehead to forehead. "You've lost your belief in the spiritual, brother. Our mother is still with us, our guardian angel. This boy has one of his own. His story made national news, and the skeptics tore him apart. There will always be nonbelievers."

"Well, his friend over there seems to believe. I'll give you that," Hector said.

"Dead or not, Mother was there for us when we needed her." Victor backed away from his brother. "You saw her too. I know it. She led us out of the fire, kept us safe."

Hector sneered. "She led *you* out of the fire. Only part of me got out."

"Her punishment for your having started it."

Hector snarled. "I only did what you didn't have the *cojones* to do yourself, big brother. That motherfucker deserved to burn."

Victor clapped him on the back. "I know. I'm sorry, bro. I shouldn't have said that. But look at us now! The Suarez brothers leading the way to a new world order. We stand on the precipice of change, my man. You know better than any of us that no fire can ignite without a spark."

He pointed at Michael, who lay near his feet. "This boy's got an angel looking out for him, and now, it's going to look out for us too."

"I hope you're right. Otherwise, we risked going out there for nothing. And you know I'm going to have to kill the kid when this is over."

Jimmy gulped and turned his back to the brothers. *These guys are crazy. Dead mothers, guardian angels... killing Mikey?* He wished he had never listened in to the conversation. *No, I should never have told them about Michael in the first place. Just one more wrong I need to make right.*

"Once we're back at the safe house, he's yours to do with as you please," Victor said.

Hector asked, "What about the other one?"

"The verdict's still out on him." Victor shrugged. "Let's see what he wants." He bounced on his toes. "Hey, Jimmy. Come here a second."

Jimmy descended from his perch and plodded over to them like a man walking to the gallows. "What's up?"

"You want to leave us, don't you?" Victor asked.

"Huh?" Jimmy blinked. The bluntness of the question startled him, and he hoped the brothers had read it as confusion. *Play it cool. Don't oversell it either way.* "I'd love to be a million miles away from Fall River right now, but where else do I got to go?"

"Look, I get it, kid," Victor said. "You don't know any of us and have no reason to trust us. But let me ask you this: truthfully, who have you ever had looking out for you out there?"

"I never said I wanted to leave," Jimmy said.

"You never said you didn't," Hector countered.

"I don't want to leave." Even to Jimmy's ears, the lie rang hollow.

Hector stepped closer. "Sure you do. It's written all over your face."

Jimmy sighed and hung his head. Victor put his arm between them and eased his brother back. So far, Victor had been nice to him. Every vibe Jimmy got told him that the gang's more eloquent leader was a whole lot better than his sinister counterpart, but he'd seen Victor murder that prisoner, Ernie, without any real provocation or reason. And Jimmy hadn't forgotten that after Victor had killed Ernie, he'd turned the gun on Jimmy.

"You have potential, kid," Victor said, smiling. "I saw it right away back at the courthouse, and I still see it now. Maurice says you did well in nabbing your friend, never tried to run or betray us. That's good. Real good." He pointed at Michael. "Your friend's going to help us get out of here. He just doesn't know it yet."

Jimmy squinted at Michael, who was sitting up, propped against a support beam. *When did he wake up? How much has he been listening to?* Since they'd gotten Michael out of the Honda's trunk, Jimmy had tried not to make eye contact with him. Doing so was like a kick to the gut. But when Victor had pointed, Jimmy's head turned before he could prevent it. Michael was scowling and staring right at him.

Jimmy huffed. *Like you have it so rough. Try living where I've been these last nine months.*

"Hey!" Victor snapped his fingers in front of Jimmy's face. "That kid's our best chance out of here. The cops have roadblocks everywhere. They're looking for us, and sooner or later, they're going to find us if we stay here. If we can see our future, we can slip past them. That's the hope, anyway. Because of you, we have that chance."

Hector's nostrils flared. "We usually have more certain help at our disposal, but—"

"I didn't ask you to come get me!" Victor said. "But would you have preferred to leave me in there to rot?"

"Maybe we'd have better luck if we all split up," Jimmy said sheepishly.

"We're not doing that!" Anger marched over Victor's face but was gone as fast as it had come. "We're the Dorchester Six." He winked at Valeria, who stood with arms crossed a few feet away, silently listening. Then he looked up at the ceiling and frowned. "Five now, I suppose. But I'm looking to recruit you and fill out our numbers again." He grabbed Jimmy's arms and shook him. "What do you say? You won't make it out there a single day without friends."

Jimmy hesitated a second then asked, "What about that guy we left behind? You're not going back for him?"

"Sleven?" Victor made a raspberry sound. "He'll be lucky to be alive, if that Rex guy got ahold of him. If he ain't dead and he ain't here, then the pigs must have got him."

"You're not going to try to bust him out?" *Like he did for you.*

"If the pigs got him, he's on his own. We were able to pull off my escape with a lot of planning and because no one saw it coming. We won't get a chance like that again."

"So what are you guys?" Jimmy asked, looking over at Hector. "Terrorists or something? Why would I want to partner up with you?"

"Terrorists?" Victor laughed, but his brother remained stone-faced. "No, man. Nothing like that, though there will always be some who call us that. We're just trying to level the playing field, make the world even."

"Even?" Jimmy asked.

Hector sighed. "I'm going to check the perimeter." Without waiting for a reply, he skulked off.

"You know," Victor said, "we take from the haves and give to the have-nots."

"What are you saying, that you're modern-day Robin Hoods?"

"Yep, except we don't wear tights, though Maurice could probably pull it off. You see, the haves don't want to give anything away. They just want more, more, more, and we've got to take it from them. They'll do anything to keep what they have, which is everything. They own the governments, the schools, the utilities, the media... fucking everything, man, from those clothes you're wearing to the idea planted in your head that told you to buy them. You think your vote matters?"

"I'm not old enough to vote yet."

"Fuck that. See? In their eyes, you already don't matter. They'll use you until they break you then toss you in the trash when you're of no further use to them. Your vote will *never* matter. You're too smart to think it will. Presidents, pshaw! Take this last election: we had two choices, Satan and Lucifer. The best we can do is hope for the lesser of two evils, but either way, we're fucked. All they care about is how fat their wallets are, and they don't give a shit how many backs they have to break to make them just a little fatter. Politicians don't represent you or me, kid. They don't represent the masses. They represent the rich and, sometimes, just themselves. They use their mouthpieces in the media—actors, actresses, preachers, and even teachers—to preach their corrupt doctrines and peddle their lies. And if you don't want to eat the shit they're shilling, they'll use their puppet governments, the army, and those pigs in blue to browbeat it into you, to stomp you into conformity or else leave you broken."

"Nice speech," Michael jeered. "Did you practice that at home in front of a mirror?"

Jimmy cringed. Michael didn't know what Victor was capable of.

"You got something else you want to say?" Victor slapped him hard enough for the sound to echo. "Little boy who thinks he knows something of the world? You don't know shit. I will take you apart so motherfucking completely, no one will know your ass from your eyeballs. I will fucking bury you!"

Michael spat some blood onto the floor. "And you think blowing it all up will solve things? You won't change a damn thing. All you'll do is kill innocent people. You *are* terrorists!"

Victor laughed. "Kid's got a mouth, huh?" he asked as he bounced on his feet, looking as though he was about to deliver Michael some more pain.

But after a few seconds, he stopped bouncing and relaxed. "Everyone wants change, kid, but no one wants to sacrifice anything to trigger it. We may be seen as terrorists now, but time will be our one true judge. The history books will remember us fondly, the fathers of a second revolution. Do you think the instigators of America's great war for independence weren't first thought of as criminals? Murderers? Terrorists? All of our founding fathers, all of the world's greatest visionaries and instruments of change, began as wanted men. William Wallace, Spartacus, Samuel Adams, Joan of Arc, Maximilien Robespierre, Simon Bolivar, Lenin, Trotsky, Garibaldi, Castro, Collins, Guevara... the list goes on and on! You can't have change without revolt and a whole lot of collateral damage."

Michael sneered. "What about Ghandi? Nelson Mandela? Martin Luther King? Bob freaking Marley? Hell, that guy who stood in front of tanks in Tin... Tinny-man Square? Revolutionaries who didn't kill innocent people."

"No one's innocent, kid, least of all some of those people you named. That's your youth talking, blinding you to the blood on your heroes' hands, the pages in the history books that have been left out. You're just a dumb kid eating up what you're spoon-fed in school and by the media. Think for yourself, man. See the truth."

Jimmy couldn't help but smile. Michael had more balls than he'd guessed. Jimmy wiped the grin off his face before Victor could turn back and see it.

Valeria sauntered over and ran a finger down Victor's chest. She gave Michael a wink and blew him a kiss. "Is it time to play?" She leaned back into Victor's arms.

"Never mind him, Valeria," Victor said. "He lives in a pig sty and probably hears that pro-establishment propaganda on a daily basis. Fucking conformist. He'll never get it. Revolution won't start unless you start it."

Michael snickered. Jimmy wished he'd stop. Michael was pushing his luck.

As if to justify Jimmy's concerns, Victor walked over to Michael and kicked him in the ribs. "Keep laughing, why don't you?" He kicked Michael again. Then again. "Hmm? I can't hear you anymore. How come you're not laughing now, huh? How come you're not laughing?"

Michael curled into a ball, coughing and scowling up at his attacker. His face was red with rage, and tears shimmered in his eyes.

"Just do what they want, Mikey," Jimmy said softly. "Then you can go home." He looked to Victor for confirmation that what he said was true.

Victor's face was bland. His placid expression gave Jimmy no indication of what he would do next.

"I can't do what they want!" Michael shouted at Jimmy. "I'm not a psychic. I can't see the future. My seizure back at school wasn't some psychic vision. It's called epilepsy, you idiot."

Jimmy shrugged and turned back to Victor. "Maybe he's telling the truth. Maybe I told him about my plan to kill Glenn and just forgot that I did. Maybe it was all just a coincidence."

"I don't believe that," Victor said. "And I don't think you do, either. We found out about him while we were checking into you. The article claimed that he gave a full account of the shooting to the school principal *before* it happened. You said you could prove it, but you wanted to go see him alone. Were those all lies just so you could get away from us?"

Yes. I saw an opportunity, and I took it. Now I'm no better off, and Michael is paying the price for it. He pursed his lips and scratched his head, trying to think of a way to get Michael and himself safely out of that warehouse. "Maybe I was wrong about him." He gave Michael a sad look. "I'm sorry, Mikey."

Michael scowled. "You're not sorry, but you're going to be. Real sorry. This isn't going to end well for you."

"Oh yeah?" Victor asked. "And how do you know that?"

"Oh, come on!" Michael said. "A prediction that Jimmy—no, that *all* of you—are going to end up dead or in jail hardly seems to be much of a prediction at all. More like common sense."

"You *do* see something." Victor stomped back over to Michael, grabbed his shirt, and hauled him onto his feet. "You are going to tell us a way out of here, or I'm going to kill you. How's that for common sense? And if that's not enough common sense for you, don't you think a judge and the foster kid of a police detective make two mighty fine hostages? Your usefulness is endless. See? I took you from the haves and gave you to the have-nots: us. You belong to us now."

"I'll never help you."

Michael said it so matter-of-factly that Jimmy was startled by its sincerity. *You're stronger than you were when Glenn dunked you in that toilet, Michael. A lot stronger.*

"You're already helping me," Victor said. "Your presence alone helps me. Soon, Hector is going to fit you and the judge—she's that muffled moaning you keep hearing from the back of the ambulance—with two of his special belts. Things will be simple then. If we die, you die."

"I don't see anything," Michael said through gritted teeth. "I can't tell the future."

"Let's give him another chance then, shall we?" Victor wiggled his finger an inch in front of Michael's forehead then poked him.

Michael collapsed back onto the floor.

CHAPTER 18

Michael stands and dusts himself off. His wrists and ankles are no longer bound, but he's wearing the same clothes he'd been wearing before Victor touched him, and before he got up, he was lying where he'd likely fallen from that touch, so he assumes he hasn't gone anywhere. Or any when.

He looks behind him and sees himself curled up on the floor, still tied up. The face is contorted, as if he is in the middle of a seizure. Jimmy and Victor are standing right in front of him, Hector and Valeria a few feet off to the side, none of them blinking or even breathing.

Time is frozen for everything and everyone except Michael. He smirks then kicks Victor in the balls as hard as he can.

"Well, that sucks," he says when his foot passes right through the gang leader, though he isn't really surprised. He turns to his friend. "You're lucky, Jimmy. You were next."

Michael looks around the warehouse, using this strange opportunity to look for a means of escape. Everything is as it was before he entered the dream or vision realm or whatever it is.

"Time is a face on the water," he mutters, quoting from his favorite book, Stephen King's Wizard and Glass. *"At least it used to be. What can I possibly see with time at a standstill?"*

"You can see me."

Michael jerks and spins around. What the Whisperer said isn't exactly true. He heard the voice clear enough, but he doesn't see anyone.

"Show yourself!" Michael says, though he's not sure that's what he truly wants to happen.

Several feet away, the air shimmers like a disturbed pond surface. He thinks he can see someone in it, someone translucent. A face on the water. *Michael blinks and rubs his eyes, hoping that shimmering air and ghostly figure will have vanished when he opens them. But when he takes another look, the figure has become solid as if it materialized out of the air itself.*

The figure wears the same dark hoodie clouding the face. In a flash, he or she or it halves the distance between them, there one second, gone and back again, much closer a second later. Like Nightcrawler, except this isn't a comic book.

"You can see me," the voice whispers from out of a cavern of darkness. The words somehow come from everywhere, echoing all around Michael.

A lump of fear rises in Michael's throat. He glances around for an exit or a weapon but sees nothing. He turns to run anywhere that isn't toward the Whisperer. A thought stops him in his tracks. The same Whisperer?

"And I can see you," the Whisperer says, appearing directly in front of him.

Michael jumps back a step. "Get away from me! Leave me alone!"

The Whisperer extends both arms, hands turned palms up. "Do not be afraid."

Michael shuffles backward and steps through his own body. He stands over his empty shell and raises his fists. "Stay back. Leave me alone!"

"I mean you no harm, Michael. I just want to talk."

"Who are you? How do you know my name?"

"Let's just say we've both been doing a little research, in our own ways."

His head pounds as though his brain is trying to hammer its way out. With each thump, his thoughts seem closer to the truth, something he's felt, something he's known but has been unwilling to admit each time he's been near the Whisperer. The idea inside his head is screaming itself so loudly now it can no longer be ignored. He has to face it.

"You... you killed my parents."

After a pause, the Whisperer says, "I was responsible for their deaths, yes."

Michael's arms fall to his sides. A question rises on a sob in his throat and comes out as a croak. "Why?"

"Does it matter?"

The answer crumbles what's left of Michael's composure. Sniffling, he shouts, "Of course it matters! I have nothing, no one... all because of you!" His heart thuds, and he gasps. Before, it was just a gut feeling, some strange idea that this Whisperer had somehow been responsible for the sideways track his life took. Now, he's heard it from the culprit's mouth.

An atom bomb explodes in his head, and he is certain of more. "You were there," he says softly. Then louder, he repeats, "You were there!" The cowl over the Whisperer's forehead shields his eyes and nose, but Michael can make out a rounded white chin that's smooth, with no stubble.

"Yes, Michael. I was there. I was there, as sure as you are here. Your parents were a means to an end. Nothing more. I didn't hurt you then, and I won't hurt you now, not unless you force my hand."

"Didn't hurt me then?" Michael wipes the spittle off his mouth with his sleeve. "You killed my parents! Do you think that didn't hurt? Do you think that made life easy for me? I've been transferred from foster home to foster home, traded like a Pokémon card, wondering if my next fake mom and dad will see me as a project to fix or a burden. Every day hurts. Every single day. You did that to me."

"I'd say I did you a favor. Your guardian now is a far cry better than your parents ever were. But we don't have much time, and—"

"Sam? How do you know about Sam?" Michael raises his fists, taking a southpaw stance, just as Sam taught him.

The Whisperer sighs. "I'm not your enemy, Michael. In fact, in case you haven't noticed, I'm the closest thing you have to a kindred spirit. I never would have guessed, not in a million years, that the one person I chose to spare would end up sharing my gift."

Michael wipes his eyes. He wants to scream, to lash out at the phantom in front of him, but he knows it will do no good. "Gift? The visions? They're no gift. And if you're the reason I get those, then there's one more way you messed up my life."

"They can be a gift, if you know how to use them. We are not so different, you and I. I've seen your past, present, and future, and I didn't need any vision to do so. I've lived it."

"Whatever it is you're selling, I'm not interested, okay? Please, just leave me and Sam alone."

"I can't do that. Not just yet. But if that's what you truly want after hearing me out, then fine. I'm coming for you now. I can get you out of here, but we must be quick. All I ask is that you stay with me long enough to hear what I have to say, to hear what I'm offering you. Will you come with me?"

Michael hesitates, evaluating his chances. Sam's coming. He knows that much is true from his vision of Jimmy's future, but Michael wasn't in that version of the future. In fact, Jimmy had implied that Michael was already dead in that scene. His captors won't keep him alive long if he refuses to help them. And maybe if he's not there, Sam won't be, either.

Michael nods. "Yes, I'll go with you."

"Good. Wake now, and be ready. I'm close."

CHAPTER 19

W*hat have I done?* Jimmy stared down at Michael's twitching body. His arms were bent like those of a T. rex, and his face was all screwed up, as if he was in a lot of pain. *I've become the bully.* "I'm so sorry, Michael."

As if he'd heard the whispered words, Michael's eyes opened. His pupils rolled into place and shrank to a normal size. He blinked several times, seeming a little confused.

Victor nudged him with his foot. "Welcome back, *compadre.*" He booted Michael harder. "Wake up."

Recognition returned to Michael's eyes. He stared up at Victor.

Victor crossed his arms. "Well?"

Michael groaned and sat up. "Well what?"

Victor shook his head. "What did you see? Can you get us out of Fall River?"

Maurice stepped closer. Jimmy hadn't noticed him before then and wondered where he had come from. Valeria moved to stand next to Victor and put an arm around his waist. Loudly chomping on some gum, she looked expectantly at Michael.

The spotlight's on you, Michael. Jimmy cracked his neck in a fruitless attempt to ease his tension. In a warehouse as big as a stadium, a mob was circling one small boy, dwarfed by towers of pallets and row upon row of mile-high shelving just beyond. Jimmy's cheeks flushed. For a moment, he was thankful all eyes hadn't been on him.

Then the guilt returned. *Come on, man. Make something up if you didn't see anything. Just tell them what they want to hear.*

Valeria said, "This fool don't know shit. You gonna off him or what?"

"Easy, babe." Victor laughed. "Let's give the kid a chance." He glared at Michael, all humor vanishing from his face. "What do you say, kid? Last chance. Can you use your psychic powers to get us out of here or not?"

"It doesn't work that way," Michael muttered.

"Val's right, Vic," Maurice said. "This twerp doesn't know shit. We risked going out into the open for nothing."

"Now wait a minute." Victor was all smiles again. "He just admitted to having visions, which means he lied before when he said he didn't." He grabbed Michael by the front of his shirt, twisting the material in his hand. "So how does it work? Did you have a vision just now?"

"Yes."

"Good. What did you see?"

"Your mother. She looks good in black."

Victor slapped Michael's ear, knocking the teenager to the ground. The whole side of Michael's head reddened. Jimmy was beginning to see a strong family resemblance between Victor and his always-scowling brother.

"These guys think you're a bust," Victor growled. "What do you say, kid? Are you a bust? Because if you are, I'm afraid we have no more use for you."

"Just let him go," Jimmy said. "I was wrong about him. He doesn't even know where we are. And I know him. He won't talk. Right, Mikey?"

Michael didn't respond. His glower never changed, and Jimmy could see that Michael lumped him in with the rest of the gang.

I'm trying to help you, you stubborn ass. Roll with it. Jimmy bit into his lower lip. *They're going to kill him.*

"Well," Victor said, kicking Michael in the hip, "are you going to help us or not?"

Michael sneered. "I wouldn't help you even if I could."

Victor rolled his eyes and clapped. "All right then." He reached down, grabbed Michael by his hair, and pulled him to his feet.

Jimmy had to look away. *It's all my fault. I should never have told them about Michael.*

Victor called out, "Hector? Where are you, man?"

Hector stepped out from behind a row of open shelving where he'd been tinkering with something. He was holding some wires in one hand and a small metal canister in the other. "What's up?"

Victor laughed. "You rigged this place, didn't you?"

On the non-scarred portion of Hector's mouth, his lip curled up into what passed for a smile on his burned face. "Why, brother, whatever do you mean?" He barked a laugh of his own.

They're crazy, every one of them. Jimmy shot a glance at Michael. *Can't you see that? Can't you see that they'll kill you? Just tell them what they want to hear already, and maybe they'll let you go home. Maybe.*

Victor waved a hand over Michael. "Take our guest to the office in the back. Do him quietly."

Jimmy gasped. "B-B-But we need him as a hostage. You said so yourself."

"I changed my mind," Victor said. "We have the judge. She'll do just fine."

"Isn't it better to have two?" Jimmy heard the whine in his own voice. He hated begging, but if he didn't do something soon, Michael would be murdered, and it would be all his fault. *What else can I do?* He felt powerless, and he hated feeling like that. That was how bullies made their victims feel. He had stopped playing the victim. *Haven't I?*

Maurice stepped in front of Jimmy. "Jimmy's right. We could need him."

"Just... trust me," Victor said with a wink.

Maurice nodded. Jimmy looked back and forth between the two, trying to understand what silent agreement they'd made. He couldn't figure out what it was.

"Good. That's settled." Victor gestured at his brother.

Hector placed the bomb parts on a shelf and walked over to where Michael lay on the floor. Michael sat up and scooted back on his butt. With a low chuckle, Hector grabbed Michael under his arms and stood him up. Maurice pulled a knife from Hector's toolbox and cut the rope around Michael's ankles.

"Move," Hector said, pushing Michael.

Michael cast a final glare at Jimmy before turning and staggering off.

"Wait," Victor said.

Hector jerked Michael to a stop and looked back.

Victor grinned. He stared past Hector, beyond the long rows of shelves behind him to the loading dock many yards away. There, tucked in the farthest corner, was a small office. "Let the kid do it."

Hector raised an eyebrow and smiled in the wickedest way Jimmy had ever seen. He was evidently pleased with the turn of events.

"He should already be back there," Victor said. "Probably coloring or some shit."

"Luther?" Maurice asked. "That's your plan? You sure, Vic? I mean, he's just a kid."

"He's my brother, and he has to grow up sometime." Victor smirked. "You're not getting all soft on me, are you, Maurice? Luther needs to pop his cherry sooner or later. Why not now?"

Jimmy fought back tears. "Victor, you don't have to do this. Michael won't say anything. I'm sure of it. Tell them, Mikey. They'll kill you if you don't. Tell them!"

Michael stared at the floor. He said nothing to save his life. It was as if he'd already given up hope.

"Shut the fuck up, Jimmy," Hector said. "Or we'll make you do it, then you'll join him."

Jimmy shuddered. "I'm sorry, Mikey. I'm really sorry."

Michael finally looked up. "Save your sorrys for someone who gives a damn."

MICHAEL DID GIVE A damn.

In fact, he cared more than he would ever admit aloud. He didn't want to be killed. It sounded painful. *Sure, life sucks. But I never really wanted to die.*

He found it easy to be strong and talk tough when anger was all he had. He had bigger things to fear than death, like the Whisperer who could talk to him in dreams. That was a neat trick. He wondered if that might be something he could pull off.

As Hector and Maurice took him at gunpoint toward the back corner of the warehouse, Michael considered running. His captors were leading him to an office where some kid was going to execute him. So either way, he was as good as dead. But he didn't run on the off chance the boy might hesitate.

About a third of the way to the far end of the warehouse, a pounding sounded at one of the garage doors in the front. Hector turned to face the sound, spinning Michael with him. Victor appeared with Valeria in tow, both with guns drawn. Victor nodded at Hector, signaling him to approach the door from the right, while he and Valeria wove their way through the pallet stacks in the front-center of the warehouse. Michael inched backward.

Hector noticed and said, "Don't move."

Michael planted his feet and stared past the stolen vehicles, the only things between him and the stranger who had come knocking. The shelving stood several feet to his left and the wall a little farther to his right. His thoughts seesawed between dreams of rescue and fears of something worse. Someone was pounding at that door loud enough to alert anyone in a one-mile radius. Hector growled and nodded at Maurice, who hugged the wall and crept toward the door with his gun held high.

Five box-shaped windows, each set apart from its neighbor by a metal square of equal proportions, formed a horizontal line across the door. Maurice stood to the right of the last one. He bobbed his head out, peeked through a small spot where the black paint coating over the window had chipped away, then quickly ducked back again. Michael couldn't see Victor and Valeria, but he assumed they were doing much the same on the opposite side. Leaning against the door, Maurice shook his head at Hector.

Boom! Whoever was on the other side of the aluminum door had hit it even harder than the previous times. Maurice jumped a little, but he stayed where he was.

"I saw you, fuck head," a man shouted. "Let me the fuck in."

"It's Benzo," Maurice said in a low voice. "What should I do?"

"He's one of the guys my brother partnered with, right?" Victor asked. "Open the door for him before the whole damn neighborhood knows we're here."

Hector threw Maurice a set of keys then ducked behind a roll of wrapping sheet, slamming Michael into it beside him. Maurice unlocked the garage door and yanked it open with a clamor akin to bashing two garbage can lids together.

"Be quiet, you fool, and get inside." Maurice waved in a weaselly young man wearing a leather jacket in ninety-plus weather and heavy black steel-toed boots. He had a tribal tattoo that looked like black flames crawling up his neck.

"What the fuck, man?" Benzo asked. "You fucked us. You fucking fucked us." He pushed Maurice, who barely budged. "Where's that son of a whore, Hector?"

"Hey," Victor said. "That *whore* is my mother too. I suggest you take it down a notch before you end up like your friends."

"So you heard, huh? Yeah, they're fucking dead because your brother fucking set us up." Benzo pulled a monster of a handgun from inside his jacket. His nostrils flared, and his eyebrows pointed south. "Your whore mother better get back to fucking, 'cause she's gonna be down two sons in about a minute."

A series of clicks echoed in the garage. Maurice, Valeria, and Hector were locked and loaded, each pointing a pistol at the newcomer. Hector hid behind Michael, aiming over his shoulder.

Now's my chance, while he's distracted. Michael surged forward, but before he could take a complete step, Hector kicked out his feet. Michael crashed to the floor, his elbow slamming against the concrete, sending dizzying pain swirling through his head. Blood trickled from a scrape along his forearm. He started to rise.

"Stay down, or you're dead," Hector said calmly.

"You're going to kill me anyway," Michael retorted.

"Yeah, but you can die with or without a bullet first shattering your kneecap."

Michael stayed down.

Ignoring the altercation between Michael and his brother, Victor laughed and told Benzo, "Settle down. You're outnumbered."

"I want to see Hector," Benzo said, pointing his gun at Victor, then at Maurice, then back at Victor. After a few seconds, Benzo sighed and tucked his gun into the back of his pants. Without it to back up his words, the man seemed small.

"Should I kill him?" Maurice asked.

"No, let me! Let me!" Valeria hopped around like a kid asking for ice cream.

"Nobody's killing anyone. Right, Benzo?" Victor asked.

Benzo nodded, seeming smaller still.

"See? That's better," Victor said. "Nice and civilized. Now, Benzo, you have a grievance you would like to share?"

"My *grievance* is with Hector. I'd like to know why the fuck the courthouse bomb went off fifteen minutes after the time scheduled for the heist."

"Luther!" Hector called, coming out from hiding while using Michael as a shield. "Get out here!"

Benzo turned toward the sound of Hector's voice. "There you are, you prick." He stormed toward Hector, swinging his arms in a wild parody of an angry gorilla that his diminutive frame couldn't justify.

"Yeah, bro?" Luther called from the office. He ran toward them. Benzo shoved his finger in Hector's face, but Hector just ignored him.

"Take my gun," he said, handing his pistol to the boy.

Luther's hands remained by his sides. He looked at Michael with suspicious eyes then asked Hector, "Why?"

"You're going to take this one into the back room and kill him," Hector said. "Do it quietly, just like I showed you."

Luther's face paled. "But—"

"No buts!" Hector scowled.

Benzo released a litany of curses as Maurice held him back. Michael tried to block them out, since his fate was being determined in a quieter conversation between a psychopath and his much-younger brother.

"Take it," Hector insisted. "It's about damn time you started do-ing your part around here."

Luther reluctantly took the gun. He held it away from him as if it were a snake. "I... I don't know if I can."

Hector shot his little brother a look devoid of warmth or kinship. "You'd better."

Benzo shook free of Maurice. He put a hand on Hector's shoulder and spun him around. "Are you even listening to me?" Benzo blurted. "What the hell, man?" Behind him, Maurice had his gun pointed at the back of the robber's head.

"Let's go," Luther said to Michael, waggling his brother's pistol.

Michael headed toward the back office, thinking his odds had just improved. *Maybe I can overpower him and get the gun.*

"What's your problem?" Hector asked from behind him.

"You set us up!" Benzo shouted.

"Now calm down, Benzo. Nobody set you up." Hector's placating tone was unlike anything Michael had heard from that brother yet. *It seems even Hector can play politician when he has to.*

"As soon as we drew our weapons, it was like a fuckin' boys-in-blue convention. The fuckin' pigs were coming out of the woodwork. We had to shoot our way out. We somehow got away but not without considerable heat on our asses. They took us down in Brockton. Tony got clipped, and Carp got pinched. Only I got away."

"So what are you complaining about?" Hector asked.

"You said there would be a diversion!"

"There were. Several." Hector chuckled. "You were one of them."

"I'm going to kill you, you ugly Picasso," Benzo said.

A gun went off.

Valeria screamed.

Michael ran. He sprinted for the back office. He heard more gunshots and could have sworn he felt bullets fly past him. *The little brat is shooting at me.* He hadn't been hit, though. *Good thing he's a terrible shot.*

He reached the office, dove inside, and slammed the door behind him. After turning the lock, he crouched and searched for a place to hide.

CHAPTER 20

Jimmy heard the gunshot. He had to bite down hard into his cheek to stave off his tears, the fresh pain ironically bringing them out anyway. *They shot him. They actually shot him.*

But the screaming wasn't coming from the direction the kid had taken Michael. Jimmy turned toward the sound. Victor lay at Valeria's feet, bleeding from a head wound. He wasn't moving.

Jimmy's brain struggled to process what was going on. One second, Victor had been standing there, laughing and flirting with his girlfriend, seemingly content to let his brother deal with that guy Bongo or Gonzo or whatever, and the next, his brain matter was splattered like SpaghettiOs all over an industrial-sized roll of sheet wrap. His blood cascaded like rainwater over Valeria's screaming lips.

Jimmy watched her, unsure what he should do. For a second, she went silent. She raised her shaking hands in front of her eyes. Her face paled, and she started screaming again.

Boom!

She fell in a slump over her dead boyfriend.

The second gunshot snapped Jimmy from his trance, and he dove behind a column of pallets just as a third blast cracked through the air. He didn't know exactly where the bullets were coming from, but given that Valeria had gotten hit in the back of her head, the shooter was somewhere behind her. The only hiding place was a huge pile of crushed cardboard boxes in the corner closest to the side entrance, the door that was blocked from the outside.

He scooted in that direction, keeping his back against the pallets. The weasel-looking guy came running up the far aisle, wheeling his gun around until it pointed at Jimmy.

"Not me! Not me!" Jimmy shouted. "Over there!" He threw a thumb over his shoulder.

"Is it the cops?" Bozo or whatever said.

"I-I-I don't know!" *This is crazy! I need to get out! I need to—*

The man took aim at the boxes.

Boom!

Bozo staggered forward, a large red disk forming in the middle of his shirt underneath his open jacket. A vertical line appeared under that as if Bozo had an ankh or a supersized magnifying glass tattooed under a see-through shirt.

A second bullet put a nickel-sized hole in his forehead, and his head exploded in human awesome sauce out the top. He fell, and Jimmy was pretty sure he was dead.

Hector skidded to a halt behind the row of shelving then dashed past the open space, diving for cover behind the ambulance. He poked his head over the hood and mouthed to Jimmy, "Where?"

Jimmy pointed at the pallets that served as his refuge.

"How many?" Hector mouthed.

Jimmy shook his head and shrugged.

Hector nodded. He placed a finger over his lips.

Another shot came. The bullet hit one of the ambulance tires, and it burst with a sound even louder than the gunfire. The ambulance jerked, and a muffled scream came from inside it.

Hector roared with rage as he retaliated with a volley of bullets from the gun Bozo had held. He must have scooped it up when he ran past the dead man. Jimmy had been too busy making himself as small a target as possible as wood splintered around him that he hadn't actually seen Hector obtain the weapon.

Not the cops. Can't be the cops. They weren't told the place was surrounded, and they hadn't been asked to surrender. They were being assassinated, picked off one by one by a skilled shooter who obviously wasn't looking to make any arrests. *Who, then?* Someone—one of the many, no doubt—the Suarez gang had pissed off seemed most likely.

What was it Mikey said? That it wasn't going to end well for me? Jimmy's breath whistled through his teeth as he inhaled. "Shit!"

He stared down the aisle toward the back. Maybe he could make it if he hauled ass, assuming he could find a way out back there. *Is that what Mikey saw me doing when it didn't end well for me? Fuck! Where is Michael, anyway? He'd know what to do.*

He looked around for an ally or another means of escape. *Where's Maurice?* Jimmy turned back toward the office, but rows of shelving blocked his view. *Where's the little kid?* He found it difficult to swallow. *Come on, Mikey. Where are you?*

He caught a glimpse of movement to his right. He almost pissed himself, thinking that maybe the shooter was headed toward him. Then he recognized the silhouette of Maurice's sculpted body. The much-smaller shadow lurking behind him meant that the big man had Luther in tow.

The pair stopped at the end of a massive shelf that almost reached the ceiling. Maurice boosted Luther up to the second tier, while Hector sent another round into the boxes. Luther climbed like a spider monkey and disappeared somewhere overhead.

Maurice crept toward the boxes and crouched behind a large waste bin. Hector moved to the back of the ambulance, out of Jimmy's sight. Together, they should have had the shooter pinned. Maurice moved in.

Now's my chance. Jimmy pushed off the column at his back and sprinted toward the back of the warehouse. He only got a few feet before the sound of more gunfire made him duck for cover beside the high shelves.

A low grunt, followed by a growl and heavy breathing, came from the near side of the box pile. "Fucker shot me." Maurice made the statement as though it were somehow inconceivable that he might be shot in a gunfight.

More shots came from where Hector was hiding. Jimmy wondered how many bullets any of them had left.

"I see him!" a high-pitched voice squealed from above. Luther fired two shots from right above Jimmy. The little ninja must have jumped across the shelves.

Jimmy looked up as more gunfire came from across the room. The shelving creaked and rocked. Luther screamed and seemed to fall in slow motion.

"Oh my God!" Jimmy ran to try to catch the boy, but Luther hit the unyielding floor before Jimmy reached him. Jimmy heard a sickening crunch that put an end to the kid's screaming.

Luther's gun hit the floor a moment later and went off. Jimmy shrieked. The bullet had hit him in the thigh, somewhere near the surface. The outpouring of blood made it hard for him to see just how bad it was. His knee buckled, and the initial shock and painless burn flowered into sparkling agony as he fell. The pain was like caffeine to his brain. He suddenly saw the hopelessness of everything.

"Luther?" Hector called. "Maurice?" Behind the ambulance, Hector was the last man standing. "Fuck this!" He dashed back down the aisle he'd come from, fleeing under a spray of bullets, leaving his brethren where they lay.

One of whom was not dead.

Luther spasmed. He tried to speak, but his body, inside and out, was a broken mess.

He's just a kid. Jimmy sucked it up and crawled over to the boy. The blood pumped more feverishly from his leg. He didn't think his wound would kill him, and making it worse seemed the least of his worries. The shooter would be coming for him soon enough. Still, he would comfort the other boy in his final moments. He took Luther's hand in his.

"Jimmy? Where are my brothers?"

"They're safe. You saved them. You're a hero, kid. Close your eyes now. Try to get some sleep."

"They *are* closed, Jimmy. I can't see anything. I'm scared, Jimmy. Is it okay... to be scared? My brothers aren't scared of nothing."

Jimmy decided against telling him how Hector had abandoned his brothers to run away. "It's okay to be scared, Luther. I'm scared too."

Another cough turned into a fit, and afterward, Luther fell quiet. Jimmy held his hand a little longer then lay down beside him, waiting to die.

"Jimmy?" Luther's voice had become so soft that Jimmy had almost missed it. The boy lurched with a wheeze, which was succeeded by a slur of rapid, phlegmy breaths.

"Yeah, Luther?"

"Do you think I'll go to hell for letting that woman get shot by my brother back at court? I... I didn't mean to."

"If you didn't mean to, you'll be all right."

Luther exhaled long and slow and didn't inhale again.

A shadow loomed over them. Jimmy closed his eyes. "Just do it already," he said. "I'm not afraid of you."

"Death comes to all," the shooter whispered. "And perhaps today it will yet come for you. But not by my hand. Michael wouldn't like that."

Michael? Jimmy shook. He clamped down on his leg just above the knee to stop it from bouncing. He expected to feel the metal nose of a pistol against his head at any moment.

Several minutes passed. He opened his eyes. The shadow had vanished without a sound, leaving Jimmy alone with a dead kid who had just needed better role models.

He buried his face in his hands and cried.

CHAPTER 21

When the shooting began, Michael hid under a desk in the office and worked at the ropes around his wrists. They hadn't been tied well, and after a couple of minutes of twisting and tugging, he wriggled his hands free with only a little rope burn to show for it.

For a while, things quieted in the main area, but as soon as he started to climb out of his rust-stained, musty-smelling hiding spot, World War III broke out all over again. The shots didn't seem to be that near, but it was hard to tell with the way they echoed through the vacant warehouse. And they didn't have to be close: the bullets moved a lot faster than he could. He would only need to step into the path of one.

Not that it would matter too much. No one would miss me. Except Sam, and all I ever am to her is a burden. And now I'm a life-threatening one? Michael wondered if the person from his visions was the cause of the chaos outside. *He said he was coming.*

"Oh, why did I ever have to go and get this stupid power?" he mumbled. "Why couldn't I have been strong like Superman or fast like the Flash?"

He straightened. *Because those guys aren't real, and you are. And comics are just stories for kids who don't want to grow up.* He loved them all the same, but he needed to ground himself in what was real if he wanted to survive. No heroes were coming to save him.

He shook his head. *But seeing visions of the future—that isn't supposed to be real, either.*

Fast footsteps were coming his way. Michael peeked over the desk just in time to see Hector racing past the window. A moment later, he heard a loud grinding noise, as if a metal drawer had been forced open. The footsteps grew softer.

Did he know a way out? Michael waited a couple of minutes then stood and tiptoed up to the office door. He rested his ear against it but heard nothing.

As he raised his head, the doorknob rattled.

Shit! Someone's right outside! Choking with fear, Michael darted for his former hiding place. On the way, he noticed a better spot and wedged himself into the corner beside the filing cabinet. A few clicks, and the doorknob turned. Whoever was entering either had a key or knew how to pick locks. Michael doubted either scenario boded well for him.

With a long high-pitched creak, the door swung open. Michael held his breath and tucked his heels under his buttocks, making himself as small as possible.

No one came into the office.

That's weird. Michael couldn't relax. *Why open a door if you're not going to use it?*

He thought about calling out but immediately decided against it. *It may be a trap. No, it's definitely a trap, but what choice do I have? I'm a sitting duck as long as I stay here.*

As tentative as a baby bird peeking over the edge of its nest for the first time, Michael crept to the door. He poked his head out into the warehouse and looked up and down the aisle, but he still saw no one.

The *thud-clink* of heavy gears turning and catching filled the air. The factory-operated metal shutters of the loading dock were opening. The shelving blocked his view of the bay, but the setting sun backlit everything else.

He stole from the room and crossed the aisle to the nearest row of shelving. He slid along it to its end. Only a short distance away, the shelving receded, and the conveyor belts began. They were massive things, as long as the moving sidewalks at airports and twice as wide. Each belt ran out a bay door at the height of Michael's sternum, where they would be in a fine position to load most freight carriers, though Michael saw no trailers parked outside them. Michael duck-walked over to the nearest belt, freedom only thirty feet away. Keeping low, he closed the distance.

"What the hell?" he whispered as he peered over the lip of the belt.

He saw a green pickup, and its bed was literally a bed, filled with blankets and pillows. Michael had an idea who had used it, and he swore right then that he was going to start wearing full-body condoms.

Just as he noticed the truck's engine was running, he realized someone was behind him. He could feel it. He turned, but before he could so much as scream, a gloveless hand palmed his face, pushing him back. Between its fingers, Michael saw the Whisperer's black hoodie.

Then his world went dark.

MICHAEL SAT UP IN THE back of the green pickup, surrounded by blankets and pillows. He wasn't tied up or anything. He planted his soles on the blanketed floor and grabbed the side of the bed. He rose to a squat without making a sound.

"I wouldn't," the driver called through the open window in the back of the cab.

Michael jerked around and saw a familiar figure shrouded in the oversized black hoodie. But the voice, *her* voice, was no longer a whisper.

"You're a woman?"

The Whisperer laughed. "Yes! Why wouldn't I be? You thought I was a man all this time? Well, I wonder if I should be offended." She laughed some more. "I'm just teasing. I wear these baggy clothes to disguise my sex, particularly when I'm working. But Michael! I thought you were more perceptive than that."

She sighed. "I guess I needn't have worried you'd recognize me if you couldn't even tell I was a woman. My breasts aren't the biggest, but... anyway, I had to stay hidden until I got a feel for you and understood why you wanted to find me. But I think it's safe to reveal myself now. You know you won't be able to link me to a crime that happened almost twelve years ago. And after I show you what I can do, you won't even want to try."

The Whisperer lowered her hood to reveal a bob of dirty-blond hair cut short around small ears. She kept her eyes on the road, and Michael could only see her profile. He looked in the rearview mirror to try to catch a glimpse of her face, but the angle was all wrong.

"Should I know you?" he asked. "Have we met before? I mean outside the day you killed my parents."

A strange feeling came over him. He couldn't remember what his mother looked like. In his dreams, he could never see his parents' faces, or much else, for that matter, though they had to be present. *And this woman, this new kidnapper, she had been there, and she had abilities kind of like mine.*

The thought was ridiculous, but he couldn't rid it from his mind. "Are you—"

Before Michael finished his question, the woman burst into hysterical laughter. "Your mother?" She laughed again, long and hard.

Michael flushed. He failed to see the humor in the question, though he was pretty sure he'd gotten his answer.

The Whisperer composed herself and turned just enough to flash him a grin. "I'm sorry. It's just been so long since I had a good laugh. But there is some merit to your question. I guess I am, in a way, though not biologically. You were reborn the day I entered your life. It's far too big a coincidence that I would spare your life, making you—and now your friend, consequently, but we both know how that ends—the sole exceptions to a rule that has always kept me protected, only to have you grow up to be just like me."

"I am nothing like you," Michael said through clenched teeth. "I don't kill people."

"Oh, shush. You are only making big of it because someone somewhere along the line convinced you that killing is morally wrong. But it's just you and me here. Are you going to tell me that Masterson fellow didn't deserve to die? How about Glenn Rodrigues? Those Suarez boys back there? Perhaps even me, in your eyes? Be honest. Every now and then, you want to sometimes, don't you?"

"Everyone thinks about it from time to time. But only psychos *do* it."

"Does that make Jimmy a psycho? How about Tessa?"

"They... they had exten-you... nating circumstances. And *they* didn't murder my parents."

"Well, you admit to thinking about it sometimes. That's a start. Not everyone thinks about it. But tell me: at those times, if you had a weapon in your hand and knew without a doubt that you could get away with it, wouldn't you take the opportunity fortune presented to you?"

"I don't—"

"Yeah, yeah, yeah." The Whisperer pounded her palm into the steering wheel.

Michael rose onto his knees. He studied the speedometer, but the numbers were impossible to read. From the vibrating needle's position, it didn't appear as though they were traveling much over thirty. He assumed they were still in Fall River, hopefully on back roads that would have stop signs and lights.

"I guess I thought we would be having this conversation in dreamland," the Whisperer said, laughing uneasily. "I set up the truck bed and everything. But of course, the one time you don't have a vision is when I touch you. Instead, you just fainted. Ha! I guess I could've just triggered...

Michael spotted what he was looking for: a lady walking her dog. He raised his hands to cup them around his mouth.

Hey!" the Whisperer yelled. "What do you think you're doing?"

As Michael opened his mouth to shout for help, the Whisperer's voice crackled through his brain like an earthquake breaking trenches through dry earth. The internal shout was accompanied by pain fierce enough to make his nose bleed.

"Don't!" was the one-word message.

The dog stopped sniffing a telephone pole and raised its head, but its owner remained oblivious.

"She won't help you," the Whisperer said. "And if you jump, you'll be tossing away your only chance to get answers." She pulled the truck over to the curb. "So please, come inside the cab, and we'll talk like two civilized individuals."

Michael sat frozen, watching her without blinking. He couldn't tell if she was playing some sort of game.

"I'm sorry I got angry, Michael. It's just that I've taken a great risk in revealing myself to you, placing my trust in you, and I was hoping you'd show me the same trust in return. I mean you no harm whatsoever. But you lied to me. Or else you're lying to yourself. If you'd had access to a gun, it might have been you standing in your friend Jimmy's shoes that day. I know your mind. I can hear your thoughts as clearly as if you shouted them. Some kills aren't immoral. Some are righteous. And some, well, are just plain lucrative."

"It's not true. I would never kill anyone," he growled. "I wouldn't kidnap someone, either."

The woman tittered. "You are not being kidnapped. Face it, Michael. I saved your life. Those Suarez boys wanted you dead. Now most of them are dead, and you are free. And all I want to do is talk. Don't you think you owe me that much?"

"Why?"

"Well, first of all, I can make your visions so much stronger."

Michael groaned. "I never wanted these visions. Why would I want to make them stronger?"

"You don't. I get it. You want to learn how to control them. I know how to do that."

Control them? That was something he did want to learn, perhaps even badly enough to hear his kidnapper out. Michael scratched his head. "All right." He hopped out of the back of the truck, opened the passenger door, and got in. After fastening his seat belt, he said, "Tell me how."

"That's the spirit!" the Whisperer said, slapping her knee.

When she turned to look at him, Michael saw her face for the first time. She had high cheekbones and glasses that made her eyes look ginormous. He was surprised that she looked familiar. "Do I know you?"

"Ha! I asked you that once not too long ago."

Michael squinted at her. "I do know you! You work in the library. You told that hot girl to help me."

She guffawed. "I'll be sure to let Katie know she made quite the impression. I'm guessing my looks didn't make the cut."

Michael blushed. "I'm sorry. I didn't mean... Wait a minute! Why the heck am I apologizing to you? Are we just forgetting the fact that you killed my parents?"

She sighed. "I suppose we need to get past that first. The library is my cover job, though I do rather enjoy it. With all the money I've amassed, it may be time to retire." She rubbed her temple. "How should I put this? Your parents were related to a job. Like you, I have scruples. I don't just kill anyone, and I do my research first. They weren't good people, Michael. They deserved—"

"To be murdered in cold blood?" Michael balled up his fists. "I don't believe that. I *can't* believe that."

"But you know I didn't pull the trigger?"

Michael studied the floor. "Yes."

"Whittaker was the target. Your father was the patsy. He was an abusive drunk. Your mother was having an extramarital affair. They made it too easy. No one was innocent. You were the only complication."

"Is that what I was to you? A *complication*?"

"I could have killed you too. But you weren't part of the plan, nor was I paid to end your life. My mentor, the same one who taught me all I plan on teaching you, helped me plan it, and I got away clean. I would be lying if I said we left your father to take the fall and go to jail for it, because we knew he would take his life as soon as he took your mother's. We may have set the scene well, but your father did all the dirty work and cleaned up all the loose ends, except for you."

"Your mentor? Someone else was involved?"

"Yes, but he's... not here, though he still talks to me from time to time."

Michael's eyes widened. *Uh-oh. She's crazy. Is this what the future has in store for me?* "So what do you really want with me? I don't believe you just want to help me with my visions out of the goodness of your heart. What do you get out of all of this?"

The librarian's brow furrowed. "That's a hard question to answer. And to be honest, I barely know you. For many years, I had forgotten all about you. But since your trial by fire last fall, I've been keeping my eye on you. I keep tabs on all reported psychics, real and fake, especially the local ones and those affiliated with law enforcement. Imagine my surprise when I looked a bit deeper into Michael Turcotte and realized you were really Michael Florentine, the little boy I spared all those years ago." She smirked and patted his leg.

Michael jerked his leg away.

Seeming unperturbed by his rejection, she put her hand back on her own knee. "I've been reaching out to you through the dreamscape ever since. Visions, or a true fugue state, are always the easier mediums, and though I sensed you often enough in the beginning before I could harness a link, your visions have been next to nil as of late." She pointed at his gloves. "I'm guessing those have something to do with it?"

Michael ignored her question. He couldn't deny that what she said she could do intrigued him. "You can reach out to people in their dreams and visions? Enter them?"

The librarian looked at him flatly.

Michael rolled his eyes. "Duh. You've been doing it all along." He huffed. "You've been watching me."

"Don't beat yourself up too much over it. It's actually a good question. But it only works with others like us."

"Others like us? How many of us are there?"

"Not a lot, but more than you might think. Most of them are crazy, though. They can't handle their gifts. Some try to suppress it, like you have, but that just drives them crazy faster when they realize they can't, at least not in the way you're going about it."

"They're crazy? And you're not? Dead people talk to you, and you kill people." He pursed his lips. "You killed my parents."

She stared at him quizzically. "Dead people don't talk to me. Where did you get that idea?" She shrugged. "As for your parents... I did kill them, indirectly anyway. Get over it."

Michael slouched. He could feel the sullenness oozing out of his face. "You want me to trust you? Fine. But first, you have to tell me what you really want with me."

The librarian smiled warmly. "Fair enough. I suppose I owe you that much, but why don't we save that conversation for when we're back at my place? For now, rest. You've been through a lot. Life's been beating you up pretty hard. I think it's time it started to go your way."

CHAPTER 22

"We wasted twenty minutes waiting for SWAT." Sam paced outside the warehouse. The gunshots reported only a few minutes earlier suggested Sleven had named the right place. "Is the owner here yet? Can we get those shutters open?"

Is anyone even fucking listening to me? She pulled the edge of the bulletproof vest away from her neck, the chafing of her skin adding to her irritation. "The caller said it was like a battlefield in there. Will you guys hurry?"

The tactical unit spread out, taking positions outside the side door and beneath the conveyor belts of the open loading bay shutters. They had the building surrounded, but their commanding officer was letting time tick by.

"Are you freaking ready yet?" she shouted to Sergeant Montgomery, a fastidious man who would not risk his team for the lives of one civilian, even if that civilian happened to be the pseudo-foster child of a Fall River detective.

The sergeant stood behind an armored truck. Although he had to have heard, he ignored her question.

Sam held back the four-letter words she had for the sergeant. She stormed over to him and poked him in the chest. "There's a kid in that warehouse who's scared and could be injured, not to mention the Justice of the Superior Court these sons of bitches took hostage. If either one of them dies because you and your men were too busy checking and rechecking your jock straps, I'm holding you personally responsible."

Sergeant Montgomery stiffened, and his face turned red. "We need eyes on top," he said, referring to the snipers scaling the roofs of the surrounding buildings.

"Be patient," Frank said, putting a hand on her shoulder. "They're closing the net. We'll find the boy and take them all down."

Sam ducked away from the agent's hand and glared at him, ready to ignite. But then she gritted her teeth and turned away. "Fuck this," she muttered as she marched to the front of the armored truck. "Michael's inside. He could be hurt. I'm going in."

"Detective," the sergeant called after her, "my men are set. We just need to open one of those garage doors."

She pushed the vehicle's driver, a baby face on a man's body, out of her way and climbed in. The keys were in the ignition, and she fired it up. "Oh, I'll open one of those doors." She threw the truck into gear. "Stand back!" In her peripheral vision, she could see the sergeant, the driver, and Frank backpedaling away from the truck. She took her foot off the brake and hit the gas.

With a screech of tires and the burn of rubber, the vehicle barreled forward. Three seconds later, it collided with the garage door and busted through it. The metal door twisted and hinged upward, creating space for SWAT to enter. With her gun up, Sam leaped out of the truck. The SWAT team fanned out around her, responding to their new leader.

She took point, glancing back only once to see Frank covering her rear. She breathed a little easier, knowing she had a skilled ally at her side. After reaching a stack of pallets covered in torn plastic wrap and dust, she took cover behind it then edged to its corner. Swinging around it, weapon at the ready, she saw no sign of the gang or its two hostages.

At another column of pallets, Sam halted. "Anything?" She waited as patiently as she could, giving the team time to report.

"I've got one!" an officer yelled from somewhere to her left. "He's been shot. There's no pulse."

"Got one over here too. He's DOA," another officer added from near her right flank.

Sam took a deep breath and swallowed her fear. "Either of them Michael?"

"Negative," both reported.

She examined a hole in the wood at her eye level. It looked like a thousand other bullet holes she'd seen. With a penknife, she dug out the bullet, gave it a once-over, then dropped it into a plastic baggie. She inched forward and rounded the pallet. On the other side, she came face-to-face with a boy of Michael's height and age, covered in blood. *Jimmy Rafferty.*

"Freeze!" The barrel of her pistol was lined up with the center of Jimmy's face. Removing her support hand, she held it up and signaled her team. "Nobody shoot!"

With a detective's eye for detail, she assessed the level of threat Jimmy posed. He held a gun but hadn't raised it. Blood coated his shirt and one leg. The blood on his leg appeared to be from a wound, but the blood on his shirt... *Oh, Jimmy. What have you done?*

"Jimmy?" Sam put her free hand out in a placating way, but she never took the finger of her other hand off the trigger. She could see a small form lumped behind Jimmy, too small to be Michael. "Are you alone? Where's Michael?"

"He's gone," Jimmy said. His eyes were swollen, and Sam guessed he'd been crying.

What does he mean 'gone'? Oh, Michael, please be okay.

Jimmy hung his head. "They're all gone."

Sam edged closer to the armed teenager. She could sense Frank circling the boy to her right. Jimmy took a step toward her on wobbly legs.

"Put the gun down, Jimmy," Sam said, trying to keep her voice calm. *Please, put that gun down, and just tell me where Michael is.* "Lower your weapon, and we'll help you. You have my word."

"I'm not going back there." Tears streamed down Jimmy's cheeks. "What I did to Glenn... that was a good thing! I don't deserve that place. I don't belong there!"

"You helped me at the courthouse, remember?" Sam asked. "We can put in a good word for you. Get your sentence commuted."

"You don't understand. That place... juvie just turns screwed-up kids into career criminals or... or... something worse. I never wanted that kind of life. I never wanted this. I just wanted to do my time in school, maybe work with animals when I get older. That place, that fucking place! They're the animals!"

Sam only half listened. She knew unstable when she saw it, and Jimmy's arm had begun to flex and tremble. With all the time they'd spent talking, her team must have had the drop on Jimmy a dozen different ways. The sudden multiple clicks confirmed that suspicion.

"Hold your fire!" she shouted. "Don't do it, Jimmy. Don't make me shoot you."

Jimmy's arm showed hesitation, but Sam could no longer doubt he would raise it. She prayed she might somehow be wrong.

"Maybe I'm just an animal too." The gun rose.

"Don't!" Sam cried.

Aim low, Sam, a voice screamed in her head. *Aim low!* Her finger pressed the trigger before Jimmy could get a shot off. Her bullet ripped through his abdomen, and he fell to the ground, writhing in pain, his gun thrown from his hand as it smacked against the floor.

She ran over and kicked the gun out of his reach.

"It... it wasn't loaded," he said, grinning with bloody teeth. "I would never hurt you."

"Where's Michael, Jimmy?"

"They took him... toward the back. Th-The office. It hurts so much. But I can die, like poor Luther." His eyes rolled back in his head, and he lost consciousness.

Sam started to check his pulse, but she noticed his chest still rising and falling. *You're not dying on my watch.* "You!" she shouted at the baby-faced officer who'd been inside the armored truck. "The place is clear. Get the paramedics in here." When the officer just gave her a confused look, she added, "Now!" and he spun into action.

"Help's coming, Jimmy," she whispered. "Hold on."

She moved past him to the small heap a few feet away. When she saw the contorted body, she covered her mouth and thought she might vomit from the terribleness of it all.

"Luther Suarez," Frank said as he came up beside her.

"Is the rest of the building clear?"

"Just about. They're clearing the office, but so far, no Michael. Victor Suarez, Valeria Perez, and Benzo Antonelli, the third man from the bank job, are dead. Maurice Thibeault has been shot twice and has lost a ton of blood, but he's alive and being taken to the hospital. That just leaves the two hostages and—"

"Hector Suarez," Sam growled. "We'd better get back there."

Two paramedics came running up with a gurney, along with the man Sam had sent back to the ambulance. "We've found the judge!" he blurted. "She was tied up in the back of the ambulance, severely dehydrated, but otherwise unharmed."

"Good work, Officer," Sam said. "Now, get this boy and the judge to the hospital ASAP. We can question them after they've been taken care of."

While the officers loaded Jimmy onto the gurney, Frank came over and patted Sam's arm. He smiled warmly. "This is good news. If they left the judge alive, why would they hurt Michael?"

Sam tried a smile that wouldn't hold. "Let's go."

When they reached the office, only one member of the SWAT team remained. "There's no sign of Turcotte or Suarez. No one could have slipped past us unseen, so they must have escaped before we arrived."

"What's that in your hand?" Sam asked.

"Copper wire," the officer said. "It looks like Hector Suarez may have been making another bomb, but we haven't found much in the way of other supplies."

"Clear the building!" Sam shouted.

The officer's brow furrowed. "We haven't seen any devices—"

"Get everyone out now!"

"All units, clear out!" the officer said into his radio. "Explosive devices suspected. Immediate evacuation ordered." The officer nodded at the other door. "This way. The loading dock is open."

The three of them sprinted toward the back of the building, the young man leading the charge. From above, Sam heard a beep, then another sounded to her left, then another, and another. The beeps sounded like those of an EKG, except the heartbeat they monitored grew faster by the second.

Soon, the beeps were so close together that they sounded like a solid tone. Sam and Frank leaped through the loading bay door as the first explosion came. The bomb must have been affixed to the ceiling because the sound came from above, and remnants of the skylights rained down around them along with some shingles and splintered wood. The officer was already across the back lot, waving for them to hurry.

"There!" Frank pointed at an abandoned trailer then took Sam's hand. "We need cover."

Boom! The second blast sent projectiles into their backs as they scooted beneath the trailer. *Boom! Boom! BOOM!*

A cloud of dust and dirt cycloned around them, and Frank threw his body over hers. They closed their eyes as the building continued to rumble, Frank holding her tightly. A tempest rocked the trailer above them, but it landed back in place. A hailstorm of debris poured down onto their makeshift shelter.

When silence returned, Sam opened her eyes, blinked several times, and coughed out some dust. Frank helped her out from underneath the trailer. Fat brown clouds as thick as London fog waved across their legs.

When the smoke thinned, she saw that the building was gone. A pile of rubble sat in its place.

"Anyone hurt?" Sam called into her radio.

"A few cuts and bruises, nothing more," someone answered.

Sam shook her head. "There goes my evidence." She pushed her hair back over her ears. "There goes my chance to find Michael."

CHAPTER 23

"How can I trust you if I don't even know your name?" Michael stared at the glass of soda the woman had poured for him—root beer, his favorite. He wondered if she knew that or if it had been a lucky guess. Cool beads ran down the glass like the sweat rolling off his lower back.

The house was plain. It screamed "assassin" even less than the woman did, if that was even possible. Drab olive-green furniture and sturdy but simple oak tables gave the place a cabin-in-the-woods-type feel, though it was dead in the middle of suburbia. They had tramped across a cracked walkway overgrown with weeds and up some railless concrete steps to a single-story house with a one-car garage the woman hadn't used. He noted the house number, 736, and had memorized most of the street signs, just as Sam had taught him, but the street the house sat on was only marked with a signless pole.

Never once did she try to force him inside or push him in any way he didn't want to go. But he knew she could shoot, and he knew she had killed. Walking away hadn't seemed a real option when he'd exited the pickup.

But now? Michael rolled his fingers on his knee. *She's offering me root beer.* He took the glass into his hands without looking at it or its carrier, focusing instead on the stacks of newspaper piled everywhere, some in neat bales held together with twine, others a loose-leaf mess. He couldn't make eye contact with his... *kidnapper? Is that right? She said I could leave.*

The woman laughed. "Somehow I doubt giving you my name is all it'll take to get you to trust me."

"No, but it would be a nice start."

"I've let you into my home." She spread her arms wide. "I have nothing to hide, not from you. My name is Ryan."

"Well, Ms...."

"Ryan is fine."

"Well, Ryan, what's with all the newspapers?"

Ryan's face lit up like the holidays. She slapped her thighs and ran her hand over the closest stack. She lifted a newspaper cutout with a picture of a smiling teen raising her hand before a judge. The article read *Daughter of Late Lawyer Follows in Father's Footsteps.* "I follow them. See? Janie Morgan is a lawyer now."

"Follow who?"

"Well... all of them."

Michael swallowed, his mouth dry. "Who's *them?*"

"Those whose lives I change."

Michael squinted at the paper. *Daughter of a dead lawyer?* "Do you mean the children of those you kill?"

"No." Ryan scoffed. "Don't be silly."

Michael smiled, not trying to hide his relief.

"Not just the children but all those impacted. Husbands, wives, kids, grandkids, mistresses... I've even chronicled the life of a spaniel that was Best in Show but lived a quieter life after I pushed her master in front of the subway."

Michael gulped and shrank away from Ryan.

"No, no," she said. "It was good, clean. And rarely has there been someone so deserving."

"Wh-What did she do? Why did you do it?"

"Well, for money, of course, but that didn't make it any less satisfying. She was one of those rich girls who think they own everything. She got together with her friends and hazed a classmate so badly on all those social media sites that their poor victim committed suicide. Their money bought them good lawyers, who got them off with community service. But the victim's family had enough money to see justice done, at least to the ringleader." She shook her head. "Shame they couldn't afford the rest."

"But... she was just a kid."

"Rotten kids grow up to be even more rotten adults." She smirked. "You're not a rotten kid. Are you, Michael?"

Michael swallowed hard again, his mouth gone even dryer. "Uh, no. No." Without thinking, he took down a large swig of root beer.

"Relax. I'm just teasing you. And I shouldn't. I'm sorry. You're nervous enough about being here without me making things worse."

Tasting nothing odd in the soda, he did relax a little. "Why do you follow them?"

"Have you ever heard of the butterfly effect?"

"Yeah, something about a butterfly flapping its wings in Africa causing a tidal wave in New York Harbor or something like that."

"Close enough. I like to think my acts have a ripple effect, not only across my mark's circle of friends, but across time. I excise cancers from healthy lives. Those who survive are made better by their loss, sometimes without ever knowing it. Take that dog, for example—the spaniel. She can now live a life of comfort without having pompous snots sticking thumbs up her butt. And Janie Morgan here"—she held up the article—"who, before Daddy's death, was content to mooch off him for all her days. Now she is strong, independent."

"Did you ever, you know, follow me?"

"Couldn't. I tried, but once you entered the foster system, you vanished. I guess I could have found you if I tried harder, but I don't like to dwell on the failures. I wish I had tried sooner, because look at you! Not a failure at all! And with such power, you don't even know."

Michael looked away. "You're right. I do want to know. How to control it, I mean."

"I know you do, Michael. And I promise to show you all I can. But first, shouldn't you call Detective Reilly and let her know you're okay?"

Michael sat up straight. "I can do that? I can call her?"

"Of course!" Ryan laughed. "Like I said, you're not a prisoner here. And she must be worried sick about you. Obviously, I hope you will use discretion in what you tell her. I guess there's no hiding the fact that I carried you away from that warehouse. She won't believe that was luck. But I'm guessing she'll believe I was there to help you if she knows I'm like you. Well, I'm not really guessing since I've already foreseen all of this."

"How can you know what I'm going to do when I don't even know it?"

Ryan just smiled and handed Michael her mobile phone.

He took it and ran his thumb across the screen. When it lit up, he stared at it for a moment then shook his head. "I don't know her number. I have it programmed into my phone."

"That's okay. We'll just wait for her. She should be here in less than an hour."

CHAPTER 24

Sam was down but not out. She knew she had just missed Michael, but if he wasn't in the building... *No, he was definitely not in the building.* She had to believe that much. The loading area had been opened. Michael had gotten out safely.

But is he safe? Where did he go? Is he with Suarez?

Scanning the force assembling around her, she snapped, "All right, listen up! We have one perp unaccounted for and a hostage, a fifteen-year-old boy who means everything to me. That means he had better mean everything to all of you too."

Bystanders were emerging from the city's dark crevices like cockroaches. Sam pursed her lips and studied her team. "Reynolds, Bertrand, you two cordon off the area and keep back the media and all these busybodies. Sergeant Montgomery, I'm sure your men won't mind assisting wherever they can."

"We're on it," Montgomery answered. SWAT stood at attention. "Two birds in the nest. The rest of you, set a perimeter. Eyes open for any sign of the suspect or the boy." He twirled a finger in the air, and his men moved as though choreographed.

"Ansari and Phelps," Sam continued, "head over to the hospital and get a statement from Judge Baker as soon as she's ready to give one. Leave Thibeault or Detective Spinx for me."

Sam faced a bulldog of man, complete with gritted teeth and hanging jowls. "Sergeant Coles, organize a team to question every single person who steps foot on, near, or away from this lot. Nobody ever talks in this neighborhood. Still, we have to try."

Coles nodded and corralled four of the patrol officers still awaiting instructions.

Sam waved a hand. "The rest of you, spread out, search the area, and report in with any sign of the missing boy or the still-living Suarez." *Not if I get my hands on him.*

She watched her men go to work. Under one guy's cap, a jagged scar bisected the officer's neckline. She recognized it, the constant reminder of the mace that had split his head open. Only in Fall River would a killer use such an antiquated weapon.

"Tagliamonte," she called.

He turned and offered a sad smile. "Yes, Detective?"

"Can you go by my place and make sure Michael hasn't returned there?" She checked her phone. "I doubt it, since he hasn't called, but we need to check."

"On it," Tagliamonte said. He hurried off.

She could almost feel Frank's ear listening in, though he shuffled and pretended not to be. With his hair and sports jacket covered in dust, he looked pretty rough, and he was massaging a kink out of his neck.

Sam asked Frank, "You with me on this?"

"Of course," he said.

"I think going back to the precinct is our best bet. I want to pull up CCTV video on all neighborhood traffic cams. Best thing we ever installed. If he left on foot, we'll have a direction. If in a car, we'll have something better."

"Hector's like a snake that crawled out from under a rock. He'll be looking for a new hole to slither into and disappear. He can't be far."

"All but one of this Suarez gang is dead or in custody. I want to get him, too, but I want to find Michael more."

"I understand."

She studied the older man's tattered coat and stretching crows' feet, wondering how badly the explosion had affected him. "You okay to drive?"

He frowned. "I'm not out of the game yet."

"Good." She tossed him her keys. "You drive. I've got to make a call."

On the way back to the precinct, Sam called Traffic Control and requested footage from every nearby traffic camera for a timeframe spanning thirty minutes before her arrival at the warehouse through the time of the explosion. Video footage waited for her in her inbox as soon as she signed on to her computer.

Sam forwarded the videos to every subordinate not already working a major case to comb through for signs of Michael or Hector. With Frank hovering over her shoulder, she opened each file and fast-forwarded them to five minutes before she and SWAT had surrounded the building. She played four videos at a time in different windows on her screen.

"That's odd," Frank said as he pointed to the window in the bottom right corner. "Can you pause that one?"

Sam clicked the pause button on the media player. The screen showed an empty road, nothing out of the ordinary and nothing to set it apart in Sam's mind from other Fall River streets. The file read Broad Street, which she knew ran into South Main.

She sighed out her impatience. "What is it? What did you see?"

"Rewind it five seconds."

Sam clicked the button that backed up the video thirty seconds.

Frank jabbed a finger at the screen. "There!"

A green pickup crossed the camera frame, moving as a small dot near the middle of the screen and getting bigger—but harder to see inside the cab—as it passed under the camera. The close-up overhead view made it look as though the bed were filled with giant marshmallows.

Squinting, Sam realized they were pillows. "Why would someone have an actual bed set up in their truck bed?"

"Could be any number of reasons, I suppose, but my thought is that if you were going to drug someone or render them unconscious, parking your pickup under that conveyor belt and throwing your victim into the back of a truck would be a lot easier than dragging him into the passenger seat." He shrugged. "Maybe I'm reaching, but—"

"No, I don't think you are." Sam maximized the window, rewound the video, then played the short scene forward again in slow motion.

As the truck came into view, she paused and unpaused the video repeatedly to obtain the best and largest image she could of the people inside the cab. The driver had on a black sweatshirt, its hood pulled low and jutting out enough to cover the eyes from the camera's angle. Though the clothes were gender nondescript and hid the shape of the body beneath them, the hand on the steering wheel was slender and hairless.

"I'm guessing it's a woman," Sam said.

"Yeah, you might be right. Not what I expected."

In the passenger seat sat a blurred boy Sam recognized as Michael. He appeared to be sleeping.

If you hurt so much as a single hair on his head... Sam gnashed her teeth. "It's him."

"What's the driver doing with her hand?"

"Steering?"

"No, her other hand."

Sam rewound the video again, and the next time through, she paid close attention the driver's right hand. With each pause, the hand stopped somewhere in what soon became obvious as a side-to-side motion.

Sam frowned. "Is she actually waving at the camera?"

"Well, it sure looks like it. But I guess it could be someone on the street. I don't know."

Sam rewound the tape again and hit Play. Staring at the video so hard her eyes were almost watering, she focused on the license plate.

A dispatcher hustled over, a flabby, unkempt man with man boobs bigger than her own. She recognized the man but didn't remember his name. He hadn't worked there long.

"Detective Reilly," he said, almost out of breath.

"Yes?" she asked, thinking the man better have a damn good reason for interrupting.

"We just received an anonymous tip, no caller ID and way too short to trace, giving us a location on Hector Suarez."

Sam glared at the dispatcher, who seemed to shrink beneath her stare. "Well? Out with it."

The dispatcher swallowed. "The address is 42 Dwyer Street."

"What were the caller's exact words?" Sam asked.

"'If you want Hector Suarez, he's at 42 Dwyer Street, but you'd better hurry.' Then he hung up."

"He?" Sam asked. "So it was definitely a male voice?"

The dispatcher nodded. "Yes, definitely."

"Nothing else?" Frank asked.

"No, that's all," the dispatcher said.

"Thank you," Sam said. After he hurried off, she rocked back in her chair and folded her hands behind her head. "What do you think?"

Frank stroked his chin. "Sounds legit. What are the odds of information leaking so soon after the warehouse explosion *and* it already being used to create a false lead? The caller was specific in naming Hector, the only one of the Suarez gang not accounted for." He leaned back against her desk, his fingers tapping the edge.

"Go," she said.

"You sure? I promised I'd help you find Michael."

"I'll follow up on the plate and leave word where I'm heading. You go to Dwyer Street, but watch your back. It's a bad neighborhood. A lot of crack houses filled with junkies who'll do anything for a chance to get high. I'll call Sergeant Montgomery and have him gather a team to meet you there."

"As soon as I've got him, I'll join up with you."

"Take him alive, if you can, in case this plate doesn't pan out and he has any idea how to find Michael."

"I'll try. Believe me, I've got a few questions I'd like to ask him myself."

Sam met his eyes and frowned. "It could be an ambush."

"If my theory is correct about these guys, I expect it will be." He stood, grabbed his tattered jacket from the back of the chair, and threw it over his shoulder. "Wish me luck."

"Good luck. Hopefully, you won't need it."

CHAPTER 25

I told you not to bring him here, the Voice said. *He knows too much now. And worse, that detective is like a dog with a bone. She won't stop with finding him. She'll look into you. She'll find out about... your condition. You talk too much when you use. I won't let her get close to me.*

Ryan lazed against her headboard, the rubber tube still wrapped tightly around her bicep, the needle discarded on the bed beside her. A warm euphoria exploded in her chest and radiated outward. Her eyes rolled up. Her chin quivered. Nothing the always-chattering Voice said would sway her. She was no longer a dog on a chain.

"Haven't I followed your rules? I've done every job, everything you've asked of me, and what do I have to show for it? I ask this one thing. One thing!"

You'd have it all if not for that nasty habit of yours.

"This 'nasty habit' is the only thing that makes life tolerable, the only thing that ever has. I had it before I had you."

You used to find joy in your work. The Voice sighed. *Maybe I waited too long to enlist you. We tolerated your drug abuse because it never affected your work—*

"It still hasn't!"

No, but it's affecting your judgment. He's just a boy. He still sees the world in black and white. When he's ready, he'll come to us. And when that time comes, he won't have that damn detective following at his heels. We've seen it all—

"So have I! You want to wait until he's like me... I mean, *really* like me. An addict. Alone. Suicidal. What kind of life will he have then?"

It's too soon, Ryan. He's jaded. He still clings to notions of morality spoon-fed by the preachings of fools. His has no mindset for the work we do.

"Then let him do something bigger, something better. Let him be better than us."

Ah, I see. This isn't about him at all, is it? It's about you.

"What do my reasons matter? He deserves a better life than the one dealt him. He can be so much more than us, so much more than *you*. Does that scare you?"

Yes, and it should scare you too.

"Ha! I'm going to teach him everything. By the time he's your age, he will be able to see infinite futures, maneuver us as a species onto the optimal path."

You'll drive him mad. Those who have tried to change too much, tried to create the perfect future, have always failed and gone mad trying. They fried their own brains with the constant seizing. They failed to understand what I thought you grasped: perfection is unobtainable. Utopia is a lie. Human nature is constant, and it is ugly.

"It can be reprogrammed. We can be fixed."

You disappoint me, Ryan. Clean yourself up. Your company awaits.

MICHAEL SIPPED HIS root beer as he scanned the room. Newspapers weren't just stacked everywhere. Some were framed. Where most people had family photos, Ryan had articles relating to the families of those she had killed. *That's fucked up.*

He let out a breath. *She did save your life, for whatever that's worth.* He tapped his fingers against his leg. *I wonder what happened to Jimmy.* He shook his head. Jimmy didn't deserve his worry.

Focus on yourself, Michael. He stared at the closed door at the end of the hall through which Ryan had vanished. From what she had said, she knew how to make his powers stronger. She could teach him how to control them. What he really wanted to know, though, was whether or not she could make them go away entirely.

Then what? I could be normal? He scoffed. Normal was something he figured he'd never be. Normal didn't happen for kids who'd seen the stuff he had. *Ordinary? Visionless? Now that doesn't sound so bad.*

Where is she, anyway? When Ryan had excused herself, he figured she had to go to the bathroom or something. But she had been gone twenty minutes already, maybe a half hour. He giggled. *Maybe she's clogged up.*

He plopped down on the sofa and sighed. Janie Morgan's smiling face stared up at him, her hand raised as she was sworn in to the Massachusetts Bar. Judging by that picture alone, he thought the woman seemed happy. People smiled for pictures. That was what they did, whether they felt like smiling or not. It was hardly enough evidence to determine that Ryan's murder of Janie's father had made her life better.

Even if it did, I don't want to kill people. I already help people where I can, and I do it without killing. He put his drink down on a coaster—he always used a coaster, ever since his one and only visit to the Masterson residence—and rested his face in his hands, trying to come up with a plan. But the plan had been made as soon as he awoke in that cab, the reason he hadn't made a break for it. He just hadn't articulated it yet.

"Learn what I can from her, learn how to stop the visions, then go our separate ways." If he had to, he'd give her up to the police. Since hiding his plans from Ryan seemed futile, he figured the plan was sound, or at least she had no objection. After all, he was still breathing.

"But what do I tell Sam?"

He heard Ryan talking in another room. *Is she on the phone? Is she talking about me?*

He stood and crept into the hall. He was a few feet from the door when her conversation became more animated.

"So have I! You want to wait until he's like me, and—"

Someone knocked on the front door of the house. "Michael? Are you in there? Open up."

Michael frowned. *Sam.*

"I SWEAR TO GOD IF SOMEONE doesn't open this goddamn door in three seconds, I'm going to kick the fucking thing in!"

Sam knew she wasn't playing by the rules. Those had long since gone out the window where Michael was concerned. *Is this what it means to be a mother?*

She had found Ryan Chambers's address in the RMV's database and sped over there, calling in Frank's backup as well as her own as she drove. Her men hadn't arrived yet. She would not wait for them.

When the door didn't open, she pulled out her gun. "Goddamn it!" She stepped back to kick in the door.

The door creaked open. Michael stood in the doorway. "She said you would come."

"Michael!" Sam pushed her way inside and threw her arms around him. "Thank God, you're all right." She resisted the urge to pull him closer, feeling him tense and tilt his head away as soon as she touched him. With considerable effort, she forced herself to back away, stand up straight, and wipe away the wetness from her cheek.

"Are you... crying?" he asked.

"I'm sorry. I... I just got caught up in the moment." She ironed out the front of her pants with her hands and swallowed hard. "I was worried about you, you know?"

"I know. I'm sorry."

"Are you hurt?"

"I'm fine. I—"

"How did you get here?"

"I brought him here," a woman said, stepping from the shadowy hall.

Sam raised her gun, but seeing the woman's hands were empty, she lowered it a little but didn't holster it. She took a quick inventory: the woman wore a tracksuit, unzipped but long-sleeved and a bit heavy for the warm day. She was thin, almost skeletal, with big eyes made bigger by the magnifying effect of her bifocals. She reminded Sam of the creepy dude from the *Lord of the Rings*, the one that kept calling his ring "Precious," except with hair like eagle wings at the farthest point down in their flap. The style had been popular once, when she was a kid maybe, but not since.

"Please, come in," the woman said. "Have a seat."

"Who are you?" Sam asked, her every impulse telling her to grab the woman by her neck. "Why did you take Michael?"

"Sam," Michael said, "she didn't take me. She *saved* me."

"What do you mean?" Sam's grip tightened around her pistol. "Did she kill all those people back at the warehouse?"

"Kill people?" The woman laughed. She scratched at the inside of her elbow through the jacket. "Of course not. I found Michael there"—she stepped closer—"running into the street, screaming for help. He flagged me down. All I know about what he was running from comes from what he told me. That and... well, perhaps I best let him tell you. You might not believe it coming from me."

"If that's true, why didn't you take him to the police? Why did you bring him here? You had better start talking."

"Detective, there's no need for—"

"Why don't we start with your name?"

"You know my name, just as I know yours, Detective Reilly. I knew you would come here for the boy."

"Ryan Chambers?"

Ryan nodded.

"Michael," Sam said, not taking her eyes off the skeleton in the tracksuit, "if you're not here against your will, why didn't you call me?"

"Because he—"

"I'm asking Michael." Sam huffed then took a deep breath. "Look, Ms. Chambers, I mean no disrespect, and if what you say is true, then it appears I owe you a debt of gratitude. But I don't know you from squat."

"She's like me, Sam," Michael said. "That's how she knew you'd be coming, and how she knew where I would be when I, uh, escaped."

Sam snarled. "What's with all these newspapers? What have you been doing, studying up on him? If you're another one of those con artists looking to exploit him, I'll—"

Michael stomped his foot. "You're not listening! She's not a con artist. She's the real thing. Can't you just trust me for once?"

Sam leaned closer to him while keeping one sharp eye on Ryan. "Michael, I do trust you. I was worried sick about you. This woman had you in her care, and by her own admission, she knew you had been taken hostage because you told her. And she didn't think to call the police? Didn't think to let you call me?"

Michael shrugged her hands off him. "She did let me call you! I didn't call you because I don't have your number memorized. And anyway, I didn't want to."

Sam stiffened. A pang stabbed her heart as real as an icepick. Her shoulders drooped. "Why? Why didn't you want to call me?"

"Because I want to stay here! I want her to teach me how to control it, so I never have to have another vision again. So I never, ever put us into someone else's danger again."

"Michael, my job is dangerous—"

"Yeah, and you don't need me making it worse."

"I chose this life. I've been at it a long time. I never really had anyone else to care for, never had someone else I was responsible for. I can see I've failed you, Michael. You're hurting, and you need help. Maybe it's time I took a little break from the force. Maybe you and I could take a little vacation. What do you say?"

"You just don't get it, do you?" Michael frowned. "You can't help me, but *she* can." He pointed at Ryan.

"He's right," Ryan said. "I can help him."

"You... just stay out of this." Sam glowered at the woman who had apparently helped Michael where she couldn't, conflicted and hating her for all the wrong reasons. She turned back to Michael. "You know I can't let you stay here."

"Whatever." Michael scowled. He crossed his arms and stared at her defiantly. "You're not my mother."

Sam's eyes watered a little, and she looked away. "Please... just get in the car."

After a moment in silence, Michael relented. Pouting, he pushed past her and headed for the car, leaving Sam alone with the Good Samaritan.

"Teenagers," Ryan said, offering a shaky smile.

"I expect to see you down at the precinct first thing tomorrow, so I can get your statement." *And figure out if I should be getting a search warrant.*

"Sure thing, Detective. I only want to help." Ryan took a step closer. "I can help."

"We'll see." Sam turned and headed out the door, repeating, "First thing tomorrow."

She got into her car and called off the backup en route. Without a word to Michael, she pulled onto the street, wondering how to repair the damage she'd done to their relationship.

He's right. I'm not his mother. I was a fool to think I ever could be.

MICHAEL STARED OUT the window the entire drive home. Sam probably thought that he was pissed at her, and if so, she was right. But he had another reason for watching the road. He was memorizing the street signs as they passed.

CHAPTER 26

Frank waited outside the run-down tenement while Sergeant Montgomery assembled his men. The building was dark and silent. The lawn was a rough graveyard of dirt and rubble. The structure was a charred remnant long since abandoned and condemned.

From the street, he danced his flashlight's beam across blackened glass and through the several breaks. Still, the light couldn't pierce the darkness within. The officers had the building surrounded. If Hector Suarez was in there, he had no way out.

Unless he's a rat. Frank eyed a slick-furred black critter as it raised its head to catch a scent, its snout wiggling as it closed its beady red eyes. As Frank's light hit it, the vermin skittered back through the hole in the foundation.

Frank could hear more of them squeaking and squirming in the dilapidated walls, under the earth, at his ankles. *I should have gotten a rabies shot before coming back here. They should level the whole damn city, bury all the rats in it. There really is nothing here worth saving.* He thought of Sam. *Well, almost nothing.*

"We're ready to move in on your orders," Montgomery said, snapping Frank from his reverie.

"On my orders?" The deference Sam had somehow gotten her men to show him caught him off guard, but he recovered quickly. "Yes. Let's move."

He drew his sidearm and skulked toward the front door. At the bottom of the steps, he nodded to Montgomery, who waved forward an officer carrying a mini battering ram. When the officer hit the door with it, the rotten wood fell apart like wet cardboard. The stench of decay blasted from the house with a whoosh. Frank covered his mouth with a handkerchief.

The officers didn't need instruction. With semiautomatic rifles and flashlights raised, they broke off into multiple directions upon entering, covering all locations at once. The team of six entered the house, followed by the sergeant and Frank. Two men ascended the stairway to the second floor. Another pair headed into the basement. The remaining couple on the first floor cleared the rooms, each heading in opposite clock directions, only to meet again as they completed their circle. Montgomery and Frank moved in a straight line to the same point between them.

In front of them stood a door and a hallway that ran left and right. Montgomery signaled his men to clear the hall as he leaned against the wall on the left side of the door. Frank hid behind the wall on the right.

Montgomery reached for the knob, pausing as his fingertips connected, his eyes on Frank. Frank nodded and brought his pistol up. Montgomery twisted the knob and flung the door open. He followed its momentum to the wall, keeping cover.

At the same time, Frank wheeled around the corner of the frame, ready to take the head off anyone who so much as farted. The room was empty, except for Hector, who was tied to a chair, his mouth duct-taped shut. He squirmed and writhed, grunting. His breath whistled as it forced its way through tiny curls in the tape.

Frank smiled. His adversary had been giftwrapped and handed to him on a silver platter. He barely had time to consider who might have done his job for him before he read the note on Hector's chest: Live by the bomb.

"Die by it?" Frank gasped. "Stand back!" He threw his arm out to block Montgomery just before the other man could step into the room.

Frank looked down. His shin rested against a strand of piano wire that curved around it. He slowly, delicately dragged his foot back. The wire vibrated like a struck guitar string.

"Thank God the door didn't open the other way." Frank laughed nervously. "Get your men out. This whole place could be rigged."

"Sir, the house is clear," an officer told the sergeant behind him.

Frank stepped over the wire and into the room.

"Everyone out," Montgomery ordered. "Call in the bomb squad, and keep everyone way back."

As the sounds of boots on musty wood diminished, Frank began to sweat. He didn't feel like dying, especially not for that lowlife Suarez. But though he wasn't a particularly brave man, he'd never shirk his duty. He couldn't hide his smile when Montgomery stepped up beside him. *I'll say one thing for Fall River's finest: they've got balls.*

"What do you think?" Frank asked.

"Hard to tell." Montgomery leaned closer to Hector. "Whoever did this to him roughed him up pretty good. I can't tell what's important and what's not with all the blood everywhere. For all I know, there could be a napalm bomb hidden under all that duct tape on his chest."

"Maybe we should ask him," Frank said, nodding at Hector. "He's the bomb maker."

Hector's eyes widened as Frank reached out a hand toward him. "Now, I'm just going to remove this tape from your mouth, and hopefully, you can tell us what we're up against."

Hector's eyes continued to bulge, but he nodded as if he understood. When Frank's hand tugged on the end of the tape, Hector did not try to pull away.

As soon as the tape was off, Hector asked, "Is it just you? Just the two of you?"

"Who else did you expect?" Montgomery asked.

Hector snorted out a laugh. Then another. Soon, he was laughing hysterically. "She's not here!" he sputtered. "You don't have to do it. It's not the right one. You don't have to do it!"

"Do what?" Montgomery asked. He looked at Frank. "You think he's lost that last marble?"

But Frank wasn't focusing on Hector's words so much as to whom he was speaking. Hector wasn't looking at Montgomery or Frank. He was looking *past* them.

Frank searched the dark corner behind them and spotted the red light of a camera on a wall mount hidden in shadow. "Oh shit!"

"What?" Montgomery looked over his shoulder.

"We need to go! Now!"

Frank and the sergeant hurdled the tripwire and sprinted toward the front door.

Behind them, Hector called out, "Wait! Don't leave me. I—"

Boom!

The blast sent Frank airborne. As he hurtled toward the sidewalk, he threw out his forearm to brace his fall.

CHAPTER 27

Michael locked himself in his room as soon as they had made it home, refusing to speak to Sam. She didn't press the issue, figuring she should give him time to come around. Michael had been through a lot. Sooner rather than later, they'd have to talk about all of it. But she couldn't yet. The last words he'd said to her had hurt Sam more than she cared to admit.

She rubbed her temples as she sat in the dark at the kitchen table, a cup of piping-hot coffee in front of her. *He has to understand. He needs to.* She covered her face with her hands but caught herself before her emotions could swell over.

Who is this Ryan Chambers? She scowled. *What reason do I have to trust her?* Though she'd never say it out loud, Sam knew she had one good reason to trust Chambers: the stranger had rescued Michael.

Yeah, but could that meek, mousy, frail woman have taken down the Suarez gang alone? Sam found it hard to imagine the skeletal librarian popping caps in gangster wannabes, but if her years on the job had taught her anything about criminals, it was that looks could be deceiving. More likely, Hector Suarez had killed the others in a double cross, or perhaps that dead bank robber had other friends that didn't end up in jail. Ballistics might tell a more complete story, but at the moment, the bullets were buried under the rubble with the bodies.

Jimmy might know something, if he lives. Or Thibeault, if he'll talk. Or Judge Baker, maybe. Her hands shook, and for the first time since she was a teenager, she craved a cigarette. She settled for adding a shot of whiskey to her coffee. *Or maybe Hector will squeal, if we catch him.*

"Damn it!" She slammed a fist against the table. "I'm not saying he can't see her," she muttered. *I just want to look into her first, do my due diligence, see what skeletons she might be hiding in her closet.*

In Fall River, everyone had skeletons, their closets stuffed full of bones. She had the obligation of looking after Michael, one she had willingly taken on and couldn't shirk, whether he liked it or not. So far, she'd done a lousy job of keeping him safe. She scoffed. *Always good at catching the bad guys, terrible at protecting the ones you love.*

When her phone rang, she answered immediately, hoping for some good news. "Reilly."

"Detective Reilly, it's Rollins. Just calling to give you the heads up that your boy from the FBI was just admitted to Charlton Memorial."

"What? Is he okay?" Sam chewed her thumbnail.

"He's stable. That's pretty much all I know. There was another explosion on Dwyer Street."

"Jesus." Sam went silent, lost in shifting thought before she could gather her focus. "And Suarez?"

"Not sure. The rumor is he went up with the building. He's not here, so either he's dead, or he got away."

"Thank you, Sergeant Rollins. I'm heading to the hospital now."

She hung up and slid her phone into her back pocket. She got up and went to knock on Michael's door. He didn't answer, but she could hear him playing a video game.

"Michael?"

No answer.

"Michael, I have to go to the hospital." She hated to leave him alone again so soon, but she knew that was exactly what she was going to do. *He'll understand.* At least, she thought he might. A faint smile crossed her lips as she had an idea. "Do you want to come with me? We can check in on Jimmy while we're there."

Still no answer.

Sam sighed and rested her head against the closed door. "Okay. I get it. But please, promise me you'll stay here until I get back. I won't be gone more than an hour, an hour and a half tops."

No sound came from Michael's room save for machine gun fire and alien growls. She shook her head and went back to the kitchen.

After grabbing her keys, she left her apartment. She locked the dead bolt behind her.

CHAPTER 28

S he's gone, Michael heard Ryan say in his head.

"I know," he answered the only way he knew how.

You coming out?

"Yeah, I'll be right down."

As if from far away, Michael heard a door close. He emerged from the daydream with his PlayStation controller in his hand. On the screen in front of him, his avatar lay dead in a pool of blood, an alien salivating over the fallen hero before burying its razor-sharp teeth into his stomach and chowing on a mouthful of intestines in an endless loop. The word *CONTINUE* followed by a question mark ran across the screen.

"Sam?" he called out. No answer. He frowned. *Abandoned again.*

Was I daydreaming? He rose and walked to his bedroom door. Opening it a crack, he peeked out. "Sam? Are you here?"

Outside his room, the apartment was dark and quiet. He vaguely remembered hearing her voice, but he couldn't recall what she'd said. Rubbing the sleep from his eyes, he figured he must have nodded off. *When was the last time I really slept?*

He tried to remember his dream. He'd been talking to someone... someone who wanted him to go outside.

"Ryan?" he called, but no one answered. Still, he couldn't shake the feeling that someone was watching, a ghost hovering beside him. He shuddered and stepped into the dark hallway.

When he found the light and flicked it on, he saw nothing out of order. The only thing missing was Sam. He had been mean to her, said some things he wished he hadn't, but he wasn't ready to apologize. *Why can't she let me have this chance to be normal?*

A knock came at the door. Michael jumped then stared at the door, unsure if he should answer it.

After a second knock, Michael tiptoed over and peeked through the eyehole. A familiar figure with a black sweatshirt, hood pulled over her eyes, stood outside, hands in her pockets. Michael was pretty sure it was Ryan, but he had experienced enough over the past couple of days to make him cautious, warier of strangers, and even friends, than he'd ever been.

"Who are you?" he asked through the door. "What do you want?"

"Seriously?" Ryan's voice came out as a whisper. "We just spoke. My first tip for you: trust in your dreams."

"What do you want?"

"You know what I want. To help you."

"Why?"

"You know why. Are we going to waste all night rehashing it, talking through this door?"

Slowly, Michael reached for the dead bolt, unlocked it, then opened the door.

Ryan pushed through it, pulling a pistol with an elongated barrel from her pocket. She drove Michael backward as she raised it toward his face.

Michael gasped. He backed away until he fell against the table.

Standing over him with her gun raised, Ryan said, "Second lesson: never trust anyone. Always ask to see someone's hands before letting them into your home." She lowered her gun. "Have a weapon of your own nearby at all times."

"Are you crazy?"

"Relax. It's not loaded."

"And how is *that* supposed to help me control my abilities?"

"My offer of help comes with a price. You'll have to learn the business end as well."

"What do you mean? Kill people? I'm not a killer."

"Not yet. But we have time."

"I... I don't think I could ever do that."

Ryan's eyes rolled up and to the left. "Shut up! He *is* ready. You just don't want me to have this."

"Uh..."

"Shut up!" Ryan stomped her foot and glared at the ceiling.

"Um, who are you talking to?" Michael asked.

"No one. At least, no one important right now." She pocketed her gun. "Come on. Let's go back to my place before that detective returns."

Michael's throat dried, and he found it hard to speak, to swallow even. "I-I-I'm not sure that's... such a good idea. I've put Sam through a lot of worry lately. Maybe I should wait 'til the morning, after we've had a chance to talk it over."

Even as Michael made the excuse, he could hear the falseness in his voice. But Ryan was beginning to scare him. He believed she could help him, but her motives terrified him. *Is she looking for an apprentice? A partner? A son?*

"Yeah, maybe it would be better if we just waited until tomorrow. I'm sure Sam would let me have some kind of supervised—"

Ryan raised her pistol again. "Enough of this. You're coming with me."

Michael laughed nervously. "What are you going to do with that? You already told me it wasn't loaded."

Ryan aimed the gun slightly to Michael's left and fired. The weapon made a slight *chew*, and the wood paneling lining the wall behind him splintered. Her lips curled mischievously. "I lied."

"A silencer?" Michael understood then why the barrel was so long. It had been affixed with the means to make his death come quietly. He raised his hands in front of him. "Please. I only think we should wait 'til Sam—"

"You asked for my help. Now you've got it. I've been watching you for a long time, watching you treat your extraordinary gift as though it's a curse. Well, it doesn't have to be. It can be a blessing. I'm going to help you see that whether you like it or not." She glowered at the ceiling. "He's ready, damn it! He just needs a little convincing. Don't you think I foresaw this?"

Michael noticed Ryan's twitching fingers. She scratched at the inside of her elbow as if fire ants were biting her flesh. She closed her eyes for a second. Michael thought about running, but before he could move, her eyes were open, staring at him with fiery rage.

She pointed at the door with her free hand, keeping the gun pointed at Michael with her other. "Let's go."

Michael wondered if she had really foreseen any of this. He began to doubt whether she had any control over her abilities at all. Maybe the voice in her head was nothing more than—

"Come on. Move." She prodded him in his chest with her pistol.

"Can I just leave a note for Sam? If she comes home and finds me gone, the first place she'll go looking is your place."

Ryan laughed. "Let her try."

"At least let me tell her I'm okay."

"You've got thirty seconds."

Michael hurried to the counter. He grabbed a pen and a pad of paper then wrote:

I stepped out. Robbie is having a party and a sleepover. So that's where I'll be. Please don't worry. See you tomorrow.

He dropped the pad and pen on the counter. Forcing a smile, he turned back to Ryan. "All set."

She raised an eyebrow then picked up the pad. Her eyes ticked to the right a couple of times as she read his message. Grunting, she tossed it back onto the counter. "Okay then. Let's go."

CHAPTER 29

S am had only been in the waiting room for fifteen minutes when Frank came strolling out. A white cast gave him a Popeye-sized right forearm. A bandage covered his receding hairline on the same side of his forehead. Other than that, he seemed fine.

When he saw her, he beamed. "Sam!" he said, raising his good arm as if going in for a hug. But as he neared, his arm fell to his side, and he nodded. "Thanks for coming, but you didn't have to."

"First off, are you okay?"

"Yeah, it's nothing. Just a compound fracture to"—he ran a finger along the inside of his forearm—"this bone."

"Your ulna?"

"That's the one. Other than that and a few bumps and bruises, I'm good to go." His smile waned. "How's Michael?"

"Found. He's home, safe." She stared at the carpet. *Then why can't I stop worrying about him?* "A woman picked him up. She claims—or Michael claims—that he escaped and flagged her down. There are some holes in their stories, but nothing other than Michael being with her links the woman to the shootings at the warehouse. I'd like to look into her more, but for now, that can wait. Where are you heading? I'll take you."

"I should be heading back to Boston sooner or later. I'm sure the agency's expecting my report."

Sam stepped closer to him. Only a couple of inches separated them as she looked up into his eyes. She rocked on her heels. "The hell with that. You can stay at my place tonight and report back in the morning. I want to hear all about what happened, and I need your help in developing an investigation strategy going forward."

Frank smiled. "All right. I know better than to argue with you. Lead the way." He waved his casted arm.

Sam turned and walked with him to her car, wondering what she had just committed herself to. As she drove them back to her apartment, Frank explained how he'd found Hector tied to a chair loaded with explosives and how he'd nearly been caught in the explosion himself. He also told her that the entire thing was being recorded.

"And you think Hector's benefactor was watching?" Sam asked.

"I do. Well, it seems whoever was watching had ceased to be Hector's benefactor or never truly was. I believe Hector was part of something bigger, something in which the rest of his gang played a lesser role or no role at all. I tried to find out more from Thibeault, but he's still in critical condition, no nonessentials permitted. Anyway, not only do I think he had help from a criminal organization, but I think... I think it's the same one."

"The Four Pi," Sam muttered, the words leaving bitterness on her tongue. For so long, she had refused to believe that the death of her partner had been caused by this mysterious evil group Frank insisted had been behind everything. She knew who killed her partner. She had been there when it happened. His was a face that would haunt her dreams forever. She bit back her anger for the man who had taken away her second father, the man who had been her mentor and friend on the job when she needed one most, when she might have veered down a baser path.

"What makes you think that?" she asked.

"It's been ten years. In all that time, we've never stopped looking for him or those who may have helped him escape. Every time we got close, he slipped away as if tipped off or having resources and the kind of friends who excel at making people disappear. He was good, sure, and his benefactors were even cleaner. But they weren't perfect. We have gathered small pieces to a massive puzzle over the years, not enough to put anyone away but enough to pin up a few faces, even an alias or two."

"Have you found *him*? Do you know where he is?"

"I told you, the Suarez gang was only part of the reason I came down here."

"He wouldn't have the nerve—"

"If there's one thing we know about him, it's that his nerve never stands in his way."

The thought chilled Sam to the bone. Her partner's killer had escaped justice more times than she cared to admit. To think he would come back to Fall River and hide in plain sight, rubbing her nose in her failures, her department's failures... She growled, her fingers tightening around the steering wheel. "Why would he come back here?"

"That, I don't know, and I haven't confirmed that he is here. But this area is his home. Maybe he has unfinished business. After all, he came back once before."

Mulling over Frank's words, she pulled into her driveway. They got out of the car, and she led the way up the stairs to her apartment.

"I want you with me on this, Sam," Frank said. "It's time we mounted the tombstone on that case, take down that son of a bitch and any others responsible for all those deaths. We both lost good men and women chasing down a ghost. It's high time our own ghosts had their chance to rest."

Sam turned her key in the dead bolt, but it wasn't locked. She drew her gun.

Frank did the same. "What is it?" he whispered.

"I locked this when I left." She hurried into the apartment, moving fast but remaining mindful of her training. She hit the light switch and swept the room, Frank on alert beside her. They split up, Frank heading toward her room as she stalked toward Michael's.

She tried the knob. His door was unlocked too. The pixelated melody of a video game floated into her ears. But when she entered the room, she found no one. After clearing it and the living room, she returned to the kitchen.

Frank was waiting. "There's a note," he said, tossing her the pad she kept on her counter.

She read it aloud. "I stepped out. Robbie is having a party and a sleepover. So that's where I'll be. Please don't worry. See you tomorrow."

She frowned. "Robbie? Robbie Wilkins?"

"Who's that?"

"Probably the closest kid Michael has to a friend. One of the bullies that dunked him in the toilet... it's a long story. Anyway, Michael's never gone to a party at the boy's house before. Michael's never gone to any parties before."

She ran her thumb over the note. "Wait a minute." Some of the pen marks were clearly heavier than others. Michael had pushed down on the pad hard to make them. She flipped to the second page and looked at the clear letters that had been etched into it.

"H. E. L. P." She threw the pad back onto the counter. "Fuck! He's in trouble!"

She scanned the kitchen and dining room for signs of where Michael might have gone or who might have taken him. She noticed a hole in the wall, close the floor, that she was certain hadn't been there before. She grabbed a screwdriver and knelt in front of it. After digging around a second, she extracted a bullet. It looked exactly like the one she had found at the warehouse.

"She has him!" Sam blurted. "I know she does." She strode to the door.

Frank ran after her, following her back out to her car. "Who?"

"The woman who picked him up." She snarled. "Ryan Chambers."

CHAPTER 30

"This isn't the way to your house," Michael said, though he hoped he was wrong.

"I'm taking you to a safe house where we won't be disturbed." Ryan glanced in her rearview mirror. She'd done it often, as if she was afraid they were being followed.

They had crossed out of Fall River. That much, Michael knew from the Now Entering Lakeville sign they had passed. He had no idea whether or not they were still in Lakeville. If not for the road itself, Michael would have believed they had left human habitation altogether because the walls of pines on either side were so thick he couldn't see anything else.

Save for the narrow strip of sky above, the only light came from their headlights. The smell of compost swirled in through the cab's partially open windows. The only sounds were the hum of the engine and the chirping of what had to be a million crickets.

Ryan slammed on the brakes when a rabbit darted across the road. A coyote followed, hot on the smaller animal's heels. "That's you." She pointed out the window to where the animals had disappeared into the forest.

"The coyote?"

"The rabbit. But we'll make a coyote out of you yet." She stepped on the gas, and they continued down the road.

"You're kidnapping me."

Ryan slapped the steering wheel. "I'm trying to *help* you."

"How? By making me a killer?"

"By teaching you how to control your ability. Teaching you how to kill and get away with it, that's just an added bonus. Trust me, you're going to thank me someday."

"I don't think I have it in me. Even if I wanted to..."

Ryan smiled, her emotions as flippant as a child's. "You don't give yourself enough credit."

She slammed on the brakes again. Michael instinctively threw a hand out to brace himself, but the seat belt did its job. He rocked forward then whiplashed back. Staring through the windshield, he expected to see another rabbit hopping in front of the car, but all he saw was empty road.

"Sorry," Ryan muttered. "Sorry." She put a hand on Michael's leg.

He stiffened. If she was trying to comfort him, her actions were having the opposite effect.

"My teacher, the man who did for me what I am trying to do for you, insists that you're not ready for this, that you will be my downfall and bring unwanted attention to the rest of us." She stroked Michael's thigh in a way that might have been arousing had she been someone else.

"But you wouldn't do that, would you, Michael? You wouldn't give us up." She turned to face him and smiled, and Michael saw for the first time how yellow and cracked her teeth were, how sunken and glassy her eyes seemed. She looked like a cross between a pale-faced witch and death itself. She had that lost sort of look that starving Somalian children shared in commercials looking for donations to stave off world hunger.

Play along. Sam will find you. She has to. "N-No. I would never tell on you."

Ryan looked upward. "See?"

Michael wondered if she was talking to him or this teacher she professed to hear. But when she looked back at him, her face was as hard as stone. The glassiness in her eyes had vanished, replaced by that animalistic sheen he had seen in Jimmy's not long ago. The eyes of a killer.

"I wish I didn't have to ask, but you do know that if you expose me, he'll find you, right? My teacher will find you."

Michael nodded slowly. "Yeah. I wouldn't do that." *I'm sorry, Sam. You were right about everything. I was wrong. Please, just find me soon.*

After turning down more dark paths and nameless roads that were impossible to keep track of even with the knowledge that his life could depend on it, she steered through a large iron gate that seemed to emerge out of the forest itself. The gate was covered in brambles and looked centuries old, gothic even, a bar to the entrance to Dracula's homestead.

Despite the gate's antiquity, the security systems were modern enough. Ryan pulled up to a card reader half hidden by vines. She took what looked like a credit card from her pocket and slid it into the machine. Immediately, the gate swung open. Michael heard no rusty squeal, so someone had obviously been caring for it.

The paved driveway on the other side was surrounded by a well-manicured lawn lined with flowers. An ornate water fountain depicting statuesque cherubs at play stood in the lawn's center. Water flowed noisily, and Michael wondered who else might be in the place.

The house was large but new and seemed to contrast with the gate and fountain. It was Victorian-style but equipped with a host of modern comforts, including a satellite dish and a two-car garage with a remote-controlled door. Ryan parked her beat-up Ford in the stall on the right beside what looked like a brand-new BMW.

Michael climbed out of the truck after she did. He thought about running and looked around wildly to see where he might head.

As if sensing his thoughts, Ryan rested an arm over his shoulder. He hadn't even heard her approach.

"Give it a chance, Michael. Like I said, you'll be thanking me later." She gave him a little push toward the door that led into the house.

I could run. I should *run.* But he couldn't shake the feeling of being watched. He surveyed his surroundings but saw no one. He imagined the barking of dogs set free as soon as he set one foot toward freedom. He walked to the door.

"Go ahead. It's open," she said.

He twisted the knob and pushed open the door. As he stepped inside, someone grabbed him from behind. A cloth doused in a strong chemical, like hospital disinfectant or ammonia, was pressed over his mouth. He struggled to breathe as he fought against the arm restraining him. Even in his panicked state, he recalled enough movies and TV shows to know what was being applied over his nose and mouth: chloroform. But it was too late. He was already starting to fade.

But why? he wondered as he tried to bite the hand holding the cloth. *I was cooperating.*

"Hush, hush," Ryan said from behind him. "Don't fight it. Everything will be all right."

Michael wanted to scream. Everything was not all right. Darkness clouded the corners of his vision. His head throbbed as if it were swelling. In a last-ditch effort, he stomped his feet and swung his arms wildly. The fight left him quickly as the darkness prevailed.

SHE FEELS THE WIND on her face. The breeze carries with it the smell of surf and the taste of salt. The roar of the waves and the cries of gulls soaring high above are the only sounds. Pleasant sounds. Her breathing slows.

She lifts her feet, and sand slides between her toes as if through the bottleneck of an hourglass. But time is frozen even if the birds, wind, and waves don't know it. There, she has found peace. The sun warms her skin, her heart, and her soul.

Laughter.

She stares at the water and smiles. Michael, only three years old, splashes a few yards away where the waves spread thin over the beach then retreat. In his hand, he holds a shovel as though it were a mighty sword. Its corresponding pail is atop his head, his helmet as he does battle against the forces of Morgana. He is Gawain, the Green Knight—Gain, as Michael calls him, his small mouth not yet able to form all the syllables—his favorite knight pulled from the kiddy versions of the King Arthur fables she reads to him at bedtime. The same stories she would have read to...

A twinge of sadness. For whom, she cannot remember, doesn't want to remember. Michael is her boy now. She watches him and laughs. Gawain was her favorite too.

A cloud passes over the sun. No, not just one cloud. The whole sky darkens. Something is wrong. Something beyond the weather. She can feel it panging hollow in her stomach.

"Michael," she calls, but he doesn't hear. He slashes the water with his shovel, giggling away. "It's time to go, Michael."

Her heart stops dead in her chest when she sees the fin, black and razor sharp, cutting across the water, heading toward Michael. It can't possibly reach him in the few inches of water he's in, but the thought does little to allay her fears. She jumps to her feet and darts to the shore. But her movements through the sand are slow, while the fin moves so impossibly fast.

It is nearly upon Michael. How the rest of it remains underwater, she cannot comprehend. A yard away from her boy, the predator submerges completely. She screams.

"It's not real, Ryan," a voice whispers in her ear.

The shark has come ashore.

She turns to face the speaker, a man old enough to be her father, who at times she wished had been more of one. Wrinkles spread across his face as he smiles softly but without a hint of weakness. His platinum hair is parted on the side, its color matching the whiskers sprouting from his ears. His skin is bronzed and leathery, every part of him indicating his age save for his eyes, which are a brilliant blue, twinkling, and full of life.

He gently grabs her arms. "This isn't real. It will never be real. You must let it go, or it will destroy you."

Ryan sniffles. A tear rolls down her cheek. "I am already destroyed."

Lightning flashes, and the shark-toothed grin behind the old-man mask can be seen, but only for a moment. "I've done all I can for you," the man says. "Don't throw away everything we've worked for on this... this fool's errand."

"This is real!" Ryan screams. "I've seen it. This will be!"

The old man sighs. "Then it is too late. The drugs have won, not your visions. Goodbye, Ryan." He kisses her forehead.

"Fine. Go." Ryan looks away for only a second, and when she looks back, the man-shark is gone. "Wait. I..."

She turns to face the water. "Michael?"

The boy has vanished. His bucket hat floats atop the waves. Ryan races to the water's edge, scanning the surf for any sign of him, but in her heart, she knows he is gone. Just like her Gawain, her Green Knight.

"Michael?" She tears at her hair and drops to her knees. "Michael!"

THE SOUND OF SOMEONE screaming his name shook Michael from sleep. Across from him, Ryan lounged in a recliner with her leg draped over the side. A rubber tube was tied around her right arm.

She jerked awake the way Sam did when her own snoring startled her. Her eyes were hazy, and she dripped with sweat, though the way her body was trembling, Michael would have thought her freezing. Her face was pale. For a second, Michael half expected to hear that strange hiss-growl zombies made in the movies.

She eyed him for a moment without saying a word, then she got up and stuck her hand in the crack on the side of the cushion. When she pulled out a long needle, Michael squirmed and noticed he'd been tied up.

Don't panic. Think. What would Sam do?

What looked like a seat belt crossed his waist. He was sitting in a something that resembled a dentist's chair. Another strap ran across his shoulders and two more over each wrist. The binds were loose, and he was sure he could wriggle out of them as soon as his audience was distracted.

"You don't mind sharing, do you?" she asked. "I promise I don't have anything. I've always been safe."

"Sharing? What do you mean?"

She winked and walked around behind him. A minute later, Michael heard the clink of a lighter flicking open. When she returned, what looked like dirty water filled the syringe. A bead of the fluid slid down the sharp metal needle. She took a step toward Michael.

"Wait!" He struggled against the belts. "What are you doing?"

"Relax, honey," she said, smiling and reaching toward his arm. "This will help you see so much better."

CHAPTER 31

Tagliamonte called out, "Detective, you should see this."

The Fall River Police Department was tearing apart Ryan Chambers's home. Rollins had gotten the search warrant with ease, even at the late hour, with the bullet found in Sam's apartment and Michael's cryptic plea for help. So far, their search had revealed nothing but newspapers. Lots and lots of newspapers.

"I found this in the bedroom. It was all by itself, like it was special or something." Tagliamonte held up an article. The title was "Murder-Suicide in the Flint."

She ripped it from her officer's hands and started reading.

"What is it?" Frank asked.

She didn't look up from the paper. "It's an article about Michael."

"Yeah, they're all over the house," Frank said.

"Not an article about Michael Turcotte, but Michael Flo—who Michael was before he was Michael Turcotte." She folded the article and stuffed it into her pocket. "Thank you, Officer."

She and Tagliamonte shared a look of understanding. He was one of the few officers who knew where Michael had come from, since he'd been one of the first responders to Michael's parents' crime scene. He nodded and went back to the search.

Sergeant Rollins hustled over with a stack of newsprint. "Detective, do you remember Muriel Costa?"

"The woman who drove her car off the pier, drowning herself and her two children?" Sam said, shaking her head in disgust. "How could I forget?"

"Yeah, her husband swore foul play was involved, that Muriel loved her children. Couldn't believe she'd done it. What about Laurence Castor?"

Sam shook her head.

"He went missing off a cruise line, presumed dead. Out of our jurisdiction. We could do little for his family, but... hold on. The article's here." He shuffled through the stack in his hands.

"I remember now." Sam stroked her chin. "Where are you going with this?"

"Well, many of these articles pertain to people, and the survivors of people, who have been murdered, committed suicide, or died under suspicious circumstances or even by a commonplace accident. At least, that's how they were written off. Others in these articles vanished altogether. There's Janie Morgan, Fisher Marko, Noah Stapleton, Eddie Cruz, Victoria—"

Sam put up her hand. "I follow you, but what do you suppose it means?" Sam had her own theory, but she wasn't one to steal the glory from one of her men who was showing stellar recall and excellent police work.

"I'd say easily a quarter of our cold cases are here." Rollins paused, found his confidence, and showed why he was next in line for detective. "She's either an amateur investigator, someone with an avid interest in local crime, or someone who has a more personal stake in the outcome of these failed investigations."

"Are you suggesting..." Frank scratched his head. "One woman? All these crimes?"

Before he could outright dismiss it, Sam spoke. "It's really not that hard to believe when we consider the facts. She's kidnapped Michael. She was present at the warehouse earlier today. If she single-handedly took out the Suarez gang, Chambers is no one to be trifled with. Add to that the foresight Michael claims she has—"

"Foresight?" Frank scoffed. "Like psychic? The FBI has worked with many so-called psychics over the years, and I can tell you from first-hand experience, they're wrong a hell of a lot more often than they're right."

Sam bit back the anger rising in her gullet. "It's different with Michael, and if he says Chambers is different, then I believe him. I'll forgive your doubt. I had it, too, once. I had to learn to accept it the hard way. A boy died because of my disbelief. But even if you doubt *him*, put your trust in *me*."

Frank bristled. "Like you put your trust in me when it comes to the Four Pi?"

Sam thought it a low blow, but she had no retort. She scowled then softened. "I was wrong. There is something bigger at play with the Suarez gang. You're wrong about this."

"I'm sorry, Sam." Frank's shoulders drooped. "I was—"

A phone rang. Everyone froze.

When it rang a second time, Sam hustled over to where the sound was coming from. A mobile phone lay a few inches under the bed. She picked it up. "Hello?"

"Detective Reilly?" The voice was clearly disguised. It grooved like a record turned slowly. "Detective Samantha Reilly?"

"Yes?"

"If you ever want to see your boy alive again, go to lot 17, plot 4, on book 1364, Lakeville."

Sam covered the mouthpiece and called out to the room. "Lot 17, plot 4, book 1364. Someone write it down! Pull up the Registry of Deeds website."

"Hurry, Detective," the voice said. "Your boy doesn't have much time."

"Wait. Who has him? How many are there?" The phone went dead. The caller had hung up.

She looked at the men staring back at her. "Well, what are you all standing there for? An extra vacation day to whoever gets me directions to that address first, even if I have to give you one of mine to make it happen. Feed it into Rollins's computer. Send backup to the address once you've got it."

She turned to the sergeant. "Rollins, we're heading to Lakeville."

CHAPTER 32

Darkness.
       Yet familiar.

Michael has been here before. But something is different. His head pounds against the wall, but he stops it. His pudgy, baby fat legs are crossed under him. He uses them to stand. The wall, with its crackled paint and sandpapery surface, is his only barrier. The blockade put up by his subconscious has fallen. He can see if he wants to.

But am I ready?

"Turn around," Sam's voice whispers in his ear, though he knows she's not here. She can't be here. Not yet.

The darkness that has shrouded his eyes for so long has lifted. He doesn't want to turn, but he must turn—he knows he must, for he may not have this opportunity again. Repressed memories want to stay repressed.

The smell of sweat and sex fills the room with an air of depravity. The clock ticks, and the radiator hums louder than all the other times he's been there. The only thumping now is that of his heart, pumping furiously in his chest.

He takes in all the air his little lungs can hold then lets it out slowly. Crying, he turns.

The muffled voices are no longer muffled. He hears them clearly and understands the words far better than his feeble three-year-old mind possibly could have at the time. Fifteen in mind, three in body, and altogether helpless to stop what will be done, to undo what has already happened.

"I know what you're thinking," says a woman in a black hoodie, her face partially covered.

Michael knows who it is. She may be younger, and she may be stronger, her frame sturdy and her voice full of confidence, but she's still recognizable. Still Ryan.

"You're thinking you could pull that gun I tucked into your belt, spin around, and take your chances by firing at me like some kind of cowboy. Maybe you get lucky. Maybe you're a hero."

She laughs and pokes Mark Florentine in the back with her own pistol. "Odds are, you won't be so lucky, and the only chance you have, the only chance I've given you out of the goodness of my heart to save your son, will go down in a blaze of glory. He dies, you die, they die. Fun times."

"Don't listen to her, Mark," *Alice Florentine says.*

Michael chokes up. That voice... I remember her voice. She used to sing to me. And she would read to me. Green Eggs and Ham.

"She's—"

His mother tries to continue, but his father snaps, "Shut up! Just shut up! We wouldn't be in this mess if you weren't such a goddamn whore!" *Mark is sweating profusely. He lifts the gun from his waistband in one trembling hand.*

"Now, hold on," *says James Whittaker, a man Michael has never seen before, though he has seen his fate.* "I have money. A good deal of it. I'm sure we can work this out."

"Sorry, James." *Ryan sniggers.* "Apparently you didn't suck them all completely dry because they still had enough to scrape together and hire me—those that you didn't drive to suicide anyway. So I've already been paid. And I never leave a job unfinished."

"Whatever they paid you, I'll double it. Triple it!"

"If I do this, you'll spare me and the boy?" *Mark asks, aiming the gun at James's bare chest. His arm shakes rapidly now, as though sparking with electricity.*

"Do it," *Ryan whispers into Mark's ear.*

Mark clenches his teeth and takes aim down the barrel. James closes his eyes.

"Daddy, don't," Michael says, though no one hears him.

Mark droops as if a heavy weight is crushing down on his shoulders. "I... I can't," he says, his voice shaking. Tears fall from his eyes.

"You can, and you will," Ryan answers. "Unless you prefer four bodies to two?"

"I can't!" Mark bellows.

But Ryan won't be denied. "Now!"

Mark cries out in despair as he empties a clip into James Whittaker. The man is dead well before the last bullet hits him. Alice's screams can be heard between the gunshots. Mark's arm falls to his side, and Ryan relieves him of his pistol.

"See? You can." she whispers. She reloads the pistol then presses it back into his hand. "Now the other."

"Daddy, please..." Michael says, though he knows they can't hear him.

His mother sits up in bed beside the fresh corpse, her hands over her eyes as she sobs. "No, don't, please..."

His father wails as he empties another clip. His mother goes silent.

"You've done well, Mark," Ryan whispers. "And they got what they deserved."

Michael remembers hearing Ryan leave at this point the last time he had the recurring vision. But this time, she lingers by the door.

"I'm sorry, Michael," Mark says. He looks directly at Michael, or perhaps through him to where baby Michael was sitting by the wall. No, his three-year-old self has left the wall and crawled to his father, as if the child knows what comes next and is trying to stop it. Fifteen-year-old Michael is a silent bystander now, watching as if a ghost in the room.

The bullet creates a skylight.

The gun falls near little Michael's hands. The toddler snatches it and returns to his spot by the wall, where he tucks the gun beneath his legs.

Ryan turns to teenager Michael. She extends her hand. "Come. What's past is past. Come with me and see your future."

His tears have run dry. He follows her out the apartment door. He hates her now and feels a strong desire to kill her for what she's done. On the other side of the door is a different world filled with grass and the smell of clean air with a tinge of saltwater. A beautiful park. Familiar.

"Is this the waterfront?" Michael can't believe what he is seeing. The park is pristine. The junkies are gone. The graffiti is gone. Even the litter is gone. "The water is still a little brown."

Ryan smiles. "We're not miracle workers, but look at this place! Fall River, twenty years into the future, restored, made better because of us."

"We did this? How?"

"We've become more than hired killers. We've taken out the trash, quite literally, and made this city into something we can be proud of." She nods toward a man sprinting their way.

Michael steps back, barely able to avoid the man, who runs as if blind. As he passes through Ryan, Michael realizes that the man can't see either of them. This is not a vision of Ryan's future.

Then whose?

The frantic, wild-eyed expression on the bald man, a business-suit-type in his late forties with a tie flapping over his shoulder, gives Michael pause. That look alone is enough to abate any hope that they somehow turned Fall River into a utopia.

The man runs to the rail, looks over it and down, and starts to climb. He hears a plink *like the sound of a tiny piston firing, and the man is on the ground in front of the rail, screaming. Blood pours from a fresh wound in his leg.*

As Michael's attention is focused on the fallen businessman, another man walks by. Holding a gun with a silencer that looks exactly like the weapon Ryan pointed at Michael earlier, this new man stalks toward the fallen one. He aims the weapon at his victim's face.

"No!" Michael shouts, running toward them with hands raised. "Don't!"

The shooter hesitates. Michael, closer now, can see the corner of the man's mouth curl into a smile. The man on the ground, who has huddled as close to the railing as he can as if he is trying to squeeze through a crack beneath it, begins to relax a little as his attacker puts his gun away.

Staring down at the businessman, the shooter raises his foot, which is clad in a heavy black boot. He stomps it down onto the man's face. He repeats the action again. And again. Michael watches in horror as the stomping goes on and on, and the businessman's face smashes inward like a pumpkin.

When the killer finally stops, he raises his head. Michael stares at him. The face is older, but it is unmistakably his own. And it's also obvious that he enjoys his work.

"What's that?" Ryan asks as she studies the sky. She cocks her head like a dog as if listening intently.

With fresh tears, Michael switches glances between her and his older, psychotic self. He assumes her voices have returned and hopes they're telling her that the future doesn't have to be like this.

"They've found us?" she asks the sky. "That can't be! The future has been set. I've seen to it all. I know..." Every part of her face begins to sag. She looks old, tired. Beaten.

Sorrow etches its way into the cracks of her skin. Michael tries to stem the pity he feels, but he can't.

"I've been betrayed," she mutters then vanishes.

Michael gapes at the spot where she had been standing. "Wait! Don't go. Don't leave me here." He looks at his older self, who starts grinding a heel into the face of a man who is clearly already dead. "Not with him. Don't leave me with him!"

CHAPTER 33

Sam's team had easily gotten GPS coordinates on the Lakeville place from the information given by the anonymous caller. A battalion of Fall River's and Lakeville's police forces converged on the house, which was hidden deep in the woods.

Sergeant Rollins took a page from Sam's book. In the passenger seat, she smiled as he plowed his cruiser through the iron gate that barred their entry. Frank barely had enough time to put on his seat belt, and his casted forearm smacked his knee. He grumbled a bit after the impact. Two more cruisers were right on their bumper.

As much as she wanted to rush things, she had to be careful. Their approach had been enough to alarm the entire estate and anyone else in the neighborhood. Michael was inside that house. She couldn't charge in with guns blazing.

So she decided to try diplomacy first, never her strong point. Sam got out of the car but stayed behind its open door and sent two officers around to the back of the building. She grabbed a mini bullhorn stored under her seat. "Ryan Chambers. All I care about is the boy. Send him out unharmed, and we'll walk away. No charges. No confrontation. No nothing. Anything you want. Just let the boy go."

Silence.

Then all the lights in the house went out simultaneously. Sam had her answer. Four more Fall River Officers and two from Lakeville were nearby, keeping their vehicles between them and the house.

"On my mark, we move in," Sam said. "Cover all entry points. Close the net. No one takes a shot without my say-so. There's an innocent boy in there. Anyone who so much as scratches him will be

224

answering to me. Termination will be the least of your worries. Am I clear?"

Rollins nodded, and several of the other officers grunted their affirmation. Still more police cars, lights flashing, pulled in behind them. A swarm of others was on the way.

"Good," Sam said. "Spread the word to the newcomers."

Rollins slid round the car and ran back toward the gate. Soon, he was out of sight.

Sam leaned into the vehicle to talk to Frank, who was still seated in the back of the cruiser. "You with me?"

"Always." He smiled easily.

Sam couldn't smile back, not with Michael in danger. "All right. We'll take point. You ready?"

"Aren't you forgetting something?"

She rolled her eyes. "Oh yeah." She opened the back door for him.

"Thank you," he said, climbing out. He drew his gun.

They crept toward the house. A bullet hit the dirt at her feet. Sam froze. She couldn't tell where it had come from. She looked at Frank. He shook his head.

"I don't have to miss," Ryan Chambers called from the house.

Sam raised her hands, her gun pointed skyward. "I just want to talk." She scanned the face of the house, every closed window, but saw no sign of Ryan or where the bullet might have originated.

"Call your men back!" Ryan shouted from a new position.

Sam turned around to see no one but Frank standing near her. The other officers had smartly taken cover when the first shot was fired. "Stay where you are," she called to them. To Frank, she added, "You too. No need for both of us to be at risk."

Frank smiled. "Yeah, I don't think so. You're stuck with me."

Sam huffed and faced the house. "May I approach?" she asked, keeping her feet rooted to the same spot. "Just me. I'm putting my gun down." Sam crouched and placed her gun on the grass. With all the lights out in the house and a fountain of halogens opening up behind her, Sam was a sitting duck relying on the mercy of a suspected killer.

For Michael, she'd risk her life a hundred times over. She stepped forward.

Another bullet broke earth near her feet, creating a small divot. Sam's breath caught in her throat.

"Stay where you are," Ryan ordered, her voice coming from a place quite a distance from where Sam thought the bullet had originated.

"Either she's constantly on the move, or she has help," Frank muttered.

"I think it's the former, which means she's not watching us every second. Maybe we can force another shot and send Rollins in while she's distract—"

"What do you want?" Ryan asked.

"We just want Michael," Sam said.

"He's not here."

"We know he's here."

"Just... go away." Ryan's voice had become shaky and had risen an octave. "It's not supposed to be like this. You aren't supposed to be here. We have so much good to do."

"She's losing it," Sam whispered. "We have to make our move."

Frank nodded.

"I won't kill you, Detective," Ryan said. "He likes you too much. But your friend—"

As the meaning of the words sank in, Sam leaped sideways and tackled Frank. A shot rang out as she collided with him, and they rolled under a row of hedges lining the front of the house.

He winced and held his arm. Blood trickled from a fresh hole in his blazer. But not a lot of blood. "It's nothing," he said. His mouth opened as though he was going to say more, but the rest of the team suddenly opened fire.

Glass shattered, and wood splintered all around her. On her knees and forearms, Sam shuffled toward the bullhorn she had dropped in the grass.

Drawing it to her mouth, she screamed, "Hold your fire!"

The barrage ended with sounds that resembled the crackling at the end of a firework display. The house creaked in protest, as if sighing under the extra weight of the bullets fired into its walls. Sam listened for signs of life inside. At first, all was silent, then an engine roared to life.

"Stand back from the garage!" an officer yelled.

The engine sputtered and died. It hadn't come from the garage. It had been faint, almost as if...

Sam ran to the front door. Frank broke the cover of the hedges and joined her. No one shot at them, which was a plus. Frank rammed his shoulder into the door three times before the jamb finally splintered. By that time, the rest of her officers were able to follow them inside.

A door leading down to a basement had been left open. Sam didn't take the bait. "Fan out! Search the house!"

She beelined through the house to the back door. Frank slammed his side against the wall beside the closed door, and Sam opened it. He swung around the doorframe and stepped onto the back stairs.

And fell through them. He screamed. He hadn't fallen far, but his pants and leg were shredded up to his thigh. He shrieked louder when he tried to pull himself out and even louder when Sam tried to help him.

Worse still, he was blocking Sam's way. Beyond him, Chambers was filling the tank of an ATV with gasoline. A pistol with a silencer rested on its seat. The two cops Sam had sent around back were crumpled on the ground between them. Another officer lay to her left. As none were moving, she guessed they were all dead.

"Sorry, Frank, but duck." Sam hurdled the FBI agent and the rest of the steps. She pointed her gun at Chambers. "Freeze!" Gun held out in front of her, she walked toward Chambers, being careful not to trip on the dead officers.

When Sam had gotten within a few feet, Chambers straightened and nonchalantly tossed the gas can aside. She made no attempt to go for the gun. "You shouldn't have come here. I wouldn't have hurt him." She sniffled. Her eyes were bloodshot. "I would never have hurt him."

The side of the house exploded. The men inside began shouting. Sam glanced back as debris showered her. The damage had only blown out a small portion of the wall, nowhere near Frank, who was still stuck in the booby-trapped staircase.

"Frank, are you oka—fuck!" Her gun flew out of her hand along with a portion of skin between her thumb and index finger. Wincing in pain, she covered the wound with her other hand and squeezed it shut. When Sam looked up, Chambers's gun was aimed at her face.

"Gas oven," Chambers said. "Oldest trick in the book." She moved her jaw forward and back. "I just..." She paused to wipe snot from her upper lip with the back of a trembling hand. Between the shaking, the red eyes, the teeth grinding, and the scratching, she appeared to be under the influence of some heavy-duty drugs. "I just wanted my boy back. I would never have hurt him. Never hurt him."

She sniffled again. "You shouldn't have come here." The gun shook in her hand. How she had managed to shoot Sam's gun hand even at close range seemed nothing short of miraculous.

"Urrrrr!" Chambers groaned. She pulled at her hair. "Can't kill you. That would hurt him." She turned around and hopped on the ATV.

Sam rushed forward and speared her off of it. She landed on top of Chambers, but they continued to roll, ending up side by side on their backs. From the ground, Chambers swung her arm at Sam, slamming the butt of her gun into Sam's forehead. Sam saw floating blobs in front of her eyes and tried to blink them away. When her vision cleared, she saw Chambers getting to her feet. She scrambled after Chambers and grabbed the other woman's ankle as she started the ATV. Chambers kicked her in the ribs.

Sam let go of her attacker in favor of protecting her body from a possibly debilitating injury. When the woman pulled her foot back for a second kick, Sam wrapped her arms around Chambers's leg and yanked her off the ATV. Sam climbed on top of the fallen woman and landed a right then a left to Chambers's face. When she raised her right fist again, Chambers had the gun between them.

"No," Chambers said flatly. "Get up."

Sam climbed to her feet. She raised her hands.

Chambers pulled the trigger. At the last second, she had shifted her aim to shoot around Sam, probably to keep encroaching officers at bay.

"Detective Reilly," Rollins called from inside the house, "are you hurt?"

"I'm fine!" Sam shouted. "Everyone stay put."

"Good girl," Chambers said. "Now back up."

Sam took a few steps back.

"You don't know how lucky you are, Detective." Chambers jumped on the ATV and, through a hail of gunfire, sped off down a trail that led into the woods.

Sam ran after her a few feet before realizing she would never catch her. By the time she turned back around, Rollins and another officer had managed to pull Frank out of the stair trap. His leg looked like a lion's scratching post, but he could walk on it.

"This just isn't my day," Frank said.

Rollins called Sam over. "We found the boy. Paramedics are preparing to move him now."

Sam hurried into the house. "Where? Where?" The blue uniforms parted as if she were Moses and they the not-so-Red Sea.

"He's got a pulse," the officer said as she approached. "But it's weak."

Michael lay in a reclining chair, his eyes twitching beneath their lids as if he was dreaming. Calling his name and gently shaking him, Sam tried to wake him, but he didn't stir.

"What's wrong with him?" she asked.

Officer Paltrow held up a needle in a gloved hand. "Looks like she injected him with something."

"I'll kill her," Sam said.

She threw Michael over her shoulder in a fireman's carry, her pride and stubbornness not allowing her to buckle under the boy's weight. She managed to get him to the door, where a gurney awaited at the bottom of the front steps.

"Sam," Frank said softly, "let them take him."

She relented, and a couple of paramedics took Michael from her. They carried him down the steps and laid him gently on the gurney.

"Suspected heroin overdose," Paltrow told the paramedics as they started checking his vitals.

"Administering Narcan," one paramedic said as she reached into her kit.

Sergeant Rollins hustled over to Sam. "We're looking at maps to see where that trail goes. It probably has so many branches that she might come out in any of the neighboring towns."

Sam turned to Frank. "Follow her. Get that fucking bitch."

Frank nodded. "Take care of him," he said, nodding at the gurney.

CHAPTER 34

*S*he is vaguely aware of the needle in her arm. There. Not there. There again. "It wasn't supposed to be like this."

Tears. Emptiness. The hollowness of her insides fills with the heavy weight of loss. "Not like this. Never like this." Her eyelids flutter. Her arm throbs. But it's her heart that hurts the most.

"Gawain..."

Her visions are cruel. The heroin is supposed to block this particular one, but not this time. She is transported back to her beginning, where her visions began.

Her car has broken down on the highway. Smoke rises from under the hood.

"Fuck," she groans as she rests her head against the steering wheel. She knew she should have gotten the car looked at, but she didn't have the money.

The AC dies. The piece of junk didn't cool down the car very well, but at least it had been something. Sweat beads on her forehead, and her palms are clammy. As she pulls the keys from the ignition, they slip from her hands. Leave them, she thinks, not wishing to expend the energy, their usefulness depleted.

Her baby cries. Her little knight.

"I know, honey." She pulls out her cell phone and calls for roadside assistance. She relaxes a bit when she hears that the technician will arrive within an hour.

She opens her door and places a bare foot on the pavement. Immediately, she raises it again. The pavement is blistering hot, the midday sun beating down on it as if trying to cleanse the world through fire.

She sets her sandals just outside the open door and steps into them, using the inner door console for support. She exits the car, squeezing through the small crack she made with the door in fear of oncoming traffic. A truck passes inordinately close as she is sliding out, and she presses her back to the car as she closes the door.

She turns around and sees her baby crying in his car seat. She smiles and makes faces at him. "It's okay. Mommy's here." She reaches for the handle of the back door.

The door won't open. She panics and tries it again and again, squeezing it as if pumping the handbrake on a ten-speed.

She inhales, calms down, and reaches the front door. It, too, is locked. "What? How?"

She replays her steps getting out of the car then gasps, realizing she must have hit the button that locked all the doors when she used the console to stand. Peering in, she sees her keys on the floor and her phone on the passenger seat.

Her baby cries louder in the back seat.

"No," she mutters. She looks around for a rock or anything to break the window. "Don't panic. You'll only make things worse. Don't panic."

A car nears. "Hey!" she yells, waving her arms wildly. "Hey!"

The asshole drives by without even slowing.

She turns to the back window and punches it. "Don't panic!" The skin over her knuckles splits, but she punches the window again four more times until she hears a crack.

But the noise isn't the window breaking.

Her hand folds forward, and she screams. Then she laughs through tears of pain and fear when she sees another car approaching. She tries to flag it down one-handed. Like the first, this car shows no sign of stopping. She steps into the road, directly in its path.

Brakes screech. The smell of burning rubber fills the air. The car swerves but still manages to clip her, sending her flying. Her head con-

nects with her own car's front fender, and she continues to roll into the tall grass beside the road.

She sits up. Her own injuries are nothing. She has succeeded. The car has stopped. Its driver will find help for her baby.

"Don't panic!" She cackles through her tears. She expects to hear the sounds of a door opening, footsteps approaching. Instead, tires spin in gravel as an engine roars. The car speeds away.

"Get up," she mumbles around a mouthful of dirt and blood. "You have to get up."

She rises to her hands and screams, the pain in her wrist shooting into her brain like bullets. She collapses facedown as darkness sweeps over her vision.

Her teeth clench hard. Foam spills over her lips as her body jerks violently. Her thoughts shake loose, and she's left only with raw emotions: confusion, panic, fear. Her heart pumps at a pace it can't possibly maintain.

And eventually, it slows. When her convulsing stops, thoughts creep slowly back into her mind.

Thoughts of her dead son.

"Why?" she screams out from the nothingness, her voice echoing as if she were lost in a cave. "Why are you showing me this?"

The darkness retreats. The sounds of gulls crying and waves crashing flow into her ears, carrying her off to a better place, a vision of her own construct. A place where a three-year-old boy plays in the surf, a bucket-turned-helm on his head.

Her little Gawain.

She is in her chair, watching her son as he laughs and frolics. She scans the water and sees no fins. Still, she knows the shark is present.

"You betrayed me," she says, the words dying on a gentle breeze.

"The heroin betrayed you," her teacher says, emerging soundlessly from behind her, as if he's always been there.

She glances at her arm, clean and unscarred, bare in her sleeveless sundress. A flash of night, a needle in her arm, a tube around her bicep.

There. Not there. There again.

Gone. She begins to scratch and twitch.

"Relax, child," her teacher says. "I'm sorry what I had to offer was not enough to ease your loss and dull your pain. Here"—a needle materializes in his hand as if out of thin air, the syringe filled with fluid—"let me help you take away your pain. You can live here in this place forever."

Ryan turns her arm up and offers it. Her eyes roll back as the needle pierces the vein.

CHAPTER 35

Michael rubbed his eyes as he emerged from restless sleep, still exhausted. He felt as if he had completed six consecutive decathlons, and his mouth was bone-dry.

Sun beamed through slits in drawn venetian blinds. A television was mounted high up on the wall. The bed seemed to have an endless supply of pillows, so many tucked under his head and shoulders he was almost sitting up. A remote lay beside him, its cord suggesting it was meant for the bed rather than the TV.

Michael processed those details slowly, but the IV jammed into the back of his hand, its other end connected by a long thin tube to a saline bag hanging overhead, alerted him to his situation. That, and the doctor standing silently at his bedside.

Michael stiffened, the hairs on his neck standing on end. "You scared me."

"Sorry," the doctor said. He was an old man with shiny white hair and a dark tan. "Just wanted to have a look at you."

Memories flooded Michael's consciousness, and he focused on what he could last remember. "Ryan," he said, poking the inside of his elbow. It was tender, bruised. "She injected me with—"

"Heroin," the doctor said. His piercing blue eyes twinkled. "No stepping stones for you, son. Straight to the hard stuff." He laughed.

Michael frowned. He didn't find the joke very funny, and it seemed odd that a doctor would say such a thing.

"Anyway," the doctor said. "It's over. She can't hurt you now. I told her you weren't ready."

"I didn't want any part of it. I—" Michael froze, replaying over what the doctor had just said. He wondered if he had heard him correctly. "What did you just say?"

"She can't hurt you now."

"No, after that."

"I told her you weren't ready." The doctor smiled. "Whoa," he said, apparently noticing Michael's unease. "If I had wanted to hurt you, I could have easily done it in your sleep. Or a thousand other times. You're safe now."

"So, then... what do you want?"

"Like I said, mostly just to get a look at you, let you know I'm out there, in case you ever decide you're ready."

Michael recalled the future Ryan had shown him, the vision of himself and the awful things of which he was capable. He gulped. "And if I'm never ready?"

"So be it. No harm will come your way. But you should know that Ryan never lied to you. We *can* help you control your gifts. We *can* bring you into something larger than yourself."

"Yeah, she showed me what you can do, what you would turn me into."

"She showed you what she wanted you to see, what the drugs made her think you wanted to see. What the drugs convinced her to be true. When I found her, she'd already had... a tough life. The drugs were an escape. I was foolish to think I could wean her off them, show her that our work could be her new drug. She'd stop using for while then relapse. One time, she even stopped for a few years, but each time she relapsed, it became harder and harder to sober her again. What's worse, it affected her work. She got confused, sloppy. She got to where she couldn't tell the difference between some drug-infused dream and a true vision. Needless to say, her usefulness was on the decline."

"So you what? Killed her?"

"We terminated her employment." The doctor sighed. "I won't trouble you with semantics. But what she showed you... it doesn't have to be like that. Think about it. What's the one thing even you already know about visions of your own future?"

Michael pursed his lips as he thought. "I don't know. I can participate in them?"

"And could you participate in Ryan's vision of your future?"

"No."

"Then how can you be sure the man you saw was even you and not some figment of Ryan's confused hopes and dreams?"

Michael mulled that over. "I can't, I guess." He studied the doctor more closely. "How do you know all this?"

"Let's just say I've been watching Ryan for a long time. Watching you too. It's my job to keep tabs on recruits and potentials, and not just out here in the *real* world, if you know what I mean."

"Sorta," Michael said. "I think."

"Well, it will all make sense if you decide you want to join others like you one day, if you want to learn to use your powers rather than be used by them. It's been nice meeting you, Michael. Truly. If you change your mind, you'll know how to find me." He turned to leave.

"Wait," Michael called.

The doctor kept walking.

"How will I know how to find you?" Michael asked the empty room. He lay back down.

Five minutes later, Sam barged through the door and ran to his side. "The doctor told us you were awake. I've been here the whole time." She sat in a chair by his bed and reached for his hand.

He tucked his arms beneath his pillows to avoid contact. "Yeah, I can tell," he said, laughing. "You look like shit."

Sam stared at him, a dumbfounded expression on her face, which was blotchy and pale. Then she burst into laughter.

Michael laughed with her. He knew that despite all the crap he had put her through, the nasty things he had said, and despite her failings in turn, they were going to be okay.

He peered around her at the door she'd left open. "Us?" he asked. "You said 'the doctor told *us.*'"

"Oh, shit." Sam wiped her eyes and whispered, "I almost forgot about Frank."

She got up and went into the hall. When she returned, she was followed by a thin man who reminded Michael of the first host of that America's stupidest videos show, or whatever it was called. *Or was it the second host?*

"Good to see you well, kid," the man said.

"Who are you?" Michael blurted.

"Frank. I'm... a friend of your mother's." He put his arm around Sam, who looked down and blushed, no doubt waiting for Michael to correct the man.

Michael didn't say a word.

After a moment, Sam said, "Frank's with the FBI. He helped chase down the Suarez gang to that warehouse and helped me find you last night. We've actually worked a couple of cases together."

"FBI, huh?" Michael huffed. "Guess I better delete all those videos from my computer."

"Michael!" Sam feigned shock then chuckled. To his credit, the agent laughed too.

"Anyway," she said, nudging the agent, "tell Michael what you told me."

"Well, when we found you at that house, Sam stayed by you every step of the way. Chambers escaped by ATV through the woods, not the most inconspicuous escape vehicle. Had she kept to the woods, she might have been able to escape completely. But she headed back into Fall River and went right to the waterfront."

"Why?" Michael asked, though he had an idea.

"I don't know," Frank said. "I gave up long ago trying to figure out why crazy people do what they do—or junkies, for that matter. Needless to say, we got about a thousand reports of an ATV driving through the city. By the time we tracked her to the waterfront, she was dead. We found her sitting there on a bench, loaded up with so much heroin I can't even imagine how she took it all. I mean, she was—"

"Frank," Sam said.

"Yeah, uh, sorry." He cleared his throat. "Anyway, you won't have to worry about her ever again."

Michael frowned and looked away.

Sam leaned toward him. "Michael, I know you wanted her to help you, and I'm sorry that it ended this way. I really am."

Michael started to cry. "No, *I'm* sorry. I should have listened to you. I shouldn't have been so stupid. She could have killed me or... or turned me into something worse. I just wanted to believe she could help me. I wanted so badly to believe she could make my visions go away."

"It's okay, Michael," Sam said, squeezing his shoulder. "We both made mistakes. We grow, we learn from them, we move on. And we'll do it together."

Frank stepped back to the door. "I should go."

Sam nodded. "I'll walk you out."

"Bye, Michael," Frank said. "I am truly glad to see you're okay."

Michael nodded politely and faked a smile. He was not okay, and he began to wonder all over again if there would ever be a time when he would be. For the moment, he would settle for coping.

As they stood just outside his door, he could hear every word of their conversation.

"What's next for Frank Spinney?" Sam asked.

"Investigate the Hector Suarez abduction. Follow up on some other leads. *He's* at the center of it all; I just know it. I could use your help on this, Sam, and I'm sure I can get all the necessary clearances to make it a reality. I can probably even make it official, *Agent* Reilly."

"I'm sorry," Sam said flatly. "But I've decided to take a leave of absence. I can never forget what happened to my partner, and I'll be cheering you on from the sidelines every step of the way. But there's a boy in there who needs me, who's maybe needed me for a long time, and I haven't been there for him. It's past time I changed that."

"You sure you can just walk away? I know how much this case means to you."

"No, I'm not sure. But I have to try, for both our sakes. Goodbye, Frank."

"This is hardly goodbye. I have a feeling I'll be in your neck of the woods for the next several months. So... see you around?"

Michael could hear something like hope in her voice when she responded, "See you around."

EPILOGUE

"So, do you think you'll be getting out of here soon?" Michael asked, his smile shaky.

"I don't know." Tessa shrugged. "People have been disappearing left and right. I suppose my turn will come soon enough."

Michael grimaced. The way she said that didn't seem quite right, but he chalked it up to his paranoia. "How are you? Do you feel any better about... things?"

"You mean about being trapped in a nuthouse?" Tessa tried to smile but failed. Something heavy was weighing on her heart, something more than the usual.

The last thing Michael wanted to see was Tessa taking a turn for the worse. He bit back his frustration for her sake. *How is she ever supposed to heal if they keep treating her like she's broken?*

He changed the subject. "I missed you," he said, reaching out with a gloved hand.

She tilted her head and gave him a smile that seemed genuine. "I've missed you too."

A year older than Michael, Tessa was maturing quickly. He caught himself leering at her breasts, definitely bigger than the last time he'd been able to see her. Even in her pajamas, he could see the difference. She caught his stare. They both blushed and averted their eyes.

He'd always found her cute, but she was becoming sort of hot, not a good thing in a place like Brentworth, where the supposedly subdued male population outnumbered the females two to one. He, on the other hand, still looked like a little boy. He still didn't need to shave, and he had barely any hair on his chest.

241

"Um, so how's Jimmy?" Michael asked. "I asked to see him too, but—"

"He doesn't want to see you."

"What? Why?"

"He blames you for putting him in here."

Michael jerked back in his chair, almost toppling over. He scoffed. "That's crazy. He's the one that put *me* through a bunch of shit, and he's mad at me? That's bullshit. If not for me, he'd be back where he was before he escaped—a felony in itself, by the way—not spending his time flirting with you."

Tessa pouted. "He's not flirting—"

"I'm sorry. I shouldn't have said that. He... ugh! He just pisses me off."

"He seems to think this place isn't as nice as it appears."

"What do you mean?"

"Like I said, people have been disappearing."

Michael's eyes widened. "I didn't think you meant that literally! What the fuck? You think something's up?"

She waved her hands at the table between them. "Keep it down."

Michael bit his lip. "You're scaring me." He leaned closer and whispered, "What do you think is going on?"

"I don't know really. Just people are here one day and gone the next."

"Couldn't they just be getting discharged?"

"I thought that, too, at first. But at the rate they've been vanishing lately, you would think these doctors have found a miracle cure."

"That doesn't mean—"

"At night, I sometimes hear screaming."

Michael slumped. "All right. Sam should be outside. I'll go get her, and you can tell her everything you know."

"Are you crazy? I shouldn't even be telling you this. If something strange is going down, they're probably watching me as we speak. They'd definitely be watching me if a cop came to see me."

Michael ran a hand over his face. "She's not a cop right now."

"Whatever." Tessa's eyes darted around wildly as her knee bounced against the table. "All I'm saying is that I think there are bad people here, people worse than Father."

Is she paranoid now too? Michael frowned. "And Jimmy thinks this too?"

"Forget it. I shouldn't have said anything."

Michael couldn't just disregard it, but he figured he shouldn't push it. "All right. For now. But if you see anything else weird, you'll let me know?"

Tessa nodded like a bobblehead. "I should be going."

Where does she have to go? "Okay." Michael stood.

She came around the table and kissed the side of his head. He cringed, but no vision came, which was odd.

"Take care of yourself, okay?"

He nodded. "I will."

"Same time next week?"

"You know it."

She smiled, but he didn't think she meant it. *Maybe she doesn't want me to visit.* He sighed and watched her go down the hall until she was out of sight.

When he exited the meeting area and went to the security checkpoint, an orderly put a hand out to stop him. "Whoa, kid," he said. "I can't let you exit. Not that way. Not right now, anyway. New intakes being processed. You can either wait here or head out the back." The orderly pointed down the hall to his right.

Michael headed that way, which took him toward an older wing of the building. The fluorescent light flickered overhead. The hall was lined with boxes, a gurney missing a wheel, and some older equipment.

Sunlight seeped through the cracks around a double door at the end of the long hallway. An Exit sign was above it. *The light at the end of the tunnel.*

He passed a yellow caution sign and noticed the freshly polished floor between him and the door. Ahead, a maintenance man wearing earplugs swayed to music only he could hear. He bent and scraped something off the floor beside his industrial-sized floor buffer.

The man looked familiar. Michael felt a creeping uneasiness. *And that smell... Pine-Sol?*

He quickened his step toward the exit, his fear growing for some reason. Past the maintenance man, the hallway clutter gave way to free space, a large area with a two-color-schemed wall. *White wood on top, blue tile on the bottom...*

He was in his vision. "Oh no... Sam!"

His heart thumped in time with his pounding feet as he sprinted to the door, ready to plow through it despite its bold-faced warning of "Emergency Exit only. Alarm will sound when opened."

He remembered the axe and slammed his elbow into the glass encasing it. After ripping the weapon free, little crystals of breakaway glass dusting his arm and T-shirt, he charged outside.

Blinded by the sun, he nevertheless continued to run to the spot where his vision had told him Sam would be. The air was so humid and thick that Michael choked on it as he drew it in too greedily. A coughing fit followed.

Leaning against her car with her arms crossed, Sam gaped at him. "What's the axe for, Michael?"

Raising the axe over his head, he sprinted toward her, roaring out all the pain and rage that had been festering inside him.

Sam shrank back. The man in the plastic Indian Chief mask stepped out from the tree line, silently and stealthily. They locked eyes for just a second before the man ran straight at Sam.

Still too late? Michael urged his muscles to work harder. *I can't be.*

He cried out when he saw that he was. Worse, he had distracted Sam from seeing the man coming. The weapon in the masked attacker's hand slammed into Sam's side.

Sam spasmed and made a guttural noise. She fell against her car then slumped to the ground.

Michael screamed. *So fast. I've never seen anyone move that fast.*

He reached them and swung the axe with all his might.

And put it through Sam's back window. He kept his eyes on the murderous bastard who had just stabbed the woman he'd promised to use his visions to protect.

Behind the mask, the man was laughing. "Whew! That was close, kid! If I didn't know better, I'd think you were trying to kill me."

Michael sizzled with hate. He was trying to kill the man, and for half a second, he worried if he might have liked it, if he might actually be like the man Ryan had shown him. He refused to look down. He couldn't for fear that what he might see there would tear him apart. No, he had to keep Sam's attacker back.

He watched the man's eyes through the holes in the mask as he raised the axe in a double-handed grip as if he were stepping up to the plate in a baseball game. *I have to protect Sam. If it's not too... no, I have to protect Sam.*

Michael prepared to swing with everything he had if the man so much as feinted in his direction. The man's speed told him he'd only get one shot. He would have to make it count, commit to it, anticipate where the man would be before he got there.

But the man didn't move.

"What are you waiting for?" Michael growled.

Sam groaned, but Michael kept his eyes on the man.

"Some other time, kid. But soon, real soon." The man darted away.

Michael lowered the axe and looked down. To his relief, he saw no blood.

"That asshole zapped me." Sam raised a hand. "Help me up, would you?"

He took it and pulled her to her feet then into his arms. "I thought... I thought he stabbed you."

"Don't worry. It was just a stun gun and not even that strong of one. Guess he didn't really have enough time to get it in good and long against me, thanks to you. It hurt enough, though, the son of a bitch. Did you get a good look at him?"

Michael shook his head.

"No?"

"He... he was wearing a mask."

Sam scanned the woods, her fingers dancing on her holster. "Did you see where he went? I'm going to nail that..." She paused, perhaps noticing Michael's trembling lip at the same time he did. He bit down into it.

Sam sighed and hooked her thumb toward the car. "Get in."

He ran around the other side and jumped into the passenger seat. He slammed the door shut and locked it. The man was gone, but that didn't mean he couldn't come back. Holding back tears, he looked up at Sam as she plopped down beside him.

"I'm not going anywhere," Sam said, as if reading his thoughts. She grabbed the radio and called for backup. She smiled kindly, a smile she seemed to reserve just for him. "You know, you kind of looked like a badass with that axe in your hands."

"Heh, whatever." Michael almost smiled back. "Fall River's claim to fame: axe murdering. But... I know what you're doing."

"What am I doing?"

"Trying to make light of the fact that someone just tried to kill you."

"He wasn't trying to kill me. He just stunned me," Sam said, eye-balling the tear in her blouse. "At most, my skin will be a little irritated for a while where he jolted me."

"Not yet, anyway. Do you think he'll be back?"

"Probably."

"Do you know who he is?"

"I don't know, Michael. In my job, I make a lot of enemies." She pursed her lips and checked the rearview and side mirrors for the third time.

"Sam, you can tell me."

She pushed her hair behind her ears. "I don't know who he was, but Frank—that FBI Agent you met when you were in the hospital—he suggested that maybe... God, I don't even want to think about it."

He heard the sound of sirens. "What?"

"It's... it could be someone from my past. Someone I swore to put behind bars a long time ago. He's bad news, Michael. Worse than Masterson, worse than that whole Suarez gang even." She shuddered then straightened. "You know what? Frank's just being paranoid. That was a long time ago, and *he'd* be a fool to come back here."

Michael knew he was being placated. He studied the underbrush at the forest's edge. He gasped when Sam put her hand on his shoulder.

"Hey," she said. "We're safe now. You saved my life just then, you know? Again." With a hand not quite as steady as she probably wanted him to believe it to be, she swiped her hair behind her ears again. "Thank you."

Michael blushed and shuffled his feet. "Sam?"

"Yeah?"

"Do you think it had anything to do with me?"

"No, I honestly, genuinely do not think it had the remotest connection to you."

"What about to what Tessa was talking about?"

Sam frowned and studied him closely. Her eyes were like an eagle's swooping in for a field mouse. "What did Tessa say?"

"It's... ah, it's nothing. I'm jumpy, and she's paranoid."

"After what just happened, I'd say you have good reason to be."

Michael bit into his lip. "Will it ever stop?"

"Now that I've taken an indefinite leave, it should. We've still got most of the summer ahead of us. Why don't we get as far away from this place as we can and not come back until school starts up again?"

"I like that plan."

"Any place you're dying to go?"

"Any place is better than here."

Two patrol cars pulled in beside the car, their sirens deafening.

When the officers killed the noise, Sam pushed open her door then looked back at Michael. "I'm sorry. I have to go and fill them in on what happened. You'll probably have to give a statement, but that can wait." She stepped out of the car and bent down to look at him. "Just let me take care of this real quick. Then we'll go where no one will find us. No killers, psychopaths, or all-around douchebags anyway, I hope." She winked and walked away.

Michael folded his hands on his lap and sighed. They weren't going anywhere. Sam was a cop first and would be until it killed her. And someone out there was looking to end her career sooner rather than later.

Dear Reader,

We hope you enjoyed *Hearing Evil*, by Jason Parent. Please consider leaving a review on your favorite book site.

Visit our website[1] to sign up for the Red Adept Publishing Newsletter to be notified of future releases.

---

1. http://bit.ly/SMYH1u

Acknowledgements

T hank you to the various members of Bristol County, Massachusetts, law enforcement and court officials who helped me in the
making of this book and for your service.

About the Author

In his head, Jason Parent lives in many places, but in the real world, he calls Rhode Island home. The region offers an abundance of settings for his writing and many wonderful places in which to write them.

In a prior life, Jason spent most of his time in front of a judge... as a civil litigator. When he tired of Latin phrases no one knew how to pronounce and explaining to people that real lawsuits are not started, tried, and finalized within the 60-minute time frame they see on TV, he traded in his cheap suits for flip-flops and designer stubble. The flops got repossessed the next day, and he's back in the legal field... sorta. But that's another story.

When he's not working, Jason likes to kayak, catch a movie, travel any place that will let him enter, and play just about any sport (except for the one with that ball tied to the pole thing where you basically just whack the ball until it twists in a knot or takes somebody's head off). And read and write, of course. He does that too sometimes.

CPSIA information can be obtained
at www.ICGtesting.com
Printed in the USA
LVHW032318210821
695820LV00010B/662